As an enemy plots
to destroy the agency...
A YEAR OF LOVING DANGEROUSLY
continues....

Russell Devane aka Steve Trace
Strong and strapping—
a man who knows how to get the job done.

*Masquerading as another man—and romancing
the enemy's daughter under false pretenses—were
all in a day's work. Until Russell tempted fate by
falling for the fresh-faced goddess he was
forbidden to claim!*

Lise Meldrum
An Amazon beauty with a cloud of
luxurious auburn hair, rose-petal-soft skin...
and a secret yearning for love.

*All her life, love-starved Lise had been searching
for a man like "Steve" to make her feel feminine,
desirable, cherished. But what would she do once
she uncovered his shattering deception?*

"Simon"
Scarred inside and out, this ruthless traitor
felt the tide turning in his favor...
until he discovered he'd been double-crossed.

*When his daughter aligned herself with the
enemy, Simon vowed there would be hell to
pay. For he would stop at nothing to exact his
revenge...including sacrificing one of his own!*

Dear Reader,

You've loved Beverly Barton's miniseries THE PROTECTORS since it started, so I know you'll be thrilled to find another installment leading off this month. *Navajo's Woman* features a to-swoon-for Native American hero, a heroine capable of standing up to this tough cop—and enough steam to heat your house. Enjoy!

A YEAR OF LOVING DANGEROUSLY continues with bestselling author Linda Turner's *The Enemy's Daughter.* This story of subterfuge and irresistible passion—not to mention heart-stopping suspense—is set in the Australian outback, and I know you'll want to go along for the ride. Ruth Langan completes her trilogy with *Seducing Celeste,* the last of THE SULLIVAN SISTERS. Don't miss this emotional read. Then check out Karen Templeton's *Runaway Bridesmaid,* a reunion romance with a heroine who's got quite a secret. Elane Osborn's *Which Twin?* offers a new twist on the popular twins plotline, while Linda Winstead Jones rounds out the month with *Madigan's Wife,* a wonderful tale of an ex-couple who truly belong together.

As always, we've got six exciting romances to tempt you—and we'll be back next month with six more. Enjoy!

Leslie J. Wainger
Executive Senior Editor

Please address questions and book requests to:
Silhouette Reader Service
U.S.: 3010 Walden Ave., P.O. Box 1325, Buffalo, NY 14269
Canadian: P.O. Box 609, Fort Erie, Ont. L2A 5X3

Linda Turner
The Enemy's Daughter

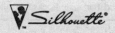

INTIMATE MOMENTS™
Published by Silhouette Books
America's Publisher of Contemporary Romance

Special thanks and acknowledgment are given to Linda Turner for her contribution to the A Year of Loving Dangerously series.

 SILHOUETTE BOOKS

ISBN 0-373-27134-4

THE ENEMY'S DAUGHTER

Visit Silhouette at www.eHarlequin.com

Printed in U.S.A.

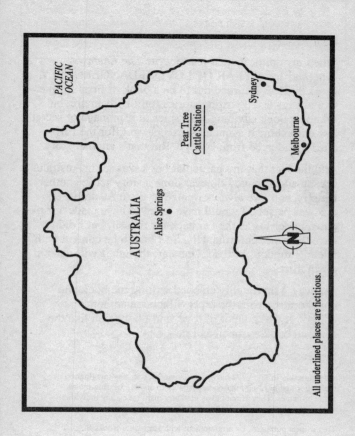

PACIFIC OCEAN

AUSTRALIA

Alice Springs

Pear Tree
Cattle Station

Sydney

Melbourne

All underlined places are fictitious.

Dear Reader,

When my editor invited me to write *The Enemy's Daughter* for A YEAR OF LOVING DANGEROUSLY, I was thrilled. It turned out to be a book of firsts for me. I've always loved writing stories full of adventure, but I'd never done anything with spies or espionage or secret law-enforcement agencies—except work for the FBI after I graduated from college. But that's another story.

And the fact that my particular book was set in Australia was an added plus. I'd never done a story set in another country, and I've always wanted to go to Australia, so this was perfect. I would have loved to have made a trip down under to see the Outback for myself, but I didn't have the time, unfortunately. So I had to be content with reading about it, instead. One day, though, I will make it down there.

Anyway, I thoroughly enjoyed writing the book and collaborating with the other Silhouette authors and editors. It was a labor of love, and I hope you like the finished book as much as I do.

Sincerely,

Linda Turner

Chapter 1

For as far as the eye could see, the land was a vast, endless stretch of lonely plains that resembled the high desert of New Mexico. An occasional eucalyptus dotted the landscape with its thin, spindly branches, and small arid plants that needed little moisture in order to survive thrived under a hot sun that burned in a cloudless sky. And covering everything was a veil of choking red dust kicked up by a dry wind that blew steadily from the north.

Staring out at the haunting land that was the Australian outback, Russell Devane had, before he'd accepted this particular mission, thought he was a man who could take in stride whatever nature threw at him. After all, his job as an operative for the secret organization SPEAR had taken him to the farthest reaches of the globe. He'd withstood the bone-numbing cold of the Arctic and the blistering sands of the Sahara, all without complaint. But he could see already that nothing in his past had really prepared him for the vastness of the outback and its drastic

temperature changes. It was the tail end of summer—fall
was just days away—but the temperature had to be a hundred and twenty degrees in the shade. And it wasn't even
noon yet!

Just thinking about working in that kind of heat all day
long made him sweat, but he grimly resolved to get used
to it. He had to. In a few minutes, he would be arriving
at the headquarters of the Pear Tree Cattle Station, where
he would assume the identity of Steve Trace, the station's
newest cowboy and an associate of Art Meldrum, the
owner of the place.

To the rest of the world, Art was an absentee landlord
who left the running of the huge ranch in the hands of
his daughter, Lise, most of the time. Only Russell—and
his fellow SPEAR operatives—knew that Art was actually
an alias for Simon, the traitor who'd spent the last eight
months trying his damnedest to destroy not only Jonah,
the head of SPEAR, but the agency itself. And he was
slippery as an eel. Time and again, just when SPEAR
operatives were sure they had him in their grasp, he'd
managed to slip away.

Not this time, Russell promised himself, his gray eyes
steely as he thought of how Simon had evaded capture
just days ago on the Caribbean island of Cascadilla. The
bastard had, in fact, never even put in an appearance on
the island. Thanks to the real Steve Trace, a kidnapper
and thug who'd been hired sight unseen by Simon, he'd
been warned he was walking into a trap if he came to
Cascadilla. So he'd run home to the outback, where he
could lie low in the bush, and he'd never known that the
real Steve Trace had died soon after he'd gotten word to
him he was in danger.

SPEAR had made sure that no one knew of Trace's
death, making it easy for Russell to step right into his life.

Pretending to be Trace, he'd used Trace's cell phone and discovered through the phone's address book that Simon was using the name Art Meldrum in Australia. He'd immediately called him and given him a sob story about needing a job. Not suspecting a thing, Simon had told him to come to the station, which was just what Russell had figured would happen. After all, Simon had narrowly escaped capture thanks to the quick thinking of Trace. The least he owed him was a job.

So here he was two days later, right in Simon's own backyard, and so damn close to the bastard, he swore he could smell him. And Simon didn't have a clue what kind of trouble was coming his way. Russell hoped he enjoyed his freedom because it was just about to come to an end.

The station headquarters came into view then, just a dot on the horizon that grew steadily larger with every passing mile. Long moments later, the mailman Russell had hitched a ride with just outside of Roo Springs pulled up before the main house in a swirl of dust. "Here you are, mate," he said, frowning at the house. "The place looks deserted."

Russell had to agree. Set in the middle of the barren plain without so much as a single tree to offer shade, the large, two-story frame house appeared empty. There were no cars in sight, and nothing moved but the dust stirred up by the wind.

Shooting him a frown, the mailman arched a dark brow at him. "You sure you're expected? Lise usually sticks close to the house when company's coming. She doesn't get many visitors way out here in the bush."

If anyone would know Lise's schedule, Russell figured it would be the mailman. Roo Springs was the closest town to the station—if you could call a wide spot in the road with fifty inhabitants a town—and there was only one mailman to deliver the mail. There was probably little that went on within a two-hundred-mile radius that the older man didn't know about.

"I didn't know exactly when I would be arriving," Russell replied, which was the truth. "I'll just unload my stuff and wait on the front porch until she gets back."

The postman, who was as thin and scrawny as the scraggly bushes planted in the dust in the yard, looked anything but convinced. "I don't know, mate. It's a warm day, and you being a Yank and all, you should be inside out of the heat. Let me see if I can raise somebody." And with no more warning than that, he laid on the horn.

Wincing, Russell swore. Damn idiot! He'd hoped he'd have a chance to look around the place without being observed, but then again, he hadn't expected to arrive with horns blaring like the leader of a damn parade, either! This was great. Just great!

Muttering under his breath, he started to tell the old man to lay off, but then his eyes fell on the corral next to the barn on the far side of the house. His heart stopped dead in his chest at the sight of a woman nearly under the hooves of what appeared to be a wild mustang rearing on its hind legs. Frightened by the horn, its eyes wide, the horse looked ready to stomp her into the ground.

Later, Russell never remembered moving. One second, he was all set to chew out the mailman and the next, he was out of the vehicle and charging across the compound at a dead run toward the corral.

If someone had asked him then what she looked like, he couldn't have said. All he saw was a woman in trouble. Hopping the fence, he swept her up into his arms like she weighed no more than a feather and set her out of harm's way on the other side of the corral fence.

Only then did he take a good look at her, and what he

saw infuriated him. She was a big girl, five feet eleven if she was an inch, with a cloud of auburn hair that fell nearly to her waist and skin that was rose-petal soft under his hands. Tanned from working outside, her eyes as blue as the sky, she was trim and fit and had the kind of fresh-faced, subtle beauty that a lot of men often overlooked. Not Russell. In the stark barrenness of the outback, she was an unexpected treasure...that had almost been stomped into the ground by a horse that was no doubt as wild as a March hare.

Infuriated at the thought, he released her abruptly, but only to snap, ''What the hell do you think you're doing, woman? Trying to get yourself killed? Don't you have any better sense than to step into a corral with a monster like that? You could have been killed!''

Her heart still pounding from the shock of being swept off her feet by a giant of a man who'd appeared out of nowhere, Lise could only stare at him like a starstruck teenager who'd lost her tongue. For most of her life, she'd been at least eye level with every man she met—it wasn't often that she had to look up to one. But this one towered over her by at least five inches and had the broadest shoulders she'd ever seen. In a matter of seconds, he did something to her that no man had ever done before...he made her feel small and delicate. It was a heady feeling.

Then his words registered.

Outrage sparked in her eyes like a summer thunderstorm. The nerve of the man! This was *her* station, dammit, and if he thought she was going to stand there and let him yell at her like she was a two-year-old who didn't have the sense to come in out of the rain, he could think again!

''Hold it right there, mister! I don't know who the hell you think you are, but for your information, I had every-

thing under control until you came charging in here like
Indiana Jones!''

"The hell you did!''

"And Thunder's not a monster! He was just startled.
If you hadn't blown your damn horn—''

"*I* didn't! That was the mailman's idea. But don't go
blaming him. He thought the place was deserted. If you
hadn't been in the corral in the first place, this never
would have happened. Anyone with eyes can see that that
horse is wild, and you've got no business going anywhere
near him!''

That was the wrong thing to say. Lise considered herself an easygoing woman, but no man was going to tell
her where she could and couldn't go on her own station.
Her blue eyes narrowing dangerously, she almost purred
her words. "Oh, really? We'll see about that!'' And before he could stop her, she slipped through the wooden
rails of the corral fence and approached the still spooked
horse without an ounce of fear.

Behind her, she heard her rescuer swear and start to
follow her into the corral, but she never took her eyes off
the mustang. Still half wild, he could, if he chose, pound
her into the dust if she made one wrong move. She didn't.
Talking to the animal soothingly, she sweet-talked him
into letting her touch him, and before he knew what she
was about, she had him bridled.

Triumphant, she turned to her visitor with an arch look.
"You were saying?''

Russell couldn't help but be impressed, and too late he
realized he may have stepped over the line. This had to
be Lise Meldrum, Simon's daughter and the manager of
the place. He'd planned to charm her into liking him so
he could get on her good side and pump her for everything he could about her father, and here he was yelling

at her, instead! Talk about a bonehead move. What the devil was wrong with him? He was good at what he did—he didn't usually make those kind of mistakes. But then again, he didn't usually come across a beautiful woman caught under the hooves of a frightened horse, either.

Which has nothing to do with anything, a voice in his head growled. *Remember your mission.*

Silently cursing himself for the reminder he shouldn't have needed, he forced himself to relax and step into the cover of Steve Trace. For the rest of his stay in Australia, he would answer to nothing but Steve. And it would help him assume his new identity by convincing himself that his name *was* Steve—not Russell.

Giving her a teasing smile, he said wryly, "Did I say what I thought I just did? It must be the heat—it's fried my brain. Can you forgive me? Obviously you know what you're doing. Of course, I would have won Thunder's trust with some sugar before I took a chance on stepping back into the corral when he was still so skittish, but I know women like to do things their own way. And that's okay," he said, grinning when steam practically poured from her ears. "You're the boss."

Stepping over to the corral fence, he extended his hand to her over the top rail, his gray eyes glinting devilishly. "You must be Lise. Your father told me you'd be running the place. I'm Steve Trace, your new cattle drover. Or at least, I am if you don't can my hide for this stunt. You just scared the hell out of me, and I overreacted. Can you forgive me?"

Gritting her teeth, Lise looked him over, taking in his chiseled good looks, the long chestnut hair worn in a ponytail, the bold glint in his gray eyes and told herself she shouldn't forgive him. She knew his kind. He was a charming flirt who'd been talking his way out of tight situations from the time he was a little boy and he'd first learned he could get his way with a woman by flashing a smile. He was trouble, and she had a feeling that if she let him stay, he was going to give her plenty of it.

Right then and there, she should have sent him packing. It would have been the smart thing to do, and her father wouldn't have cared. *She* was in charge of running the station and had full authority to hire and fire. But she was, as usual, shorthanded. Life in the outback was harsh, and finding good men wasn't easy. The work was hard, the pay minimal, the hours long. Cowboys had a tendency to drift with the wind, never staying anywhere very long. If you found a good one, you hung onto him with both hands.

And something told her the Yank would be a good one. Big and strapping, with the shoulders of an American football player and a strength that had stolen her breath, he appeared to have what it took to do the work and do it well. And she needed him, dammit. With the annual fall roundup just around the corner and only a handful of men to work tens of thousands of acres, she could use all the help she could get.

Left with no choice, she reluctantly gave his hand a firm, businesslike shake, but if he thought she was going to let him off that easy, he was in for a rude awakening. "Of course," she retorted coolly. "As long as you understand that things are done my way around here, there shouldn't be any problem, should there?"

Just that easily, she laid down the ground rules and dared him to question them.

Not the least intimidated, Steve only grinned. "Whatever you say, boss lady."

"You just remember that, and we'll get along fine, Yank. Grab your things. I'll show you to the bunkhouse."

The battle lines were drawn. Enjoying himself, Steve couldn't help but be pleased. He liked a woman who stood up for herself, who had the confidence to hold her own with a man and challenge him at every turn. SPEAR had been able to give him very little information about Lise Meldrum other than that she managed the place because her father was gone a lot on what, to the rest of the world, appeared to be business trips. Other women might have handled the business end of the station from the comfort of an air-conditioned office and left the real work to her cowboys, but that didn't appear to be Lise's way. She wasn't a hothouse flower, but a hands-on manager who apparently worked right alongside her men, and he liked that. This mission was going to be much more interesting than he'd expected.

Adrenaline pumping through his veins, Steve thanked the mailman, who'd watched the exchange between him and Lise with a wide grin of appreciation, then retrieved his duffel bag from the back seat of the mail car. He hadn't brought much with him—he'd learned a long time ago that in his business, it paid to travel light. Sometimes you had to move fast. If you had to abandon a mission in the middle of the night, the last thing you wanted was baggage slowing you down.

"All set," he told Lise as the mailman waved at Lise and drove off in a cloud of dust. "Lead the way, ma'am."

Her eyes narrowed dangerously at that. "It's Lise," she corrected him. "Just Lise. We don't stand on ceremony around here."

He'd already figured as much, but he could see that pushing her buttons was going to be an enjoyable pastime he hadn't expected. "Whatever you say, ma'am. Your father told me I'd get along fine here as long as I followed orders. Where is he, by the way? I'd like to thank him in person for the job.''

He glanced around casually, but inside, every nerve ending was standing at full alert. He'd been on the move nonstop for the last twenty-four hours in hopes of catching Simon unaware on his own turf. One phone call to Belinda, his contact at SPEAR, and he could have backup there in fifteen minutes or less.

Any hope of capturing the bastard that easily, however, died a swift death when Lise said just as casually, ''You could if he was here, but he had to leave early this morning for a business meeting in London. I'm not sure when he'll be back.''

Yeah, right, Steve thought cynically. Who the hell did she think she was fooling? She might appear to be as honest and straightforward as Mother Teresa, but only a fool bought into that act. And Steve was nobody's fool. She was Simon's daughter, for God's sake, and probably the only person in the world he really trusted completely. Of course she knew when the bastard was coming back. She was just protecting him. Steve couldn't allow himself to forget that she would, no doubt, continue to do that at all cost.

''Then I guess I'll just have to thank him another time,'' he said easily, and silently promised himself it wouldn't be long.

They reached the bunkhouse, and she preceded him inside. Far from disappointed that things at the station weren't quite as he'd expected, Steve glanced around his new home and decided that this wasn't going to be so bad. Granted, there was little privacy, but he could find a way to work around that. Especially if it meant uncovering Simon's dirty little secrets. This was the one place in the world where the traitor felt safe. With any luck, he kept records here not only of his illegal activities, but also of the network of contacts he used around the world to carry out his evil plans. If Steve could uncover that kind of information, SPEAR could not only finally capture Simon, but finally shut down his entire operation worldwide.

"It's not the Ritz," Lise said stiffly, "but I haven't heard any of my men complaining. They have their own space, and they eat good. I make sure of that. The cook here is one of the best in the country."

Realizing he was frowning in concentration and she'd taken that for disapproval of the accommodations, he blinked, and just that quickly flashed a grin at her. "Now you're talking, boss lady. I think I'm going to like it here."

She bristled at the title he'd labeled her with, and it was all he could do not to chuckle. He wasn't teasing— he only had to look around to know that he really was going to like it there. As a kid, he hadn't been able to wait until the day he could leave the dairy farm he'd grown up on in Wisconsin, but deep down inside, he'd been missing the place ever since. Lately, he'd been thinking maybe it was time to go back. He'd worked for SPEAR a long time, and the world of intrigue and adventure could be addictive, but there was a part of his soul that ached to get back to his roots, to a place where he could relax and get back to nature. For now, this just might be that place. Granted, he still had to be on guard, and the outback wasn't Wisconsin, but there was something about the whisper of the wind across the dry, parched, endless land that called to him. It wasn't home, but it felt like it.

He didn't fool himself into thinking his mission—or the cover he'd adopted—would be easy. On a station the size of the Pear Tree, there was a lot of work to be done and never enough time in the day to do it all. The men put in a long day, and if Steve needed proof of just how hard the work was, he got it later that evening when the rest of the crew returned to the bunkhouse when their shift was over.

Straggling in, their faces baked as brown as the land by the hot, unforgiving desert sun, they were dirty and sweaty and sporting various cuts and bruises. They wanted a shower and food, in that order, and nothing was getting in their way. Taking time only to greet Steve and introduce themselves, they headed for the showers, then the dining hall.

Far from offended, Steve knew they would loosen up some after they had a chance to clean up and fill their bellies, and he was right. The long table in the dining hall of the bunkhouse had barely been cleared off before Nate, the oldest of the six cowboys, pulled out a deck of cards. Thin and wiry and weathered from years spent working in the elements, he had the kind of face that didn't give away his age. With a thatch of gray at his temples and brown hair that was naturally thin, he could have been anywhere from thirty-five to fifty.

His faded blue eyes twinkling with a challenge, he held the pack of cards to Steve. "You up to a game of poker, mate?"

Liking him immediately, Steve grinned. "Well, now, that depends. I'm not much of a gambler. How about you?"

He shrugged. "I lose more than I win, but I'm willing to give it a try if you are."

Steve watched smothered grins spread through the rest of the cowboys and knew he was being set up. Not bothering to hide his grin, he'd expected as much. He was the odd man out and a Yank, to boot, and if he'd been in their shoes, he would have done the same thing. The way a man played poker said a hell of a lot about him.

Pulling out a chair across the table from the older man, he said, "I'm in. Name your stakes."

Chairs scraped on the old wooden floor as the others quickly joined in, someone pulled out a bottle of whiskey, and the game was on.

It didn't take long for his companions to figure out that Steve was no slouch when it came to cards—or for him to realize that they could hold their own with him when it came to bluffing. Especially Nate. He could be holding everything from a royal flush to nothing but a pair of deuces, but you'd never know it from the easygoing grin on his face.

And that made him a very dangerous man indeed, Steve acknowledged. When you couldn't tell what someone was thinking, you didn't dare turn your back on him. He knew that, accepted it and didn't intend to forget it. But that didn't mean he didn't thoroughly enjoy pitting his wits against Nate and every other man there. From the way things were looking, first with the daughter, then Nate and the rest of the hands, this mission was going to be a hell of a lot more fun than he'd expected.

Losing his second hand in a row to the older man, Steve watched him rake in winnings that at the outset of the hand he'd been sure were his, and he could do nothing but swear good-naturedly. "You've got a hell of a way of losing there, *mate*. You ever let anyone else lose?"

"Not if I can help it." He chuckled. "I kind of like it this way."

"I can see why you would," Steve drawled, amused. "Just don't get too comfortable. Things are about to change."

Far from perturbed, Nate only grinned. "I wouldn't go spending my winnings just yet, if I were you. From where I'm sitting, you haven't got any."

"The night's not over yet," Steve retorted, his own grin wide. "Deal."

With nothing more than that, the challenge was issued and the stakes were raised. Enjoying himself, Steve won the next two hands, then lost three. But he couldn't complain. The game stayed friendly, and it gave him a chance to learn more about Lise and her elusive father.

Tossing his ante into the middle of the table for the next game, he said with studied casualness, "I guess things are pretty easy around here when the boss is away, huh? How long's he going to be gone?"

In the process of taking a sip of his whiskey, Chuck, the youngest of the group, nearly choked. "What are you talking about? The old man doesn't give a rat's ass about what's going on around here. He's not here half the time. Lise is the one who keeps this place going."

"And she does a damn good job of it," Preston, the quiet one of the group, said proudly.

The others nodded in agreement, and there was no question that Lise was respected by all of them. "She's a good boss," Nate said. "I never worked for a better one."

"No kidding?" Steve said. "This place must be half the size of Texas. You sure her boyfriend's not helping her? That's an awful lot of responsibility for a woman alone."

Fishing for more information, Steve threw the bait out and didn't have to wait long for a response. "Lise ain't got no boyfriend," Frankie, a big, balding hulk of a cowboy, said with a crooked grin. "Never has, as far as I remember."

"Wait a minute," Barney said. A short, husky man with a tattoo of a mermaid on his arm, he had a wicked grin and the very devil in his eyes. "Don't go forgetting old man McEnnis. He was sweet on her there for a while."

"Sweet, my eye," Nate retorted. "The old geezer didn't have any teeth! And he died the next week! That ain't no boyfriend. That's a nightmare!"

Everyone laughed at that, including Steve, even as he filed away the information for future use. So Lise didn't have a man in her life, and from the sound of it, never had. That would make romancing her a hell of a lot easier, if that's what he had to do to find out more information about her father.

In her father's study in the main house, Lise sat at his oversize desk and was frowning at the ranch books when there was a knock at the study door. Glancing up, she smiled at the sight of Tuck standing on the threshold with his hat in his hand, looking for all the world like an overgrown kid being called on the carpet before the schoolmaster. He was a big man, nearly as tall as she, with a round face and an easygoing nature that made him a favorite with just about everyone. That didn't, however, mean he was soft. Far from it, in fact. He could be tough as nails when he had to, and knew the cattle business inside and out. Which was why he was her right-hand man. She could always depend on him to tell it to her straight when it came to anything concerning the station.

Closing the station books, she sat back in her chair and motioned him inside. "Have a seat. Is that the list of supplies we need for the roundup?"

"Yeah. Sorry it's so late. I meant to have it to you by this afternoon, but I couldn't get Cookie to give me a list of the provisions he wanted to take. You know how he is. He never can make up his mind until the last minute.'' Handing over the list to her, he took the seat across from her desk and sighed in relief as the cool air of the air-conditioning washed over him. ''Damn, that feels good! The heat's really been getting to me this year. I don't know how I'm going to stand the roundup. It's going to be hotter than hell out there in the bush.''

Making no attempt to hold back a grin, Lise had to laugh. For as long as she could remember, the fall roundup was held the same time every year. And every year, Tuck complained about the heat. Anyone listening to him would think he was a whiny baby who didn't have a bit of stamina, but every year, he toughed it out with the best of them and weathered the heat just fine.

''You love it and you know it,'' she teased. ''What about the rest of the men? Are they all ready? How's Frankie's foot? He didn't seem to be favoring it as much today as he has been.''

Just last week, Frankie's horse had stepped on his foot and he'd been hobbling around ever since. ''It's better than it was,'' Tuck replied, ''but it's still tender. It should be better by next week. Even if it's not, we've got the Yank to pick up the slack, so we should do fine.''

Her pulse kicking into high gear just at the memory of how he'd made her feel, Lise frowned. ''You think he'll be able to handle the work?''

He laughed. ''Are you kidding? He's big as a house! And from what you told me about the way he hauled you out from under Thunder's hooves, he's not only strong, he keeps his head in an emergency. You must have thought so, too, or you wouldn't have hired him.''

She couldn't deny it. Like Tuck, she'd thought he was just what she needed in a cowboy. Now she wasn't so sure. There was something about the man that disturbed her, and she couldn't for the life of her say what it was. For now, though, she was reserving judgment on Steve Trace, though she had no intention of admitting that to Tuck.

"It's not like we've got a flood of cowboys beating a path to our door in search of a job," she said dryly. "Beggars can't be choosers. Sometimes, you've got to take what you get till something better comes along. Not that he's not going to work out," she amended quickly. "At this point, it's too soon to tell. But at least we've got another hand for the roundup, and right now, that's our main concern."

If he didn't work out after that, she thought, she'd send him packing. They'd be shorthanded again, but somebody would come along eventually. They always did.

The next day started early. Long before daylight, the men were up and dressed and wolfing down bacon and eggs and homemade biscuits in the dining hall. Feeling like he was back home again in his mother's kitchen, Steve bit into his first biscuit of the morning and groaned in appreciation. Lise hadn't been kidding when she said she fed her cowboys well. His mother was an excellent cook, but even she never made biscuits like this. "Damn, this is great!"

Looking up from the four biscuits he was slathering with real butter, Frankie grinned. "If you think this is good, wait till the roundup starts. You're not going to believe what Cookie can do on a campfire."

In the process of taking another bite of his biscuit, Steve stiffened slightly. "What roundup?"

"The one that starts a week from Monday," he retorted. "Didn't Lise tell you about it yesterday when she hired you? The summers are so hot, we have a roundup every year at the beginning of fall to check out the cattle and watering holes. The whole crew goes.''

''Including Lise?''

He nodded. ''Yep. We load the horses up in trailers, along with all the gear, and head out for a couple of weeks in the bush. It's just like being in the Old West. It's great!''

Steve didn't doubt that it was. But he wasn't ready to leave the compound yet, dammit. Certainly not for two or three weeks! He had to get inside the house and search it, and he couldn't do that if he was miles away, traipsing around the bush playing cowboy.

There wasn't, however, a hell of a lot he could do about it without blowing his cover. He'd come there pretending to be down and out and in need of the job Simon had promised him, and when the boss said you had to go out in the bush, you went without complaint. Damn. Now what was he supposed to do?

''Hey, that's my biscuit!'' Chuck bellowed when Barney snatched the last one in the pan right out from under his nose. ''You've already had five, you pig! Gimme that!''

''Not on your life, junior. You just ate four, yourself. This one's mine.''

Furious, the younger man looked ready to punch him, and Steve wasn't sure if it was because Barney had stolen the last biscuit or because he'd called him junior. Either way, Steve knew an opportunity when he saw one. Grinning at the two men, he drawled, ''Geez, fellas, they're damn good biscuits, but you don't have to fight over them. Here, Chuck, take mine.'' Tossing him the last one on his plate, he rose to his feet and grabbed the empty biscuit pan. "I'll get a hot one from the kitchen. Anybody else want one?"

When five hands went up, including Chuck and Barney's, he had to laugh. "If Cookie can keep up with you guys, he must be some cook. I'll be right back."

Chuckling, he strode out, but his smile died the second the door to the dining hall closed behind him and he headed for the house thirty yards away. He was taking a chance, making a move when Lise and the cook were both there, but what other choice did he have? With the roundup starting in a matter of days, he was running out of time.

Another agent would, in all likelihood, have had a game plan in place before he even thought about stepping into the house, but Steve had never operated that way. He was a roll-with-the-punches, fly-by-the-seat-of-his-pants kind of guy, which was what made him a damn good agent. He didn't act—he reacted—and nine times out of ten, his instincts were right on the money.

That didn't mean the old ticker wasn't pumping out the adrenaline as he approached the door. Every nerve ending was on alert, his muscles tense, though he liked to think he hid it well. His gait easy and relaxed, he opened the back door as if he had every right in the world to be there.

Not sure what to expect, he stepped inside and found himself in a small back hall. Stairs directly in front of him gave access to the upstairs, and to the right, a swinging door obviously led to the kitchen. Through the door, he could hear pots and pans rattling as Cookie sang to himself in an off-key baritone.

So he hadn't heard him come in, he thought with a soundless sigh of relief. Now, where the hell was Lise?

Standing perfectly still, he cocked his head and thought he caught the faint strains of what sounded like the weather channel coming from a television upstairs. Pleased, he smiled slowly, his gray eyes glinting with satisfaction. So Cookie was tied up in the kitchen with the dishes, and Lise was upstairs. He couldn't have planned it better if he'd tried. He couldn't do a search now, not when either one of them could walk in on him at any second, but at least he could discover the floor plan. Then if he had to search the place in the middle of the night, he wouldn't run into a lamp or something and wake the household.

The question was, which way did he go first? Hesitating, he stared down the hall, then to his left, and wondered which led to the study. He knew there was one— last night when Tuck had returned to the bunkhouse and joined the poker game, he'd mentioned that he'd been talking to Lise in the study. It was there, no doubt, that Simon had concealed records of his illegal activities.

Five minutes, Steve thought grimly. He didn't care how well the bastard had hid them, give him five minutes and he felt sure he could find them.

Tossing a mental coin, he decided to explore through the door to the left, but before he could make a single move, he heard a noise at the top of the stairs. Freezing, all senses on alert, he glanced up, ready to explain that he was there for biscuits and didn't know where the kitchen was. But the words never left his mouth. He took one look at Lise in her nightgown and robe, her waist-length auburn hair flowing past her shoulders, and his mind went completely blank.

Chapter 2

She had no right to look so captivating so early in the morning, he thought with a frown. After all, it wasn't as if she'd been expecting him and had set out to knock the air out of his lungs. The gown and robe she wore covered her body like a sack and were hardly flattering. But still, he was somehow seduced. It was her hair, he told himself. A woman with hair like that could tempt the devil himself. And Lord knew, he was no saint. All too easily, he could picture her naked in his bed, her fiery locks spread out, giving him tempting views of her body as she smiled and held out her arms to him.

Then his gaze lifted to her face, and he realized it was a hell of a lot more than her hair that attracted him. She had an innocence about her, a total lack of awareness of her own beauty that he found incredibly appealing. With no effort whatsoever, she reached out and grabbed his attention just by breathing, and she didn't even seem to know it.

But he did, and alarm bells were going off all over the place in his head. *Watch it,* a voice cautioned in his ear. *Remember who the lady is and why you're here. You may have to seduce her before it's all said and done. If you don't keep your head about you, you may end up losing it. This is Simon's daughter, for God's sake!*

It took nothing more than that to pull him up short. Silently cursing himself for momentarily losing sight of his mission, he jerked himself to his surroundings—and his very precarious position. If she'd come down five seconds later, she'd have caught him boldly exploring the house.

He watched surprise widen her eyes, then suspicion, and didn't give her time to wonder any longer just what the devil he was doing in her back hall. Turning on the charm to distract her, he grinned at her. "Well, if it isn't my lucky day. Good morning, boss lady. Were you looking for me? All you had to do was whistle, and I'd have come running."

Stopping dead in her tracks at the sight of him, Lise felt the physical stroke of his eyes and couldn't, for the life of her, understand how he made her so breathless with just a look. Growing up around cowboys, she'd seen his kind all her life. She knew better than to take anything he said seriously.

Not, she reminded herself, that she had any personal experience with flirtatious cowboys. The ones she knew had never even noticed she was a woman, and that had always been fine with her. She knew bull when she heard it, and she'd always wondered how the women in town and at parties could fall for one load of manure after another.

Now she knew.

Caught in the trap of his boyish grin, her heart was

fluttering like a schoolgirl's, and that irritated her no end. Her delicately arched brows snapping together in a scowl, she growled, "Stuff it, Trace. What are you doing in my house?"

Not appearing the least bit offended, he held up the empty biscuit pan he'd brought with him from the bunkhouse and winked at her. "The boys want more biscuits. I'd rather have you."

She should have laughed at his outrageousness and put him in his place—it would have been no more than he deserved. But there was something about the glint in his eye that made her all too conscious of the fact that she stood before him in nothing but her nightgown and robe. Her mouth suddenly as dry as the outback itself, all she could manage was a nod toward the door on his right. "The kitchen's through there," she said hoarsely. "Excuse me. I need to get dressed."

Turning, she fled up the stairs, leaving Steve staring after her in a way that may have flattered her immensely if she'd only turned around and looked. She didn't.

"Did I hear somebody say something about biscuits?"

Jerking his gaze from the top of the empty stairs, Steve turned to find a short, rail-thin Aboriginal watching him with small black eyes that missed little. Obviously, the man had seen Steve gazing after Lise like he'd never seen a female in her nightclothes before.

His smile rueful, Steve made no apologies for his behavior. "There's something about a woman who can put me in my place that really turns me on," he said honestly. Holding out his hand, he grinned. "Hi. I'm Steve Trace. You must be Cookie. Do you think you could give my mama your recipe for biscuits? I've never eaten anything like them in my life."

He spoke nothing less than the truth, though he would

have said the same thing if the biscuits had been as hard as rocks. In order to do his job, he needed to gain the confidence of everyone who could help him discover more information about Simon, and Cookie was right at the top of the list. A trusted servant who had his own room *inside* the house, he, unlike the cowboys, was in a position to know everything that was going on with Simon and his daughter.

He wasn't, however, a pushover. If he was flattered by Steve's compliment, he didn't show it. He shook his hand, but only briefly. "I don't give out my recipes," he said curtly. "Come in the kitchen. I just took another pan of biscuits out of the oven."

Not waiting to see if he followed, the other man pushed through the swinging door, leaving Steve silently swearing behind him. His last chance to look around now gone, he was left with no choice but to step into the kitchen.

Standing in front of the mirror, Lise adjusted the collar of her cotton blouse for the third time in thirty seconds, only to realize that she, Lise Meldrum, was primping! "Oh, God!" she whispered. Horrified, she swore and quickly dropped her hand, leaving her collar just the way it was.

"Quit being a ninny," she scolded her image in the mirror. "The man's playing with you and you're falling for it. Look at yourself, for heaven's sake! You've got lip gloss on!"

Wincing, she couldn't deny it. She'd definitely taken pains with her appearance, but not because she was trying to look pretty for Steve Trace, she assured herself. She was going into town later for supplies for the roundup, that was all, and she didn't want to look like a hoyden. What was wrong with that? It wasn't as if she was dressing for Steve. She had work to do in the study that would keep her busy all morning, and the trip to town and back would take all afternoon. If she was lucky, she'd be able to avoid him not only for the rest of the day, but from now until they left for the roundup. After all, organizing a roundup took a lot of work, and even though she'd been doing it for years, it didn't get any easier. Between now and the morning when horses and men were loaded into trucks to begin the trek across the bush to the wildest regions of the station, she'd work every night until midnight and be up at dawn. She had too much to do to waste a single second between now and then thinking about Steve.

Her chin set at a determined angle, she turned from the mirror, and hurried downstairs to the study. She had letters and e-mail to answer from charities and youth organizations she contributed to every year in her father's name and that took all of her attentions. By the time she finished, it was noon and time to leave for town. Quickly dialing the bunkhouse she wasn't surprised when Tuck answered. They spoke every day, rain or shine, about what needed to be done that day, and she didn't know how she would have run the place without his help.

"I'm leaving for Roo Springs in five minutes," she told him. "Send one of the boys over to go with me. I'll need help loading everything."

"Sure thing," he said easily. "Oh, and don't forget to add metal fence posts to the list," he reminded her before she could hang up. "After that storm we had last winter, we're bound to need them."

"I forgot about that," she said, quickly jotting a note at the end of the extensive list of supplies she had to buy. "At the rate we're going, I may have to make two trips to town and back just to haul everything."

"Take the diesel," he suggested. "It holds more."

"Good idea. As soon as I gas it up, I'll be ready to go."

Her mind on everything she had to do, she checked one last time with Cookie to make sure she had his final list, then grabbed the keys to the diesel truck from a hook by the back door. The second she stepped outside the blistering heat of the day hit her in the face.

And she loved it. She always had. She'd been born and raised there, and the heat and wind and grit was as much a part of her as the color of her eyes. Given the chance, she would have parked herself in the porch swing and relaxed just by watching the wind blow. As usual, however, she didn't have the time. Tomorrow, she promised herself, and climbed into the truck to drive it over to the gas tank behind the barn.

She had a little over a quarter of a tank of gas, but it was over a hundred miles to town, and there was no place between there and home to buy anything. She had a cell phone, of course, if she got into trouble, but she could just hear Nate and Tuck and the rest of the boys, as she liked to call them, if she ran out of gas on the way to town. They'd never let her hear the end of it.

"I must be living right. Is that smile for me, boss lady?"

Caught up in her reflections, Lise jerked her attention to her surroundings to find Steve leaning against the pickup bed on the opposite side of the truck. Watching her pump gas, he had that little grin on his face that she swore he wore just to irritate the hell out of her.

"What are you doing here?" she demanded.

But even as she asked, she knew. He was the most expendable cowboy she had, the one who didn't know his way around the ranch yet and hadn't a clue how things were done in the bush. And no one had time to teach him. Which was why he was the perfect one to go with her to town. He was big and strong and could load the truck without breaking a sweat—and he could be gone for hours and would never be missed.

"And here I thought you'd be thrilled we were going to spend the day together," he replied teasingly, flashing his dimples at her. "Now I'm hurt."

A quick retort sprang to her tongue, but she bit it back, refusing to give him the satisfaction. No, she told herself grimly. She wasn't going to let him push her buttons so easily. So she ground her teeth on the sassy words and said instead, "I don't have time for your jocularity. Get in the truck, Trace. It's time to go."

"Whatever you say," he said with an easy grin. "You're the boss."

It was, Lise decided, going to be a long day.

It wasn't, however, until she slid behind the wheel and joined him in the cab of the truck that she realized just what she'd been set up for. The diesel wasn't one of those little midget trucks that was only big enough for two small people. It was big and roomy and had a cab that could, if necessary, hold up to four regular-size adults.

The problem was, Steve wasn't a regular-size adult.

Lise knew she was no slouch when it came to size, but Steve made her feel like one of those small, delicate women who couldn't open a door without using both hands. Lord, he was big! Her heart thumping in her chest, she would have given anything not to notice, but he made that impossible. Seated on his side by the window, with nearly three feet of space between them, he seemed to fill the cab of the truck.

And it wasn't fair, dammit! she thought as she drove out of the compound and forced herself to stare straight ahead at the road. Without sparing him a single glance, she was aware of everything about him. The irritating man didn't have an ounce of fat on him. He was just big. He shifted on the seat, stretching out his long legs, and she could practically feel the muscles in his thighs ripple.

Swearing silently under her breath, she tightened her fingers on the wheel and sternly ordered herself to ignore him. She might as well have told herself not to breathe. He was a man who was at ease in his own skin and comfortable with who he was. Slouching in his seat, he looked like a big, lazy jungle cat lounging in the sun. She wasn't, however, fooled by the deceptive pose. She knew better than most how fast the man could move when the situation called for it. With no effort whatsoever, she could still feel the strength of his arms as they'd closed around her when he'd swept her out from under Thunder's hooves yesterday.

Her heart lurching at the memory, she reached over and turned the air conditioner from low to high.

Arching a brow at her, Steve grinned. "Hot?"

A blush climbed high in her cheeks. She trained her eyes straight ahead. "It's a little stuffy in here. The truck was sitting in the sun and hasn't cooled off yet."

His grin broadening, he murmured, "I see."

Afraid he did see all too clearly, she pressed her lips together tightly. If he thought she was going to trade cryptic comments with him all the way to Roo Springs, he could think again.

Silence didn't bother her. She could drive the entire way without saying another word.

It was a good plan, but she quickly discovered that Steve wasn't the least perturbed by her lack of encouragement. Content to carry on the conversation by himself, he settled back in his seat with a contented sigh and said,

"You know something? I think I'm going to like it here. It reminds me of Wisconsin."

She'd sworn she wasn't going to respond, no matter what he said. And she wouldn't have—if his statement hadn't been so outrageous. Jerking her gaze from the road, she looked at him incredulously. "I'll be the first to admit that my American geography isn't the best, but isn't Wisconsin up north? By Canada?"

His dimples winking at her, he nodded sagely. "Yep. I grew up there."

"And Wisconsin looks like this?"

When she glanced pointedly at the desert landscape that stretched as far as the eye could see, he had to laugh. "Not exactly. We've got a lot more trees and it's a hell of a lot cooler. But we've also got cows. My parents own a dairy farm there, and I was milking cows almost before I was old enough to walk. I bet you were, too."

She couldn't deny it. "We only had a few we kept for milk, though."

He laughed as he told her about his childhood. "God, it was cold in the winter! The snow would pile up higher than the house, and sometimes it didn't melt again until spring. But my brothers and I had a great time growing up. As soon as we finished our chores after school, we'd go ice fishing or play hockey on an outdoor rink my dad built for us."

Lise was captivated by how Steve's face was alight with memories, his gray eyes sparkling, as he told her about good times and bad, including when the winter storms were so bad that they lost half their cows to the cold. But then there were the summers when there were fireflies to catch and camp outs in the woods and the nights he and his brothers laid out in the grass and oohed and aahed over meteor showers high in the heavens above.

And in spite of all her best intentions, Lise found herself smiling and remembering in turn. Oh, she had never seen snow, and even in their worst winter, they'd never lost a single cow to the cold. It was the summers that were bad in the outback, the summers that could kill. She'd only been a child, but she could still recall vividly the summer that was so dry the watering holes dried up. Dozens of cows died of thirst before the ranch hands could get water to them.

She doubted that Steve had any experience with a drought or could understand why a summer rain usually meant a party, but still, they were kindred souls. As children, they'd both listened to the lonely lullaby of a cow lowing. And if he was anything like her, when twilight fell and the dew turned the air cooler, he would think there was no sweeter smell on earth than the fresh earthy scent of the land.

"I can remember frying eggs on the patio out back and going swimming at nine o'clock at night," she said quietly, her eyes trained on the road and the past at the same time. "I went on a walkabout once with Cookie—or at least *I* thought it was a real walkabout—but I was just six and we were only gone for four hours. But he taught me all about life in the bush, the dangers and the magic of it, and I loved it."

"He's been here that long?"

She nodded. "Since before I was born."

"And what did your mother say about him taking you off for four hours? Was she worried?"

"She died in a riding accident when I was five," she said simply. "I don't remember that time period very well, but I think that's why Cookie took me on the walkabout. I was lonely here all by myself except for my nanny, and he felt sorry for me."

Steve had read what little information SPEAR had on her; he'd known her mother had died some time ago. But he'd had no idea she'd died when Lise was so young. The poor kid.

Instantly sympathetic, he frowned. "What about your father? Surely he didn't leave you here with the nanny and cook when you'd just lost your mother. You weren't much more than a baby!"

The very idea outraged him, but she only smiled ruefully. "And he had just lost the only woman he ever loved. He adored her. Maybe if I'd taken after her more, he would have stayed, but even at five, it was obvious that I wasn't going to be small and petite the way my mother was. He had business interests that called him away, and to be perfectly honest, I think he jumped at the chance to go. He was never happy here after Mama died. That's why he still never stays very long. He misses her too much."

If they'd been talking about an ordinary man, Steve might have believed that. His own father would be devastated if his mother died first. But Art Meldrum was no ordinary man. He was Simon, a traitor without an ounce of conscience who was out to destroy Jonah—the man at the helm of SPEAR—any way he could, and bring down the entire secret organization. A man like that was incapable of love. He was a monster without a heart, and although Lise had, no doubt, had an incredibly lonely childhood, she'd been blessed every time the bastard had found an excuse to leave the station.

That wasn't, however, something she was ready to hear. So he said instead, "Then he should have taken you with him. You were just a little girl, and you'd already lost one parent. You shouldn't have lost the other one, too."

Suddenly focusing on something else she'd said, he scowled. "And what the hell do you mean, your father would have stayed if you'd been small and petite? There's nothing wrong with you the way you are!"

She was, in fact, damn well just the right size, as far as he could see. He'd never understood why anyone would look twice at a woman who was little more than skin and bones. Give him a real woman to fill his arms, not one he constantly had to worry about crushing.

"I never said there was," she said stiffly. Annoyed, she gave him frown for frown and wanted to kick herself for confiding in him. Her relationship with her father was no one's business but her own, and she didn't normally discuss it with anyone. But then again, she'd never met anyone who was quite so easy to talk to. He made her forget that he was not only an employee, but little more than a stranger. She'd have to watch that in the future.

"Anyway, when did this conversation become about me?" she demanded irritably. "We were talking about you. So what brought you to Australia besides a job? I would have thought cowboy jobs were a dime a dozen in the States, so it had to be something else besides that."

Steve didn't so much as flicker an eyelash. Giving her a slow, intimate smile, he replied, "That's easy, darlin'. I'd always heard the women Down Under were something to see, so I thought I'd check them out for myself. So far, I'm not disappointed."

Rolling her eyes, Lise sternly ordered herself not to be flattered. He'd only been in the country two days, and as far as she knew, he'd spent that time hitchhiking to the station. Which meant, in all likelihood, that she was probably the only woman he'd met so far. So much for compliments. It was easy to look good when you were the only female in sight.

"Then I guess that makes this my red-letter day, Yank," she retorted mockingly. "I'll be sure to mark it on my calendar for prosperity."

Far from offended, he just laughed, and that only irritated Lise all over again. There was nothing so frustrating as a man who refused to be insulted. Damn the man, why did he have to be so likable? Couldn't he tell she wanted nothing to do with him?

Yeah, right, a sarcastic voice drawled in her head. *When was he supposed to realize that? Before or after you told him your life story?*

Clamping her teeth on an oath, she swore she wasn't going to say another word the rest of the way to town, and she was acutely aware that Steve seemed to enjoy watching her struggle to keep that promise to herself. Openly studying her, he made no attempt to hide his grin when a kangaroo bounced across the road a hundred yards in front of them and she had to press her lips tightly together to keep from making a comment.

Damn, she was something! he thought in growing admiration. Strong and sassy and spunky. He liked that in a woman. She stood up for herself and didn't take garbage from a man. She had no idea how that appealed to him. Delighted, he almost told her this wasn't the way to discourage him, but where was the fun in that? Settling back to enjoy himself, he let the silence stretch between them and wondered how long it would be before she broke it.

He didn't have to wait long.

The wind suddenly picked up speed, and in the time it took to blink, they found themselves driving through the middle of a small dust storm. Swearing, Lise immediately lifted her foot from the accelerator, turned on her lights and slowed to a crawl. "I hope another roo doesn't jump out in front of us," she muttered, peering through the dust that surrounded them like fog. ''I can't see a damn thing.''

''I guess you have a lot of dust storms out here,'' he said casually, his eyes dancing with amusement as he glanced at his watch to see how long it took her to realize she'd broken her silence. ''There's nothing to block the wind.''

''It's something you learn to live with,'' she retorted. ''When I was a kid, we got hit with a bad one one year when we were on roundup. It was awful. We ate dust for three days afterward.''

''You were out in the bush when it hit? What'd you do?''

''There's nothing you can do but keep your head down and your face covered and try to get to shelter. The trick is not to get turned around in the storm. Sometimes it's better to just hunker down and wait it out right where you are.''

''Sounds like a blizzard, only in reverse. I bet that blowing sand can hurt like hell.''

''It feels like you've been rubbed raw with a piece of sandpaper,'' she replied, grimacing. ''It gets between your teeth and in places you don't want to th—'' Apparently realizing just how personal the conversation had grown again, she snapped her teeth shut.

Glancing at his watch, Steve chuckled. Three minutes. And Roo Springs was still eighty miles away. If she kept *not* talking to him at this rate, he'd know everything there was to know about the lady by the time they reached town.

Roo Springs might have been classified a town by outback standards, but it was really little more than a wide spot in the road collecting dust. There were no springs, no pond, not even a water tower to justify the place's name. There was a grocery store, a hardware and station supply store, as well as a vet who worked out of his home. A small bank and post office shared the only brick building in town, and a gas station and restaurant made up the rest of the business district, if you could call it that. With a dozen or more houses huddled in the dirt, it looked hot, weather-beaten and miserable.

Steve hadn't seen much to recommend the place when he'd hitchhiked through there on his way to the Pear Tree Station, and a second visit did little to change his mind. If there'd just been something besides a few dusty gum trees to add a little more color, he might have found it more appealing, but there was nothing. No greenery, no flowers, no color. Baking in the late morning sun, the entire town was nothing but a dull reddish-brown blob.

In spite of that, however, it was a booming little metropolis, and it was easy to see why. Gas stations were few and far between in that region of the outback, and cars and pickups were lined up halfway down the street, waiting for their chance to fill up. And those who didn't need gas were stocking up on groceries and ranch and household supplies.

When just about everyone they passed recognized Lise and threw up a hand in greeting as she drove past, Steve was surprised. She was over a hundred miles from home! But when he thought about it, he realized it only made sense. When you lived out in the middle of nowhere, you had to go where the stores were for supplies. Lise had probably been coming to town with Cookie for groceries since she was a little girl—and so had the rest of her neighbors.

"Looks like you're pretty popular around here," he told her as he opened the door to the station supply store for her. Following her inside, he arched a brow at the sight of the man across the store from them. "Who's the tall skinny dude at the counter? He's so happy to see you, he looks like he could kiss you."

Apparently surprised that he'd opened the door for her, she glanced up and nearly burst out laughing when she saw who he was talking about. "Fred kiss me? I don't think so! He's just happy to see me because he knows I'm going to spend a lot of money in here."

Far from amused, he frowned. "Don't sell yourself short. Why wouldn't he want to kiss you? Is he married?" When she shook her head, he growled, "Then what's his problem? You're a damn attractive woman. Is he blind or what?"

He made no effort to keep his voice down, and he didn't care if everyone in the store heard him.

Color stinging her cheeks, she looked as if she wanted to sink right through the floor. "You don't understand," she whispered. "Around here, I'm just one of the guys."

Steve could already see that for himself. And he didn't like it one little bit. As Lise walked up and down the aisles collecting the supplies she would need for the roundup, none of the men who greeted her even tipped their hats at her or showed her the least courtesy. When he'd opened the door for her, at least two more men could have done the same thing before he caught up with her, but they let it slam shut behind them without even offering to hold it partially open for her. Steve had never seen anything like it in his life. What the hell was wrong with Australian men?

Irritation glinting in his gray eyes, he almost asked her, but he never got the chance. Their cart filled with the smaller items on her list, they stopped in the fencing department to see about getting metal fence posts and wiring

brought to the loading dock so they could transfer it to
the truck. Before they could find a clerk, however, they
found their path blocked by a group of cowboys telling
jokes.

Greeting Lise with a broad smile, a lean, bronzed man
who looked as tough as boot leather said, "Hey, Lise, did
you hear the one about the chicken farmer and the sex
education teacher? The teacher had this thing about feath-
ers...."

Encouraged by wide, expectant grins and masculine
chuckles, he began to tell a joke that should have never
made its way outside a locker room. Outraged, Steve
couldn't believe his ears. Was the jackass raised in a barn,
or what?

Not caring that he was sticking his nose where some
people might think it didn't belong, he growled, "Hey,
buddy, watch your mouth. There's a lady present."

That should have been enough to shut the other man
up. Instead, he looked around and said, "Where?"

The loser wasn't joking, Steve thought incredulously.
The man didn't even look at Lise, but instead glanced
around to see if another woman had walked up while he
wasn't looking.

Infuriated, Steve wanted to tear him apart. "What do
you mean, *where?*" he thundered. "I was talking about
Lise, you bastard!"

To his credit, the other man suddenly realized what
he'd said and had the grace to cringe with embarrassment.
"Oh, God, Lise, I'm sorry! I don't know what I was
thinking of—"

"It's okay, Gene," she said huskily, quickly stepping
in front of Steve before he could deck him. "No offense
intended, none taken. Excuse us, will you? This is my

new drover—Steve Trace. We need to talk outside. *Now,*
Steve!''

She didn't give him time to argue, but simply grabbed
his arm and dragged him to the front of the store to pay
for the supplies they'd collected. The second she finished
paying, she hustled him outside and whirled on him, her
blue eyes sparking fire. ''What the hell was that all
about?''

''That's what I'd like to know! You should have let
me pop that jackass. He deserved it.''

''That *jackass*,'' she said through her teeth, ''happens
to be a very good friend of mine.''

''Some friend!'' he retorted. ''Does he always insult
you that way?''

''He wasn't insulting me!''

''No? Then what would you call it?''

He looked so indignant that Lise couldn't help but be
touched. But he couldn't go around hitting people just
because they didn't treat her the way he thought they
should treat a woman. ''Look,'' she sighed, ''I appreciate
the Sir Galahad routine, but you really don't have to protect my tender sensibilities. Gene wasn't being intention-
ally rude. He just doesn't think of me as a woman. And
neither do the rest of the guys. And that's okay. It's more
important that they treat me as an equal.''

''They can treat you as both while I'm around,'' he
snapped, ''or they're going to find themselves picking
themselves up off the floor. Now that we've got that settled, why don't you bring the truck around to the loading
dock so I can load this stuff and we can get out of here?''

Rolling her eyes, Lise could see that there was no ar-
guing with the man. ''Fine. Just try not to get in trouble
while I'm gone, okay? I'd have to bail you out, and that

wouldn't make me very happy, and you don't want to see me when I'm not happy.''

Grinning, he said, ''I'll be an angel. I promise.''

When Lise snorted at that, he winked at her and just that easily made her heart thump crazily in her breast. *Angel, my eye,* she thought, irritated with herself as she turned and fled for the truck. The man was a handsome devil and too good-looking for his own good. If he thought he was going to take her in with just a wink and a boyish grin, he could think again. She wasn't that stupid.

Satisfied she had her emotions under strict control, Lise drove the truck around to the loading dock and backed into place. Before she'd even turned off the motor, Steve had pulled on the work gloves he'd brought with him and started loading the fence posts and barbed wire into the back of the truck.

''Here, let me help you,'' she said as she quickly joined him. ''You can't do that all by yourself.''

''No.''

She was already reaching for some of the fence posts. She had hardly picked two of them up before he took them away from her. ''Hey, give me those! What are you doing?''

''Loading the truck,'' he retorted. ''That's why you brought me along, remember? So why don't you grab a seat in the shade and let me do my job?''

Lise couldn't believe he was serious. ''Don't be ridiculous. I can help.''

''Maybe so, but you're not going to. I'm perfectly capable of doing it myself.''

His jaw set at an angle she was just beginning to realize was as immovable as Gibraltar, he gave her a hard look and just dared her to argue with him further. She told herself he was kidding, but there was no glint of laughter in his steely gray eyes, no smile on his mouth. Obviously not caring that they might be drawing the eye of everyone on the store's huge loading dock, he glared at her, silently daring her to pick up so much as a box of nails from the supplies still waiting to be loaded.

Standing toe to toe with him, she should have told him she was the boss and could load any damn thing she wanted. It would have been the wise thing to do. After all, who was supposed to be giving whom orders? But the darn man didn't play fair. He'd done it again, made her feel like a dainty, feminine woman, and she didn't know how to handle it. Without a word, she found a seat on a nearby wooden crate to watch him work.

That's when alarm bells clanged in her head. What was she doing? she wondered wildly. Just because the man had opened a few doors for her and wanted to wrap her in cotton like a china doll didn't mean he was interested in her. No one had ever looked twice at her before, and she didn't expect that to change just because this cowboy had walked into her life. He might have told her stories about his childhood, but what did she really know about the man himself? Nothing. For all she knew, he was just a charming drifter who never stayed anywhere long and left a string of broken hearts behind him. He wouldn't break hers, she promised herself. She wouldn't make an idiot of herself over him and have every cowboy within a hundred miles laughing at her.

That didn't mean, however, that she couldn't enjoy watching him work. With an ease that stole her breath, he picked up a heavy role of wire as if it weighed no more than a matchbox and tossed it into the bed of the truck. Muscles rippled in his arms. His back strong and straight, his broad shoulders handling the task with no effort whatsoever, he didn't even break a sweat. Fascinated, Lise had to admit that he really was something to see.

Chapter 3

From the outside, the Flamingo Café looked like a dive that would blow away in a stiff wind. Constructed of rusty corrugated tin with faded pink flamingos painted on the side, the entire building leaned slightly to the left. It had no class and very little eye appeal, and Steve loved it. The second he followed Lise inside, he couldn't help but grin. Everywhere he looked, there were pink flamingos.

"This is great!"

Surprised, Lise arched a brow. "You like it?"

"Are you kidding? It reminds me of a place back home—the Lily Pad." He laughed just at the thought of it. "God, I'd forgotten about it. It was wild! There were frogs everywhere, from all over the world. And the best frog legs you ever tasted in your life. On Friday and Saturday nights, they had a band, and you could forget about getting a table if you didn't get there by seven o'clock."

"Don't tell Mabel about that," she warned as a waitress arrived to show them to one of the few empty tables in the space. "She's the owner," she explained when he lifted an inquiring brow. "And she's always trying something new—which is how she got hooked on flamingos to begin with. Someone gave her some as a gag, people commented on them, and the next thing you knew, the place was full of them. If she thought she could do the same thing with frogs and actually sell frog legs, the place would turn into a zoo."

From what Steve could see, it was that already. Every available inch of space was taken up by either a table or a flamingo, and whatever Mabel was serving, the locals were eating it up with a spoon. Picking up a menu, he flipped it open and blinked. Beef Wellington, steak tartar, grilled fresh salmon with dill sauce. Who would have thought it out here in the middle of nowhere?

Glancing up from her own menu, Lise smiled slightly. "Mabel likes to surprise people. Believe it or not, she studied in Paris. You name it, she can cook it."

Steve didn't know about the other items on the menu, but he soon discovered Mabel knew what she was doing when it came to the salmon. Taking his first bite a few minutes later, he groaned as it all but melted in his mouth. Swallowing, he told Lise, "Do you realize I've only been in this country two days. Two days! And I've already had the two best meals of my life! This is incredible."

Suddenly noting that she'd hardly touched the beef Wellington she'd ordered for herself, he frowned. "What's the matter? You're not eating."

"Nothing," she said with a shrug. "I'm just not as hungry as I thought I was. I ate a big breakfast."

Steve didn't doubt that—he had, too. With Cookie's cooking, who could resist pigging out? But breakfast was hours ago, and they'd left the station just as lunch was about to be served. Since they'd arrived in town, they'd been so busy collecting supplies that they hadn't even had time for a candy bar, which was why they'd decided to have an early dinner before heading back to the station. Neither one of them had had anything to eat in hours.

"Are you feeling all right? You look a little pale. You're not sick, are you?"

He studied her with sharp eyes that missed little. Her gaze quickly dropping to her food, Lise silently cursed her expressive face and tried not to squirm. No! she wanted to cry, she wasn't all right. Damn the man, why did he have to be so comfortable to be with? In spite of her best efforts to keep her guard up with him, he had a way of sneaking past it when she least expected it. Who would have thought he would like the Flamingo? The men she knew cringed every time they walked into the café, though they had no complaint with the food. And then there were his manners.

The man was a drover, for heaven's sake. A stockman, a cowboy who bummed around the world in search of work. He could have been crude and rough and boorish, but he was nothing like that. He not only opened doors for her, he did it for every other woman he encountered, and he didn't even seem to realize it. It was ingrained, as was his flashing smile and the way he carried heavier items for her without her having to ask for help. And she found that incredibly appealing—and far too dangerous for her peace of mind.

She should have brought someone else with her to help her—anyone else. The other men didn't flirt with and tease her. They didn't make her constantly aware of the fact that she was a woman. They didn't make her wonder what it would be like to kiss them....

Suddenly realizing where her thoughts had wandered, she stiffened, her cheeks heating with embarrassment. If he guessed what she was thinking, she'd die right there on the spot. "I'm just tired," she said stiffly. "This time of year's always hectic, and I haven't been getting enough sleep. I'll be fine once I get my second wind."

That sounded good, but Steve wasn't buying it. Over the course of the day, she'd grown progressively quieter and more withdrawn, and he found himself missing the woman he'd ridden into town with. For the life of him, he didn't know what had happened. Had he said something he shouldn't have? Something that made her suspect his real reason for being there?

Frowning, he thought over everything he'd told her from the moment he'd met her yesterday, but he wasn't surprised when he couldn't think of anything he'd said that she would find suspect. After all, he'd been in the business a long time—he didn't make those kinds of mistakes. He protected his cover at all costs. Which meant that something else had to be bothering her, something she didn't want to talk about that had nothing to do with him.

"Maybe dessert would make you feel better," he suggested. "The chocolate praline cheesecake sounds good."

He didn't know another woman who would have turned that down, but Lise was apparently made of sterner stuff than that. Pushing her barely touched beef away from her, she wrinkled her nose at the suggestion. "No, thanks. I don't have much of a sweet tooth."

That effectively ended the conversation. He finished his meal. There was nothing left to do after that except pay the bill and head back to the station.

The ride home was nothing like the one to town. There were no childhood stories, no teasing, no laughter. The minute they got in the truck, Lise turned the radio to a

news station, adjusted the volume to one that made conversation difficult and kept it that way for the next two
hours.

Another man might have been discouraged, but not
Steve. Settling back, he took advantage of the fact that
she kept her eyes trained straight ahead on the road.
Openly studying her, he said loudly, "You know, sometimes it helps to talk to somebody when something's
bothering you. It helps you get a different perspective."

"Nothing bothering me," she retorted.

"Oh, really? So you're always this quiet."

For the first time since they'd left Roo Springs, she
took her eyes from the road long enough to spare him a
glance. "Not everyone has to fill the silences with chat-
ter."

As far as zingers went, it was a good one. Impressed—
and not the least insulted—he grinned. "That was good,
boss lady. So is that what I'm doing? Chattering? Some
women find it quite endearing."

For a second, he thought he saw her lips twitch, but
then she tossed her head and sniffed. "There's no ac-
counting for taste, is there? I guess that's what makes the
world go round."

"I heard it was love."

"You can't believe everything you hear," she said with
a shrug. "It'll get you in trouble every time."

That was the first cynical statement he'd heard her
make, and he had to wonder where it came from. Was
that really what she thought of love? If so, he couldn't
say he blamed her. Stuck out here in the bush, she hadn't
had very much positive reinforcement when it came to
relationships. In spite of the fact that her parents had supposedly adored each other, Simon had virtually abandoned Lise to the staff after his wife died and hadn't had

much to do with her since. What had that told her about love? That she wasn't good enough? That she couldn't expect to be loved if she wasn't small and petite?

That was the biggest load of bunk Steve had ever heard in his life, and if he could have gotten his hands on Simon at that moment, he didn't think he could have been held responsible for his actions. No one had a right to do that to a child.

One day soon, before his mission was completed and he left, he'd find a way to tell her she deserved someone better than Simon for a father, but today wasn't the day. She'd already returned her attention to the road. Staring straight ahead, she ignored all efforts on his part to pull her into a conversation. Giving up in defeat, he, too, stared at the road that stretched endlessly before them and let the rest of the drive pass in silence.

Even though there were others at home to unload the truckful of supplies Lise had bought, she and Steve both stuck around to help. A stickler when it came to neatness and proper storage of foodstuffs, Cookie oversaw the grocery items that were brought into his kitchen and made sure everything was put away in the right spot. Then Lise drove the truck to the barn, where the ranching supplies were quickly unloaded and stacked in the storage area until they would be needed for the roundup.

Lise had been telling herself for hours that she couldn't wait to get back home and put some distance between her and Steve, but now that the day and evening were over with, she was surprised to discover she was disappointed—which only annoyed her all over again. Damn the man, what was it about him that confused her so? No one had ever stirred her emotions so easily, and for the life of her, she didn't understand why she continued to let him do it.

Frustrated, needing some time to herself to think, she turned to him stiffly as the rest of the men headed to the bunkhouse. "Thank you for your help today. I appreciate it."

She didn't look like she appreciated it. In fact, Steve thought in growing amusement, if her frown was anything to go by, she was glad to be well rid of him. And he had to ask himself why. What wasn't there to like? He was a damn good-looking man. And modest, too.

Swallowing a chuckle at his silent ramblings, he said gruffly, "My pleasure. Any time, ma'am."

Her eyes narrowed at that, but before she could come back with a quick retort, she obviously thought better of it. "Good night," she said coolly. "It's been a long day, so I guess I'll turn in."

Closing the door to the barn, Steve watched her walk to the house in the dark and found himself looking forward to tomorrow. He didn't know what was going on inside her head, but he could count on her to make the time he spent there damned interesting. If the contents of Simon's study turned out to be just as interesting, he'd be one lucky dude.

As soon as Lise reached the back porch and stepped inside the house, the porch light went out, and Steve found himself surrounded by the all-concealing blackness of the night. The other hands had gone to the bunkhouse, and for the first time in hours, he was totally and completely alone.

The house stood before him like a present waiting to be unwrapped, and as he watched the lights go out one by one, his fingers itched to find a way inside. He could search the study in the dark, and no one would be the wiser. All he had to do was give Lise and Cookie both time to fall asleep, and he could walk right inside. The door probably wasn't even locked.

But even as he considered it, he knew the timing wasn't right. When he'd slipped into the house that morning, he'd had little time to do anything except discover where the kitchen was, and the back stairs. He knew Cookie slept in the house, presumably off the kitchen, but he didn't know where. If he tried a search tonight, it would be just his luck that he'd stumble across the old cook's room by mistake, and blow his cover.

Patience, he reminded himself. A good agent didn't rush the job. There was more than one way to get into the study. With a little help from SPEAR, Lise herself would invite him in. All he had to do was set things in motion.

Pleased with the idea, he slipped through the darkness like a shadow to the far side of the barn. Hidden by the concealing blackness of the night and out of earshot of the house and the bunkhouse, he quickly pulled his wallet out of the back pocket of his jeans. To the untrained eye, the plastic card he extracted from it looked like nothing more than a credit card that was slightly thicker than normal. Instead, it was a phone that allowed him to keep in touch with SPEAR from anywhere in the world.

All his senses on alert, he peered into the darkness to make sure no one had come looking for him, but the night was quiet and still. Nothing moved, not even the leaves on the trees. Satisfied, he ran his fingers over what appeared to be the numbers of a credit card, activating the phone. A split second later, he was connected to Belinda, his contact with the agency.

Not taking any chances that he might be overheard, he murmured as if to himself, ''I wish Mom would call so

I'd know how Dad is doing. Lise wouldn't mind if I got a call on the house phone."

"Your wish is my command," Belinda retorted just as quietly. "Expect a call at ten o'clock tomorrow morning."

Not surprised when she hung up without another word, Steve slipped the fake credit card into his wallet, then headed for the bunkhouse. He'd done all he could do for tonight, and it had taken less than ten seconds. Now all he could do was wait. He might as well get some sleep.

When the phone rang at ten o'clock the following morning, Lise was at her desk in the study writing out the bills she would pay before the roundup started. Expecting a call from her father, she smiled and quickly answered it. "Hi, Dad. I was hoping you'd call this morning."

For a moment, there was nothing but a surprised silence before a woman finally said hesitantly, "I'm sorry. I obviously have the wrong number. I was looking for Steve Trace. This is his mother. I was told I could reach him at Pear Tree Station."

"Oh, yes, of course, Mrs. Trace," Lise said, surprised. "This is the Pear Tree. I'm Lise Meldrum—I manage the station. If you'll hang on for a minute, I'll find Steve for you."

"Thank you, dear," the older woman said in a voice that seemed to be on the verge of tears. "I hate to put you to all this trouble, but I really need to speak to him about his father. He's been sick, and I just need to talk to him."

Lise hated to hear that. "Please, it's no trouble," she assured her. "You're welcome to call here any time.

Hang on while I put you on hold. I'll find Steve as quick as I can.''

The second she put her on hold, she buzzed the equipment shed, where she knew Steve was working on one of the horse trailers that would be used in the roundup. "Hello," he said on the second ring. "That you, boss lady?"

Since the phone line came straight from the house, she didn't have to ask how he guessed it was her—Cookie had little reason to call the barn. Normally, she would have reminded him that she didn't go by the name boss lady, but that seemed trivial now. "Steve," she said huskily, "your mom called and is on the other line. She needs to talk to you about your dad. If you'll come up to the house, you can take the call in the study so you won't be interrupted."

"I'll be right there," he said grimly, and hung up.

He arrived at the front door less than a minute later. Lise had never seen him so somber and subdued. His gray eyes dark with worry and his mouth unsmiling, he greeted her quietly. "Where's the study?"

"In here," she said quickly and showed him to the study to the left of the entrance hall. Paneled in dark, rich wood and furnished with man-size furniture that always reminded her of her father, it was one of her favorite rooms in the house. "Take as long as you need."

She slid the pocket doors shut and never saw the smile that broke across Steve's face as he turned toward the desk. All right! He was in!

Quickly settling into the big leather chair behind the desk, he reached for the phone. "Hi, Mom. Lise said you needed to talk to me about Dad," he said, continuing the charade in case someone picked up an extension in another part of the house. "How is he?"

Belinda, as quick on her feet as he, said regretfully, "Not well, dear. Your father's caught some kind of Turkish virus that the doctors here don't seem to know anything about. I was hoping maybe you might be able to find out something about it there in Australia, since it's a different country and everything. Your uncle Wally thought maybe you might try the Internet. Do you know how to do that?"

Searching through the desk drawers as he talked to her, Steve didn't pretend to misunderstand her. The father Belinda spoke of wasn't his, but Lise's. Apparently, Simon was in Turkey, and no one knew why or what kind of trouble he was going to stir up. Uncle Wally—Jonah— was hoping that Steve might find some damning information in the Pear Tree's computer files.

"I don't know a lot about the Internet, Mom, or Lise's computer. I've never used it before, but she probably won't mind. Give me a moment to figure out how it works, and we'll see what we can come up with." Knowing that Belinda would understand that he was telling her this was his first opportunity to get in the study, he switched on the computer and quickly began searching the files.

"Damn!"

At his soft curse, Belinda said, "What is it? Bad news?"

"No," he sighed in disgust. From what he could see, there wasn't a single file that belonged to Simon. They all appeared to be for the station, though appearances could be deceptive. He'd have to go through every one of them to make sure their contents corresponded with their file names. "I just don't see anything that would help Dad. Sometimes these things are hard to find, though. I'll have to do some more checking."

''I knew you would find a way to help, son,'' she said, sighing in relief. ''I've just been so worried about your father. He's had quite a fever, and sometimes he feels like the walls are closing in on him. It's a difficult thing to watch.''

So the SPEAR operatives were closing in on Simon, and he was feeling the heat, Steve thought with a grin. Good. It was no more than the bastard deserved. That wasn't, however, something he could chance saying aloud. ''You know I'll do whatever I can, Mom, but I don't know how long it'll take. We've got a roundup starting at the beginning of next week, and everyone'll be gone for two or three weeks. I'll try to find something before then, but I can't make any promises.''

It went without saying that he would try to slip back to the house to search it if he got the chance, and Belinda knew that. ''I know you're busy, honey,'' she said. ''Don't jeopardize your job.''

Or your life.

Steve heard the message loud and clear and grinned. ''You know me, Mom. I always play it safe.''

When she only snorted, he almost laughed aloud. They both knew nothing could have been further from the truth.

Hesitating outside the closed study doors, Lise told herself she wasn't eavesdropping when she heard the deep, quiet murmur of Steve's voice. After all, how could she be? She couldn't understand a word he was saying. Not that she was trying to, she quickly assured herself. She was just staying close by in case his mother gave him bad news.

And what if she does? Then what are you going to do? a voice in her head demanded. *Rush in and comfort the poor man?*

No! Mortified at the thought, she hurried out the front door to the porch and sent up a silent prayer of thanks that he hadn't caught her lingering in the front hall like a starry-eyed teenager waiting to catch a glimpse of the new boy in town. God knows what he would have thought.

Heat climbing in her cheeks, she sternly ordered herself to find something, anything, to do so she'd stop thinking about the man. She didn't have to look far—only to the flower boxes that lined the front porch. The wilting plants—not even on a good day could she call them flowers—desperately needed a drink of water. Relieved, she grabbed the hose and went to work giving each plant a thorough soaking.

Later, she couldn't have said what made her glance into the study window. She certainly hadn't intended to. It was just...*there.* One second she was frowning at the most pathetic pansies she'd ever seen in her life, and the next, she was looking, straight into the window next to her father's desk. And there was Steve, at the computer, frowning at the screen as his fingers flew over the keyboard.

Surprised, she stood there for what seemed like an eternity, a frown wrinkling her brow as she watched him talk to his mother on the phone. His back was half turned to her—he had no idea that she'd seen him—and before he could turn and find her at the window, she hurriedly made her way to the other end of the porch. And all the while, she couldn't help but wonder what the devil he was doing.

It wasn't that she minded him using the computer, she told herself with a frown. She'd just thought he was the type to ask first. Not only was it common courtesy, but computers were expensive and easily screwed up. She had all the station books on hers, and if he pushed the wrong keys, God knew how long it would take her to straighten things out.

Just thinking about that twisted her stomach in knots. She would, she promised herself, definitely talk to him about overstepping his bounds—but only after she was sure his father was okay. After all, she wasn't so hard-hearted that she would hit him with such a minor annoyance when his father might be seriously ill.

Her thoughts on what was going on inside her study, she didn't notice that she'd saturated her plants until water began overflowing the flower boxes. Muttering a curse, she hurried to the hydrant and had just turned it off when she heard the front door open and Steve stepped out on the porch. She took one look at the grim set of his face and felt her heart sink.

"Your father isn't—"

"Dead?" he said when she hesitated. "No, but it doesn't look good. Mom's very worried about him. He's got one of those foreign virus things."

"Oh, I'm so sorry! Is he going to be okay?"

"It's still too early to tell." Sighing heavily, he swept his cowboy hat off and ran his fingers through his hair. "His doctors are stumped on how to treat it. So Mom was hoping that I might be able to find something on the Internet." Giving her a small, sheepish smile, he said, "I hope you don't mind, but I used your computer to see if there were any doctors in Australia who'd run into this kind of thing before."

So that explained it. Relieved, Lise dismissed his concern with a wave of her hand. "Don't worry about it. Of course you can use the computer. Did you find anything?"

Just that easily, she provided the opening Steve had been looking for. "No, but there was so much to look through, and I didn't want to tie up your study any more than I already had. I would like to come back in the evening, though, if you don't mind, after I finish my work for the day. There seems to be quite a few experimental treatments being used around the world that I'd like to look into further—if you're not using the computer and it's okay with you,'' he quickly amended.

''Of course it's okay,'' she replied. ''I do have to clear up some paperwork before we leave for the roundup, but I should be able to take care of that during the day. Unless something else crops up, I don't have a problem with you using it during the evening. If my father was the one who was sick, I'm sure you'd do the same thing for me.''

Steve nearly choked at that. Simon *was* sick—in the head. He was a twisted monster Steve wouldn't go around the block to help, but that was something he kept to himself. Forcing a grateful smile, he said, ''Thanks, Lise. You don't know how much this means to me. I'll stop by after supper, then.''

The next week was wild and hectic and long. All the fluids were changed on the trucks they would be using to haul the supplies and horses into the bush, then belts were changed, coolant topped off and tuneups done. No one wanted to find themselves stuck doing mechanical repairs out in the middle of nowhere, so preventive maintenance was the order of the day. There was, however, no way to anticipate and avoid every possible breakdown, so a wide assortment of auto supplies had to be packed for the trip into the bush, plus enough coolant and oil for a small army—just in case.

Then there were the horses. They weren't delicate racehorses, but good, sturdy cutting horses. Still, a large percentage of the work would fall on them, and they had to be in top condition. They were carefully examined for health problems, especially strained tendons. Bridles and saddles were tested for weaknesses, the horse trailers readied and extra feed packed, since there was little for them to graze on out in the bush.

All in all, it was a complicated process, making sure there was enough gear and food for a two-to-three-week stay in the bush for eight people and twice that many horses. And that didn't count trying to anticipate every possible emergency that might occur. Steve gained a whole new respect for Lise, who organized the entire thing. Everything had to be coordinated, lists made and checked and checked again—because if something was forgotten, no one was coming back a hundred miles for it.

Everyone did their part to get ready for the roundup, Steve included. He worked as hard as the others in the heat, without a word of complaint. But his real work began each evening after supper, when he knocked at the front door and Lise waved him into the study.

Thankfully, she didn't stick around to see if he'd found anything that might help his father or ask for details of the new treatments he was researching. If she had, he'd have been hard pressed to answer her—because there was no such thing as the Turkish virus that supposedly had his father at death's door. Unfortunately, he wasn't able to conduct as thorough a search as he would have liked. Because every night, after she showed him to the study and left him alone to work, she left the study's pocket doors wide open so that he was in full view of anyone who happened to walk by in the hall.

Stuck, there was little he could do but work under the conditions he was presented, since he couldn't shut the doors without raising all kinds of suspicions. So with one eye on the door and the other on the computer screen, he spent hours going through each file, regardless of what it was named. And all he discovered was that Lise had been running the ranch on her own since she was sixteen years old. There was no mention of Simon anywhere, and Steve had yet to find any hidden files.

Frustrated, he scowled at the screen, his fingers furiously flying over the keys, sure he had to be missing something. Simon had owned the station since long before Lise had been born. There had to be a record of him somewhere, dammit!

The clock on the mantel struck nine-thirty, signaling that he was quickly running out of time. Work started early on the station, and by ten, the lights were usually out. Like it or not, he had to wrap things up for the night. Muttering a curse, he told himself he had time to check just one more file. It wouldn't take that long. It was marked Receipts and was probably more records concerning the station. He'd just flip through it so he wouldn't have to do it tomorrow.

With a single click of the mouse, he opened the file and expected to find feed and vet bills. Instead, old records from the construction of a cabin suddenly filled the screen. Surprised, he stiffened, his eyes narrowing sharply. What cabin? he wondered. On the plane from Cascadilla to Australia, he'd had an entire packet of information about Simon that he'd committed to memory before he'd destroyed it, and there was no mention of a cabin anywhere. Simon owned hideaways—or had the use of them—all over the world, but from what Steve had learned about him, he wasn't the kind of man to be content with a cabin. So what the hell was this?

Scowling, he quickly began to scan the information on the screen.

From down the hall, Lise suddenly called to Cookie, "Did you get the ham out of the freezer for breakfast in the morning? Never mind, I'll do it after I check on Steve. He should be almost through for the night."

She was at the study door so quickly that Steve didn't even have time to mutter a curse. Caught redhanded with a file on the screen that was, in all probability, her father's, if he didn't act fast she would discover the file and start asking questions.

"Uh-oh," she said, noting the frown he had no time to erase from his brow. "What's the matter? Bad news?"

"Just not what I had hoped for," he said gruffly as she strode across the study toward him to see what he had found. "But I'm still not giving up hope." And with smooth, unhurried casualness, he hit the save key, exited from the file and program and turned off the computer.

He gave her no chance to notice that he'd deliberately avoided letting her read what he'd found, but rose to his feet instead to distract her. "I guess you're ready to throw me out of here, huh? I don't know where the time went. It just seemed to fly by tonight."

"I hadn't noticed," she replied with a sigh as she dropped into the chair angled in front of the desk. "It seemed to drag to me. I guess you must have found something interesting to read."

He didn't deny it—or elaborate. Instead, he arched a brow at her in surprise. She wasn't a woman who had time on her hands. From what he'd seen, she always had more on her plate than any two people could handle. And she seemed to love it. Usually.

"You okay?" he asked with a frown.

She should have said yes and changed the subject to anything but herself. As closely as she worked with her drovers, she didn't make a habit of confiding in them.

After all, she was their boss, and it just wasn't good business practice. Not that she didn't consider them her friends—they were, in fact, practically family. But it was better if she kept her problems to herself.

Especially if the alternative meant confiding in Steve. She already found him too easy to talk to and laugh with. And since he'd been spending every evening of the past week doing research in the study, she was more aware of him than ever. His scent seemed to linger in the study— and the rest of the house—long after he'd left for the evening and returned to the bunkhouse, and it was driving her crazy. Lately, she couldn't close her eyes at night when she went to bed without thinking of him.

But instead of assuring him she was fine, she found herself blurting, "I'm fine. It's my father I'm worried about."

"Why? Has something happened to him?"

Caught up in the worry that twisted in her gut like a knife, she never noticed his gray eyes turn razor sharp. "Not that I know of," she replied, "but when he left last week, he said he'd be back tomorrow for the weekend. I thought he would call, but he hasn't, and now I'm afraid something's come up."

Every nerve ending jumping to full alert, Steve had to bite his tongue to keep from shouting with satisfaction. He was finally getting a break! So Simon was leaving Turkey to come home, was he? Why? Was he planning to lie low and hide out from the SPEAR operatives who were closing in on him? Or did he have some kind of illicit business to conduct here at the station, far away from prying eyes? What was the bastard up to now?

Questions swarmed in his head like bees, and he couldn't ask any of them. Instead, he kept his growing excitement carefully under wraps and said with a casualness that didn't come easily, "Does he usually call before he comes home or does he just show up?"

"He just shows up."

"Then why do you think something's wrong?"

Put that way, Lise had to wonder what she'd been so concerned about. "You're right." She sighed in relief. "Dad's not the type to report in to anyone. He never has been." Feeling foolish, she grinned sheepishly. "I don't know why I'm acting so paranoid. I guess it's just because I'd like to see him tomorrow and I'm afraid business will get in the way."

"He'll call you, won't he, if his plans change? He won't just leave you hanging."

Lise wanted to believe her father wouldn't do such a thing, but in her heart, she knew he would. He had his priorities, and business was *always* at the top of the list. She'd long since stopped wondering how far down that same list she was. What she didn't know couldn't hurt her.

That wasn't, however, something she intended to admit to Steve or anyone else. Her relationship with her father—or lack of one—was nobody's business but her own. "Sometimes things come up at the last minute, but he always calls as soon as he can," she fibbed.

"So it's safe to assume, since he hasn't called, that he'll be here tomorrow. What about the computer?" he asked with a sudden frown. "I was going to use it again tomorrow night, but if your father's here—"

"Don't be ridiculous," she said quickly. "He won't mind. Just knock on the door like you normally do."

So Simon wouldn't mind, would he? Steve wondered cynically after she left the study. They'd see about that.

Chapter 4

Lise wasn't one to make a big deal over birthdays, especially her own. They usually came and went without fanfare, and she'd never understood why other people made such a fuss about turning another year older. Years ago, she'd convinced herself it was just another day, which was just as well. Her father never commented on the day and always made a point to be in some other part of the world.

This year, however, was different. This year, she was thirty, and she felt like a kid with tickets to the circus. She tried to tell herself it was because she was entering another decade and she finally felt like an adult, but she wasn't kidding anyone, especially herself. The day was special for one reason, and one reason only. For the first time in her life—at least as far as she could remember—her father was going to spend her birthday with her.

After pulling on jeans and a T-shirt, she tied her hair back in a ponytail and didn't know if she wanted to laugh or cry. Ever since her mother had died, she'd been waiting for her father to let go of his grief and realize that he had a daughter who desperately wanted to love him. But he was always so distant, so wrapped up in his business, that she hadn't known how to get close to him. There were times when she'd even wondered if he loved her. But he must, she'd assured herself. Wasn't it written somewhere that parents had to love their children?

And she was her mother's daughter. Granted, she wasn't petite, but she had her eyes—and her smile. And her father had to see that every time he looked at her. He loved her, she'd assured herself countless times over the years. He just didn't known how to show it.

But that was all about to change, she thought with a tremulous smile. She didn't know what had happened to wake him up, but she didn't care. He would be home by dinner, not only to celebrate her birthday with her, but to spend the weekend. They were finally going to be a family.

Her eyes shining with expectation, she hurried downstairs to breakfast, but her mind had already jumped ahead to all the things she had to do. The house had to be cleaned, of course, and her father's bedroom freshened up. She didn't usually have a cake, but this year, she was baking her own—and cooking dinner. Caught up in her thoughts, she hardly touched the waffles Cookie had made especially for her birthday.

When she carried her nearly full plate into the kitchen, Cookie took one look at it and scowled. "Something wrong with the waffles?"

Not surprised by his tone, Lise just barely bit back a smile. He wasn't happy about her plans for the day and had been mumbling to himself about them all week.

"They were delicious, and you know it," she said with a smile. "I'm just not very hungry."

"You might be if you'd sit back and let someone do something for you for once in your life instead of insisting on doing it all yourself," he grumbled. "It's your birthday, for God's sake! You should take it easy and enjoy the day, not clean the house from top to bottom like a maid."

"I like cleaning house."

He sniffed at that, far from appeased. "You're not supposed to do it on your birthday, dammit! And what's all the secrecy about, anyway? Why don't you want the boys to know it's your birthday? If you'd let me tell them, they'd throw a party together by the time Mr. Meldrum got here, and you wouldn't have to lift a finger. Hell, they'd probably even clean the house for you if you'd let them."

"Which is why I'm not telling them," she retorted. "They've got enough to do without going to any extra trouble for me."

With the roundup set to begin on Monday, he knew she was right, so he let that slide. But he still wasn't happy about the situation, and he wasn't one to suffer in silence. Frowning, he muttered, "You could at least let me make your cake. And dinner, too! Or is there something wrong with my cooking all of a sudden? Is that it? Is that why you didn't touch your waffles? You're trying to tell me something?"

"Of course not!"

"Go ahead. Give it to me straight. I can take it. I'm a big boy."

Biting her lip, it was all Lise could do not to smile. "I'm not complaining, and you know it. This is just something I'd like to do myself. I don't get an opportunity to fool around in the kitchen very often. It'll be like a present to myself.''

Considering it was her birthday, he couldn't argue with that. That didn't mean he was happy about it. ''Have it your way,'' he growled. ''You're going to, anyway. If you'll excuse me, I've got some laundry to do. The kitchen's all yours.''

Her blue eyes dancing, Lise watched him stomp into the laundry room and didn't dare laugh until the door to the kitchen swung shut behind him. His nose might be a little out of joint, but she knew the second she stepped into the kitchen, he'd be there for her if she needed help. After all, he was the one who'd taught her to cook in the first place.

Before she did that, however, she had to clean the house. Usually, she and Cookie split that responsibility, but today, she would enjoy doing it herself. Grabbing the vacuum cleaner from the closet in the utility room, she worked her way through the downstairs, belting out Cher's latest hit as she went. Singing had always been a secret vice of hers, one that she kept to herself because she was so awful at it, but Lord, she loved it. Grinning, her hips gyrating, she could just imagine what her drovers would think if they could see her now.

They, however, were busy far from the house, and she could indulge herself. If Cookie heard her caterwauling, he gave no sign of it. Still sulking, he kept to himself, but Lise wasn't about to let that ruin her birthday. Finished with her housecleaning, she hurried into the kitchen to start cooking. There was never any question of what kind of cake she would make. Chocolate. It was her favorite. In spite of that, though—and the fact that it was her birthday—she would have made her father's favorite, but she didn't know what it was. Normally, just thinking that would have made her quite sad, but not today. Because things were changing. Finally!

Unable to stop smiling, she made a chocolate cake using her mother's favorite recipe, then made a cream cheese icing. Then she started on a chicken dish that was the first thing Cookie had taught her to cook. While it was baking, she hurried upstairs to take a bath and dress.

She wasn't a woman who primped, which was a good thing. By the time she finished dressing, it was five minutes to six, and her father was expected at any time. She hurried downstairs, put rice on to cook then pulled the chicken from the oven. Setting the table in the dining room with her mother's blue willow china, she listened for her father's plane, sure she would hear its familiar drone at any time. But fifteen minutes dragged by, then another thirty, and still there was no sign of him.

There was nothing to worry about, she told herself. He was just running late, as usual. He'd never been very punctual and had probably just gotten a late start. Or run into rough weather along the way. He wouldn't, of course, think to call her—he never did. It didn't seem to enter his head that she might worry.

"This time I won't," she promised herself aloud. "He's a big boy—he can take care of himself. And it's not as if the world's going to end if we don't eat dinner on time. Nobody's punching a clock. Everything'll stay warm on the stove until he gets here."

He was, she figured, bound to be coming in any moment. But another thirty minutes passed, and no plane landed at the dusty runway a half a mile from the house. Standing at the dining room window, she watched the sun sink in the west and twilight settle over the station, and she'd never felt lonelier in her life.

He wasn't coming.

Deep down in her heart, she knew it, but she still didn't want to believe it. He wouldn't just stand her up on her birthday and not even call. There had to be another explanation. Maybe he really was in some kind of trouble.

Alarmed at the thought, she hurried into the study to call him. Snatching up the phone, she punched in the number to his cell phone and waited for his voice mail to come on. Instead, her father himself answered the phone. "Hello?"

Surprised, Lise nearly dropped the phone. "Dad?"

"Lise! I'm glad you called." All business, he said, "I'm expecting some information from a telecommunications company I'm thinking about investing in, and I want you to forward the information to me in London. I'll be at the Savoy."

"You're on your way to London?"

If he noticed the surprise in her voice, he gave no sign of it. "My ETA is ten," he said matter-of-factly. "You should be getting the information I need in tomorrow's mail. Fax it to me as soon as possible. I'd like to tie everything up by Monday."

Obviously, he wouldn't be home in time for dinner— or to celebrate her birthday. He didn't even mention it. He couldn't have hurt her more if he'd reached through the phone to slap her. *Why?* she wanted to cry, but she had too much pride to let him see that she cared any more than he did. "Of course," she said stiffly. "I'll fax it as soon as it comes in."

He gave her a few more instructions about several other business matters, then reminded her again how much he needed the information on the telecommunications company he wanted to add to his arsenal of businesses. Not once did he ask her how she was doing personally or mention the station and the upcoming roundup. Ending the conversation with a brisk, "Call me if you don't get the package tomorrow," he hung up without even a good-bye.

The dial tone buzzing mockingly in her ear, Lise couldn't have said later how long she stood there, dazed, with the phone at her ear. This wasn't the first time he'd treated her so coldly—it wouldn't be the last. She should have gotten used to it by now, but she hadn't. It still hurt every single time.

Angry with herself for caring, she slammed the receiver down onto the base. "Happy birthday, sweetheart," she muttered. "Yeah, right."

The nightly poker game was loud and boisterous, and Steve was holding his own with Nate. They each had a pile of chips in front of them that would see them through the night if the game went on that long, and Steve had to admit that as far as work went, it didn't get much better than this. When he got through with this assignment, he just might make a trip to Vegas. He was feeling lucky.

His gray eyes twinkling, he watched Nate lay down three eights and chuckled as the other boys groaned in defeat. "Not so quick, old man," he said with a broad grin as Nate started to reach for the pot. "I believe that belongs to me." And with that said, he laid down three tens.

"Son of a gun!" Nate growled. "Damn you, Yank, you did it again!"

"Yep," he said, chuckling. "A couple of more hands like that and it just might make up for all the times I lost to you tonight."

"I want to know when the rest of us are going to get a little luck," Chuck grumbled. "I'm running out of chips."

"Waah," Nate teased, imitating a baby's cry.

Sore losers weren't tolerated, and the others quickly joined in the teasing. "Crybaby. What's the matter? You want to call your mama? I bet she can beat the Yank and Nate with one hand tied behind her back."

Blushing to the roots of his hair, Chuck had the grace to apologize. "I'm sorry. I didn't mean—I wasn't accusing anyone of anything. I just..."

Digging himself a deeper and deeper hole, he was floundering for a suitable explanation when there was a sudden knock at the door. Surprised, everyone looked at each other, but before anyone could rise to their feet to answer the door, Lise pushed it open and stepped inside carrying a chocolate cake.

"Hi, guys," she said with a bright smile, not even blinking at the poker chips spread out on the table. "I won't stay. I just thought you might like something to munch on during your game. I hope you like chocolate."

Setting the cake right in the middle of the poker table, she flashed everyone another smile, and before anyone could say so much as thank-you, she was gone, hurrying out without another word.

In the dazed silence she left behind, no one moved a muscle. Then Frankie blurted, "Was that Lise?"

"She was wearing a *dress!*"

"And her hair was twisted up all fancy."

"I've never seen her dressed up like that, and I've been here ten years! Did somebody die?"

"Don't be ridiculous," Barney scoffed. "Did she look like she'd just gotten news somebody died? She was smiling, for heaven's sake!"

Reeling, Steve hardly heard them. Working with Lise day in and day out over the last week, he'd thought he'd known what to expect from her. She never flirted, never dressed suggestively, never did anything that might lead her men to think of her as anything other than a sexless boss. Until tonight.

Staring at the door she'd disappeared through, Steve felt like a man who'd just been run over by a truck. From the moment he'd met her, he'd thought she was one of the most attractive women he'd ever met, but attractive didn't begin to describe the lady when she was dressed to the nines in a dress. Lord, she'd looked magnificent. The blue silk of her dress had exactly matched the color of her eyes and had molded her figure in a way that still had his mouth watering. And then there were her legs. No woman had a right to have legs that went on forever. She wasn't model-thin, but what man would want her to be? She had curves, the kind a man longed to touch, and tonight, there wasn't a doubt in his mind that she'd haunt his dreams.

But even as his mind began to tease him with images of her seductively approaching him in his sleep, he couldn't forget her smile when she'd presented him and the others with the cake. At first glance, it appeared normal enough, but the more he thought about it, the more he realized something wasn't quite right. He'd seen her real smile, and it was nothing like the strained one she'd clung to as she'd rushed out the door. And unless he was very much mistaken, her eyes had been dark with pain. Someone had hurt her, and he didn't have to ask who. Simon. She'd obviously been waiting for the bastard all day, and he'd never shown up.

Silently cursing him, he pushed to his feet and growled, "Excuse me. I need some air."

Heading straight for the house, he expected to find her in tears somewhere, crying her eyes out. Instead, she was in the kitchen, dumping what looked like a perfectly good baked chicken in the trash.

A wise man might have backed quietly out of the room and left the lady alone until she'd calmed down. Steve, however, stood just inside the door and said quietly. "Are you all right?"

Turning to the sink, she slipped the empty baking dish into hot, soapy water and never spared him a glance. "I won't be using the computer tonight. It's all yours."

"Would you like to talk about it?"

"No."

"Sometimes it helps."

"It won't change anything."

Steve had to agree with that. "It doesn't matter if it changes anything if it makes you feel better." When she only sniffed, he crossed the kitchen to join her at the sink and help her with the dishes. "Does this have something to do with your father?"

Her mouth compressed into a flat line, she reached for the scouring pad and began to scrub the baking dish, determined not to say a word. But the hurt and resentment building up inside her were too much, and suddenly, the words came tumbling out in a rush. "He promised to be here for my birthday, so I went to all this trouble, and where is he? On his way to London! He didn't even call to tell me he wasn't coming. I don't think he even remembered. And it hurts, dammit! I just wanted him to spend one lousy birthday with me. Just one!"

To her horror, tears suddenly welled in her eyes, and her voice cracked with emotion. She knew if she didn't get out of there right then, she was going to cry. And that was the last thing she wanted to do in front of Steve. She already felt too vulnerable where he was concerned. If she fell apart in front of him, she'd never be able to look him in the eye again without remembering that.

"Excuse me," she said thickly, quickly turning away. "I forgot something in the dining room."

She took two steps, but that was as far as she got. He moved like lightning, and in the next instant, she plowed right into him.

"Steve!"

"Easy," he murmured, gently closing his arms around her. "It's okay. You're going to be okay."

Fighting tears, she should have stepped back while she still could, but it was already too late for that. His arms felt so strong and sure around her, and she couldn't hold back her tears any longer. They spilled over her lashes and trailed down her cheeks, and she didn't have the strength to fight them anymore. She hurt too badly. With a broken sob, she buried her face against his chest and cried.

"That's it," he murmured huskily, tightening his arms around her. "Just let it out, sweetheart. It's okay. There's nobody to see but you and me."

Later, she couldn't have said how long she cried. She couldn't seem to stop. Time and again over the years, her father had disappointed her, and she'd always told herself it didn't matter. She was wrong. It did.

Hurt, she pulled back to look at Steve in confusion. "Why does he treat me this way? I'm his only child, but he acts as if he couldn't care less about me. Am I that unlovable? Or am I just being unreasonable, expecting him to drop everything and fly halfway across the world to celebrate my birthday?"

"Would you do it for him?"

"Of course," she said simply. "If I had the chance.

Especially for a milestone birthday. I turned thirty today.''

And the bastard hadn't even bothered to put in an appearance. No wonder she was so upset. She was his kid, for God's sake! How could he treat her with such total disinterest?

He wanted to tell her then that she was wasting her time crying over the man—he obviously didn't have a heart—but she wouldn't listen. She loved a man who didn't exist, and Steve knew the best thing he could do to help her was to put the son of a bitch in jail. In the meantime, he could give her something to think about.

"Let me get this straight," he said with studied casualness. "You'd fly to God knows where for your father, but if you expect him to do the same, you think you're being unreasonable. Is that what you're saying?"

"Well, no, not exactly," she said, hedging. "It's just that he's so busy—"

"And you're not?"

"Of course I am, but—"

"But you don't think you're lovable," he finished for her. "That's what you said," he said when she opened her mouth to object. "And I don't know why. Don't judge every man by your father. You're a wonderful person. Surely you know that."

He'd only meant to make her feel better. Instead, he made her cry again. Tears blurred her eyes and spilled over her lashes, and he felt like a heel. Without a thought, he reached for her. "Oh, honey, don't."

He told himself he was just going to hold her until she stopped crying, but holding her this close was wonderful. He should let her go. But he couldn't. Not yet. Not when he only had to lower his head the slightest degree to kiss her.

With a will of their own, his eyes dropped to the sensuous lines of her mouth, and just that easily, temptation stirred. It seemed like he'd been wanting to kiss her from the moment he'd met her. Giving in to the need, he leaned down and covered her mouth with his.

An experienced man, he'd thought he knew what to expect. It was just a first kiss, just a taste. It shouldn't have been anything more complicated than that. But the second his lips touched hers, nothing was quite that simple. Heat sparked between them, setting nerve endings sizzling, and suddenly, he felt like a teenager again, kissing Mary Jo Patterson for the first time. Awkward and hungry, he didn't know what to do with his hands.

Her head reeling and her heart thundering in her breast, Lise told herself she had to stop this before it went any further. She was his boss, and she didn't go around kissing her cowboys! It just wasn't done. But instead of pulling free of his arms as she should have, she found herself clinging to him instead. And she loved it. No man had ever made her feel so small before, so cherished, so feminine.

It was wonderful, exciting and far more dangerous than anything she had ever imagined. Even as she realized that she wanted nothing more than to melt in his arms and give herself up to the magic of his kiss, alarm bells clanged in her head. What in the world was she doing? He was a cowboy, an employee, someone she'd known only a week, for heaven's sake! She didn't even know if she could trust him, yet she was already more attracted to him than she'd ever been to a man in her life. And that scared her. How had he gotten past her defenses so quickly?

Swallowing a sob, she stepped back while she still could. "Don't! I can't—"

He made no attempt to reach for her again, but dropped his arms and took a step back. For once, there was no teasing in his gray eyes as they met hers. "I shouldn't have done that," he said huskily. "You just looked so sad and unhappy and it's your birthday. I'm sorry. I just wasn't thinking."

She'd secretly hoped he was as attracted to her as she was to him, but that hope died a swift death with his words. He'd only kissed her because he felt sorry for her. Hurt, she found herself fighting tears all over again, but her bruised pride wouldn't let them fall. Straightening her shoulders, she accepted his apology with a smile that didn't come easily. "It's okay, Steve. Don't beat yourself up over this. I'm not offended."

"Are you sure? You've had a rotten birthday, and I just made it worse. Why don't you let me finish up the dishes? If Cookie won't mind," he said hurriedly. "It's the least I can do. You can go watch TV or take a bath or something. You know...relax."

If the day hadn't been one disappointment after another, she might have done just that and spent what was left of the evening reading the new mystery she'd bought when she and Steve were in Roo Springs. But the last few hours had been an emotional roller coaster for her, and she was exhausted.

"Thanks for the offer," she said huskily, "but that's not necessary. And not because Cookie would mind— he's pouting because I wouldn't let him cook my birthday dinner for me. He's already gone to bed, so I'm just going to let these things soak overnight."

Hanging the dishcloth on a nearby rack, she checked to make sure that everything else had been put away, then sighed. "I'm really tired. I think I'll go to bed, too." She started to step past him, then added, ''I meant what I said about the computer, Steve. Use it as long as you like.''

Quietly wishing him good-night, she slipped out of the kitchen and hurried up the back stairs to her room.

Left alone, Steve couldn't believe it. Ever since Lise had started letting him use the computer, he'd had to constantly look over his shoulder every time he stepped into the study. Frustrated, he'd begun to wonder if he was ever going to get the chance to search the place in peace. And now Lise had practically handed him her father's secrets on a platter. He should have been doing cartwheels down the hall. Instead, all he could think of was that moment when he'd pulled her into his arms and kissed her like there was no tomorrow. It was a moment that would haunt him for weeks to come.

Need clawing at him, he found his imagination wandering upstairs to find her. She wouldn't be in bed yet, but probably changing into her nightgown. It would be something simple and chaste that wouldn't even hint at the passion in her. He could see her now....

Suddenly realizing that he was standing in the middle of Simon's kitchen fantasizing about his daughter when he could be searching his study, he swore softly, cursing himself for a fool. Idiot! If he wanted to dream about Lise, he could do it after he'd completed his mission and helped put her father in jail. She would, of course, have nothing to do with him once she realized he was the one responsible for Simon's downfall, but he couldn't worry about that now. His loyalty was to SPEAR, not Simon's daughter.

Disturbed that he had to be reminded of that, he made his way to the study on silent feet and quietly slid the pocket doors shut. They didn't offer him much security, since he didn't dare lock them, but they didn't open as easily as a swinging door. If anyone so much as touched them, he could be seated at the computer and diligently searching for a cure for the fictional Turkish virus before the doors slid open.

Satisfied that he was as secure as he could be considering the circumstances, he quickly went to work, starting first with the computer and the financial file he'd discovered yesterday when Lise walked in. It only took him a matter of seconds to find it again, but the receipts he'd discovered yesterday didn't make any more sense today. They were for a cabin that had been built well over twenty years ago at the station. Simon's name wasn't mentioned anywhere, but Steve didn't doubt that he'd had the cabin built—probably as a temporary home until the main house had been built. In all likelihood, the structure had been torn down years ago.

Disgusted, he exited the file, unable to find anything the least bit suspicious about it. He had a sinking feeling that the rest of the files would turn out to be just as innocent, but he searched them all, nevertheless. And came up with absolutely nothing. Swearing, he turned off the computer after an hour, but refused to be discouraged. All right, so Simon wasn't stupid enough to leave damaging information on his computer for just anyone to find. That only meant it had to be somewhere else in the room.

And there were lots of places in the study to hide damning records. One entire wall was lined with books that could conceal a safe or offer hiding places themselves. Slowly, methodically, he went through them all one by one, making sure there was nothing behind them or in them before returning them to the exact same spot they'd occupied on the shelf before he'd touched them. Then he started on the bookcases and other furniture that was tastefully placed about the room. He looked for hidden drawers and compartments, false bottoms, even a secret room behind the fireplace. And still, he came up with nothing.

Frustrated, he was forced to concede there was nothing there. That didn't mean, however, that he was giving up. The station was the one place Simon came to lie low when he needed a safe haven. His records had to be somewhere on the property. The question was where. The station was huge, and easily covered ten thousand square miles, if not more. And Simon no doubt knew it like the back of his hand. If he wanted to hide something, there were plenty out-of-the-way places no one ever went to. With no clue where to begin searching, Steve knew it could take him months, possibly years, to find what he was looking for. "Damn!" There was little more he could do in the house except take advantage of the privacy to call Belinda and report in. Taking a seat at the desk, he quickly produced his phone card and punched in the correct code. "Hi, Mom," he said quietly. "How's Dad?"

"Still suffering from the Turkish virus, as far as the doctors can tell," Belinda replied just as cautiously. "Were you able to find anything on a cure?"

"There seems to be a new treatment in London that might work, but I wasn't able to find out too much about it. There's nothing on the Internet."

Knowing Belinda would know he meant he'd found nothing on the computer, he started to tell her that he didn't expect to find anything in the places he'd been looking when a floorboard suddenly creaked outside the closed door in the hall. He froze.

Later, he couldn't have said how long he sat there without moving a muscle. He kept talking to Belinda, but she was too good an agent not to realize something was wrong. "If you're having problems, you should have told me," she said, reading his mind.

"I wouldn't say it's a problem exactly," he said as he quietly rose from his chair and soundlessly made his way to the door. His heart pounding and his cover possibly blown, he moved lightning quick and shoved open the double doors. The hall was empty; quiet echoed throughout the house. If anyone had been there within the last ten minutes, there was no sign of it.

Slowly, carefully, Steve released the breath he'd been holding, but he didn't relax his guard completely. He wouldn't do that until the day he left the Pear Tree Station far behind. "Problems seem worse at night," he told Belinda. "Your imagination plays tricks on you."

"It sounds like it might be time for you to try a different tactic in your research," she said pointedly.

He didn't pretend to misunderstand. Before he'd come to Australia, his mission had been spelled out to him in code. By telling him to try a different tactic, Belinda was instructing him to move to step two—the seduction of Lise. If he couldn't find information on Simon any other way, he would have to get it from his daughter.

Swearing silently, he wanted to balk at the order. As much as he was attracted to Lise, he'd hoped he wouldn't have to go that far. He liked her, dammit! If he was going to take her to bed, he wanted what they shared to be personal and private and just between them, not something ordered by the agency so he could complete his mission. God, what a lousy state of affairs! he thought, only to grimace at the pun. Why did he have to like her so much? It made everything so damn complicated. He couldn't trust his judgment where she was concerned. He wanted to believe she was as innocent as she appeared, but what if she took after her father more than he thought? It could all be a ruse.

And he didn't mind admitting it scared the hell out of him that he might have misjudged her so completely. He considered himself a damn good agent—he didn't get taken in by his hormones or a pretty smile, and it was high time he remembered that.

"You know I'll do whatever I have to to help Dad," he said grimly. "I'll call you back as soon as I have any new information."

He would, he assured himself, seduce Lise without guilt if he had to. But only as a last resort. First, he intended to check as many places on the ranch as he could. As soon as he hung up with Belinda, he quickly glanced around the study to make sure his search of the place wasn't evident. He took pride in the fact that he'd left no trail that could be followed. Everything was in its proper place. He'd even worn gloves to make sure he didn't leave his fingerprints anywhere but where they were supposed to be—on the computer keys. Then he quietly slipped upstairs.

The house was silent as a tomb. Standing at the top of the stairs, Steve gave his eyes time to adjust to the darkness and saw that only one door was closed. The one, he assumed, to Lise's bedroom. A mere shadow in the night, he stepped soundlessly to the paneled door and pressed his ear to it. Through the wood, he heard a soft snore and grinned in the darkness. So the lady snored, did she? One day, he promised himself, he'd tease her about that.

For now, though, he had to search the rest of the house and every outbuilding in the station compound. Quietly making his way down the hall, he slipped into each room and searched it. Two were guest rooms and were virtually empty of anything of interest. He found Simon's room at the end of the hall.

Even in the dark, he could see that the room looked like it belonged in a four-star hotel somewhere. A king-size mahogany poster bed dominated the room, its rich wood gleaming in the moonlight that spilled in through the windows. An arrangement of dried flowers sat on one nightstand, and on the other was a picture of a petite woman Steve assumed was Lise's mother. It was the only personal item in the room.

Swearing, Steve couldn't believe it. This was the bastard's bedroom, for God's sake! And there was nothing in it. Nothing! No clothes in the dresser or closet, not even a comb in the bathroom. And that said far more about the man than he probably realized. The jackass didn't even trust his own daughter. Why else would he make sure he left nothing there that might give some hint as to who and what he was?

And Lise loved this man. That still amazed Steve. Granted, he was her father, and it was only natural to love the only parent she had left, but how could she have any feelings for someone who never allowed her to get close to him? How could she love someone she didn't really know?

Not sure if he would ever know the answer to that, Steve was left with no choice but to admit that the house was a total wash. He had little hope that he would find anything in the outbuildings surrounding the compound, but he had to check. Soundlessly, he drifted downstairs and slipped out the front door.

The night sky was cloudless and brilliant with stars and a full moon. Glancing at his white shirt, Steve cursed himself for not having the sense to wear a black T-shirt. At least then he could have blended into the shadows. As it was, he stuck out like a sore thumb. Normally, that might not have mattered. It was late, and everyone had long since gone to bed. But he hadn't forgotten the creak he'd heard outside the study door. And he damn sure hadn't imagined it. His gut told him someone had been trying to slip up on him unaware and would have succeeded if it hadn't been for one misstep. Even now, that same person could be watching him, probably at Simon's orders. And he didn't have a clue who it was.

His face set in grim lines, he strode boldly into the moonlight and headed for the bunkhouse. If someone was watching him, let 'em look. After all, he had every right to be out and about at that time of night. Lise had given him permission to work on the computer as long as he liked, and he'd only just now finished. What was suspicious about that?

His strides sure and easy, he stepped into the bunkhouse. In contrast to the house, it was far from quiet. In the dark, six cowboys snored like lumberjacks sawing wood—or at least they appeared to all be asleep and snoring. For all he knew, any one of them could have made it back to the bunkhouse right before he did and was pretending to be asleep. All his senses on alert, he stood there for the longest time, waiting for someone to move. No one did.

Knowing he was taking a chance, he quietly stepped outside again, this time to check the barns and outbuildings. Slipping from the shadows of the bunkhouse porch, he darted to the barn and disappeared into the all-consuming darkness of its interior. From deep inside, he stared with narrowed eyes at the door to the bunkhouse. Five minutes passed, then ten. The wind played with a nearby bush, but the door remained shut. Adrenaline pumping through his veins, he faded deeper into the barn and silently went to work.

An hour later, he returned to the bunkhouse without a sound. Not surprisingly, he'd struck out in the barn and the other outbuildings. And that could only mean one thing. He had no choice but to romance Lise in order to find out what she knew about her father's traitorous activities. It wouldn't be easy. Because not only couldn't he trust her or himself when he touched her, he also couldn't trust whoever had been listening outside the study earlier.

Chapter 5

Long before dawn on Monday morning, the station was a beehive of activity. The wind had picked up during the night, blowing dust everywhere, but the drovers hardly noticed as they bridled horses and loaded them into trailers so they could be trucked across the station to where the roundup would begin later that day. Breakfast—consisting of sausage and biscuits—was eaten on the run, but no one complained. Everyone wanted to get an early start, while it was still relatively cool. Even though the slightly cooler temperatures of autumn were practically upon them, the heat in the bush could be unbearable, and they had a long way to go. If they were going to reach their destination before nightfall, they would have to leave within the hour.

Working to get his favorite mount loaded into one of the horse trailers, Steve saw that Lise was helping Cookie pack perishable food supplies into the propane-operated refrigerators in the chuck wagon, a specially constructed trailer that carried the cooking equipment. Not surprisingly, she was halfway across the compound from him and showed no sign of coming any closer. Ever since he'd kissed her the night of her birthday, two days ago, she'd avoided him like the plague.

It couldn't continue, of course. Especially with the roundup starting. Everyone would be going, leaving the house and compound deserted—and Simon the opportunity to slip back home without anyone being the wiser. SPEAR would have radar trained on the place and know the second someone flew in, but Simon was a slippery devil, and Steve wasn't taking any chances. Simon might have disappointed Lise on her birthday, but Steve couldn't believe he'd come back to the station without letting her know. She had to have a cell phone. Simon was bound to call her. And when he did, Steve planned to know about it. And the only way he could do that was by getting close to her again.

She didn't make it easy. Once he loaded his mount into the trailer and saw that the cowboys had the rest of the horses ready to load, he hurried over to help her with the large box of fresh produce she carried out of the house. "Hey, let me take that," he said, reaching for it.

That was as far as she let him get. "I've got it." Edging around him before he could take the box, she nodded toward the corral. "Tuck could use some help with the gray mare. She's going in next, and she hates trailers."

She wasn't ordering him to help the other man, but she might as well have. Thwarted for the moment, he smiled ruefully. "Sure. No problem, boss lady."

Winking at her, he had the satisfaction of watching her eyes narrow dangerously before she stormed past him with her chin in the air. Grinning, Steve went to help Tuck, but he kept his eye on Lise, watching for another

chance to help her. She seemed to know what he was up
to and gave him no opportunity. Then, with a rush of last-
minute activity, everything was loaded and packed and it
was time to leave.

The men began piling into the trucks, but Steve held
back, biding his time until all the vehicles were full except
one—the truck pulling the chuck wagon. With its double
seats in the cab, there was plenty of room for Lise, Tuck
and Cookie. And one more. Pleased, he strode over to the
truck and slid in beside Lise in the back seat before she
could guess his intentions.

Startled, she stiffened like a porcupine. "What do you
think you're doing?"

"Riding with you. You don't mind, do you, ma'am?"
he asked innocently. "All the other trucks are full."

She didn't like that *ma'am* one little bit, but he had to
give her credit—she hid it well. For just a second, her
mouth thinned slightly in irritation, but then she reined in
her temper and flashed him a cool smile. "Of course I
don't mind. There's plenty of room."

The second the words were out of her mouth, Lise wondered how she could utter such a bold-faced lie without
a smidgen of guilt. It was true that the truck was large
enough that each bench seat easily held two average-size
adults with no problem, but the second Steve slid in beside her, she felt crowded. And it had nothing to do with
his size.

It was the man himself, damn him. He had to know
how impossible he was to ignore, especially after the way
he'd kissed her the night of her birthday. She'd hardly
slept at all since then, and it was all his fault. Every time
she'd closed her eyes, he was all she could think of. Even
now, she only had to look at him to feel his arms around
her, holding her, offering a comfort she hadn't expected.

And then there was his kiss. How could she have known the man could kiss like that? He'd stirred a need in her she hadn't known she had, making her want to kiss him again, to melt against him and make love...

Suddenly realizing where her thoughts had wandered, she stiffened, mortified. What in the world was wrong with her? she thought wildly. She didn't do this. She wasn't the type of woman who fantasized about her drovers—or any other man, for that matter. Her mind didn't work that way. Or at least it never had before. But then again, there'd never been a man like Steve in her life before.

Ignore him, a voice in her head told her. *He's nothing but a flirt, and if you're not careful, he'll hurt you.*

Staring straight ahead, she promised herself she wouldn't give him so much as the time of day, but she'd set herself an impossible task. Every time she drew in a breath, the fresh, clean, spicy scent of him teased her senses. And then there was the way he moved. He shifted in his seat, trying to find room for his long legs, and his knee accidentally brushed against hers. With nothing more than that, he set her heart pounding.

And somehow, he knew it. She could feel his eyes on her, and she knew he was grinning. Heat climbing in her cheeks, she stared straight ahead, desperately trying to ignore him. She was fighting a losing battle.

Angling slightly to face her, he said, "I've heard we've got a long ride ahead of us."

Another woman might have been taken in by the innocent comment, but his tone was just a little too casual for Lise's peace of mind. He was up to something, and only time would tell what it was. Cautiously, she said, "We'll reach the first campsite late this afternoon."

Impressed, he whistled softly. "I didn't realize the station was that large. I guess I've got time for a nap then, don't I?''

She didn't particularly want to sit next to him while he slept, but a sleeping Steve was a much less disturbing one than a flirtatious one. Her eyes still trained straight ahead, she shrugged as if she couldn't have cared less. "If you like. Don't let me stop you."

"You can take one, too, you know. You can even stretch out, if you want to. I'll scoot over, and you can put your feet in my lap."

His grin flashed wickedly in the pale light of dawn when Lise scowled at him, and from the front seat, she could hear Tuck choke on a laugh. And Steve was eating it up with a spoon. Apparently not the least concerned that she gave him a hard look that would have sent any one of her other cowboys scurrying for cover, he only winked at her.

Oh, he was enjoying himself! she fumed. He thought he had her right where he wanted her. Well, they'd see about that!

"Gee, Steve, that's so sweet of you," she said dangerously. "But do you really think there's room in your lap for my feet and your ego, too?"

Openly eavesdropping from the front seat, Tuck burst out laughing. "She's got you there, Yank."

Not the least embarrassed, he grinned broadly. "The lady had me the moment I laid eyes on her. What do you think I've been trying to tell her?"

"Then you were out in the sun too long yesterday," Lise retorted, silently cursing her wildly beating heart. "You've obviously scrambled your brains."

It was the only explanation. She knew who and what she was, and she wasn't the kind of woman a man lost his heart to. Steve might enjoy flirting with her, but she didn't intend to let that go to her head. After all, who else was available? She was the only woman for a hundred miles in any direction.

"C'mon, darlin'," he drawled, pretending her words struck him right in the heart and pained him. "Don't be that way. I know you're crazy about me."

If any other man had said such a thing, he would have sounded ridiculously conceited, but Steve had that damn spark of mischief in his gray eyes that poked fun not only at her, but at himself. And suddenly, it was all she could do not to smile.

"Yeah, right." She snorted, struggling to hold on to her frown. Damn him, why did he always have to make her laugh? "If you believe that, you're worse off than I thought. Cookie, I think you'd better stop and fix him an ice pack. He must be suffering from heatstroke."

Everyone laughed, but Lise saw the look that Tuck and Cookie exchanged, and she could hear the gossip already. *Lise and the Yank are sweet on each other. You should have seen them in the truck. They couldn't stop teasing each other.*

Swallowing a groan at the thought, she opened her mouth to set the record straight, only to close it with a snap. No, she thought, gritting her teeth on the words before they could escape. If she did that, she would only protest too much and stir up more speculation. She'd do better to keep her mouth shut and let the rumors die a natural death.

When she turned her attention to the road in front of them and refused to let him goad her into saying another word, Steve knew exactly what she was doing. It was, however, too little, too late. Tuck and Cookie had already summed up their relationship and come to their own conclusions. By the time they set up camp for the evening, every cowboy on the station would know about the sparks flying between him and Lise.

And that would only make his job easier, Steve thought in satisfaction. He knew cowboys, and down deep, they were romantics. Once they knew he and Lise were interested in each other, they'd take every chance to throw the two of them together. That would give him plenty of opportunities to seduce Lise and find out more about her father.

Then there was the guardian Steve suspected Simon had planted at the station to watch over Lise. He still didn't have proof that the man actually existed, but he knew he hadn't imagined the floor creaking outside the study the night of Lise's birthday. Someone had been trying to listen through the door, the same person he was sure was reporting to Simon everything that was going on at the station. Simon wasn't a man who left anything to chance. He paid attention to the smallest detail, which was why he'd been able to avoid capture for so long. He wouldn't leave the station—or Lise—unprotected from his enemies. He wasn't that careless.

So he had his own man planted among the cowboys. The question was, which one was he? They all appeared to be extremely loyal to Lise, but no one knew better than Steve just how deceptive looks could be. He himself was not who he appeared to be. So who did he have to watch out for? Tuck was big and strong and, as Lise's right-hand man, the logical choice for the job, but he was far too obvious to be Simon's man. Which meant it could be any one of the others.

Whoever he was, there wasn't a doubt in Steve's mind that he would get in touch with Simon as soon as the word got out that Steve was giving Lise the rush. After all, Simon's man, too, probably had a phone that could call anywhere in the world. Steve didn't care how he contacted his boss—he was more concerned with how Simon reacted to the news that his only daughter was being pursued by a man Simon believed was involved in Simon's illegal activities. If the bastard had an ounce of feelings for her at all, it just might bring him running in concern. And that's when Steve would have him.

If Simon cared enough about Lise to make sure she was okay, Steve reminded himself grimly. From what Steve had heard of the terrorist, he didn't care about anyone but himself. If he didn't show, that didn't mean, however, that Steve's mission would be a total washout. There was still Lise. She was a sharp woman who missed little. She had to know more about her father's activities than she was letting on. He had to find a way to gain her trust so she'd drop her guard and talk about it.

That would take time, and he appeared to have plenty of that. They drove for hours, stopping only to unload the horses so they could feed, water and exercise them before they loaded them back in the trailers and resumed their trek north. And the farther they drove, the hotter it got and the more barren the landscape became.

Steve should have hated it. They seemed to be a thousand miles from nowhere when they reached the far northern boundary of the station and finally stopped to set up camp for the coming night. And in every direction, as far as the eye could see, there was nothing but red sandy dirt covered by thin clumps of grass and spindly shrubs with little color.

There was, however, a wild beauty to the place that appealed to Steve in a way he couldn't explain. With nothing to stop the wind, it swept across the desert with a low moan that seemed to call to his very soul.

Climbing out of the truck to stand beside him, Lise

watched him size up his surroundings and assumed he saw little there to like. "You'll get used to it after a while. It's not all bad. The nights are incredible. You can see every star in the sky."

"The days look like they're pretty incredible, too," he said huskily, gazing at the clouds that feathered the sky on the western horizon. "I can't wait to see the sunset."

"You're serious!"

He smiled at her surprise. "I like wide-open spaces."

He was, in fact, looking forward to exploring, but there wasn't time for that now. There was a temporary corral to be erected for the horses, tents to be put up, dinner to make and serve, all before nightfall. They'd have to hustle to get it all done before dark.

Without anyone having to be told what to do, they all went to work. The horses were the number one priority, so they were dealt with first. While some of the men helped unload them from their trailers, Steve, Tuck and Nate quickly began constructing the corral. The sun had already begun to drop in the west, but it was still hotter than hell. And Steve loved it. Civilization was a million miles away—there wasn't so much as a telephone pole anywhere in sight—and all too easily, he could imagine how the first English settlers must have felt when they explored this part of Australia. A lot of them would have hated it, but there were others who stayed and flourished here. Had he been among them, he would have been one of the ones who stayed.

There was something about the place that called to him. He couldn't say why. It was nothing like the farm he'd grown up on—it was far too primitive and desolate. So what was the attraction? he wondered. Maybe it was because he'd become so dissatisfied with his work lately. He'd become an agent because he thought he could make a difference in the war of good vs. evil, because the challenge of that—and the adventure—appealed to him. But lately, one mission ran into another. The adventure was running thin, and the bad guys always seemed to be winning. And he'd only just begun to realize that even when his missions were successful, there always seemed to be something missing. His work took him all over the world, but he never felt at home anywhere.

Until today. Until he stepped out of the truck and heard the wind as it swept across the bush, calling his name.

You're losing it, man, a voice said dryly in his head. *Where's your hat? Maybe you have been out in the sun too long.*

Grinning ruefully, he adjusted his cowboy hat on his head and knew he was thinking just fine. Whatever was going on in his head, it had nothing to do with the sun. The changes were within himself, and sooner or later, he was going to have to deal with that. For now, though, this was where he was, where he belonged. Nothing else mattered.

The corral was assembled in record time, and the horses were let loose in it, then watered and fed. Watching them, feeling like he'd somehow stepped back in time to the Old West, Steve never noticed that the sun was sinking lower in the sky until he heard the clang of tent poles as the other men began erecting the tents. Tearing his gaze from the horses, which reminded Steve of the wild mustangs he'd once seen run free across a Montana plain, Steve wasn't surprised to see Lise right in the middle of the tent builders, directing everyone where to set up their tents.

Unable to take his eyes from her, he wondered if she knew how completely she belonged here. From the first moment they'd met, he'd realized she wasn't one of those hothouse flowers that wilted under the heat of the sun.

Oh, no, not Lise. Strong and proud and in her element, she was like a sunflower that took whatever nature threw at it and still lifted its face to the sun. And she didn't have a clue how attractive that was—how attractive *she* was. Just looking at her, he ached to kiss her again. Promising himself he would soon—and not because of his job, dammit!—he started toward her. He could tell by the nervous look on her face that she saw the glint in his eye.

"You can set your tent up over by Frankie's," she told him, nodding toward the far side of the circle of tents where the big, balding cowboy was pounding spikes into the sunbaked ground. "You'll find everything over in the truck by the chuck wagon."

If she expected an argument, she would be disappointed. Without a word, he strode over to the truck for his tent, ropes and stakes. From the corner of his eye, he saw her sigh in relief, and he couldn't help but grin. He just loved it when she tried to boss him.

His gray eyes twinkling, he ignored where Frankie labored on the opposite side of the campground and marched to the spot right next to where Lise intended to erect her tent. "Actually, I like it over here better," he told her with a mocking grin. "You don't have any objections, do you?"

When she gave him a look that could have killed at sixty paces, it was all Steve could do not to laugh. The lady objected, all right. Her eyes met his, and all too easily, he could see that she was remembering that kiss they'd shared the night of her birthday, and she was determined to keep him at a distance. And they both knew why. Because she was as attracted to him as he was to her. That, however, wasn't something she was about to admit, especially when every one of her cowboys was within listening distance.

Instead, she shrugged. "Why would I?"

"You know," he teased, "I was just asking myself the same thing. And I couldn't come up with a single reason you wouldn't want me next door. After all, I asked myself, what's not to like?" His eyes dancing with mischief, he teasingly counted off his attributes. "I'm clean and friendly, you can take me just about anywhere and I know how to behave. I'm conscientious, dependable and a good worker. And," he added modestly, "I've been told I'm a damn good kisser. What do you think? Want to kiss me and find out?"

Since she knew just exactly how good a kisser he was, she could only suppose he was asking so the others wouldn't suspect he'd already kissed her. And yes, she thought with a groan, she did want to kiss him again, and it was driving her crazy. No one had ever made her feel this way before, and she didn't know what to do about it. He was playing with her and loving every minute of it, and she would have liked nothing more than to give him a taste of his own medicine. And she would—just as soon as she figured out how to do that.

"No, thank you," she said, frowning in disapproval. "I think you've forgotten who you're talking to, Mr. Trace. Or did I misunderstand?"

Undaunted, he only grinned. "I'll behave, ma'am. I promise."

He would do nothing of the kind, but Lise had come to expect nothing less from him. And if the truth were told, deep down inside, she wanted him to tease and flirt with her. But that was something she had no intention of telling him. Struggling to hold onto a frown, she said coolly, "See that you do."

Grinning, he saluted her. "Yes, ma'am. Anything you

say, ma'am, if it means I can sleep next to you. Do you snore?''

The other cowboys burst out laughing at that, and Lise found it impossible to hang on to her frown. Her lips twitching, she chuckled. ''I guess that's something you're just going to have to find out for yourself, Yank. In the meantime, neither one of us is going to be able to sleep tonight if we don't get these tents up.''

She didn't have to tell him twice. The second she moved to erect her tent, he was there to help her, then he started on his own. Lise told herself that the only reason she returned the favor and helped him was common courtesy, but she knew it wasn't true. No one had ever made her laugh the way he did or feel quite so alive. When he set out to be charming, he was impossible to resist. Later that would bother her, but for now, she couldn't worry about that. Drawn to him like a moth to a flame, she enjoyed the moment.

By the time camp was set up for the night, sunset was still half an hour away, and dinner was cooking on the huge gas-powered grill that was built into the chuck wagon. Cookie had steaks sizzling, and the tantalizing scent of the grilling meat permeated the camp. Lunch had been nothing but sandwiches wolfed down during a short break, and everyone was starving.

Hot and dusty and sweaty, Lise was as hungry as the men, but she was more concerned with taking a bath than eating. Grit seemed to cover her from head to toe, and all she wanted to do was wash her hair and put on something cool and clean. She could eat later.

The decision made, she stepped into her tent and zipped open her duffel bag. Pulling out her lightest khaki pants and a white cotton blouse, she added underwear and a towel, then grabbed her toiletries bag. Imagining the water of the nearby springs cooling her skin, she hurried outside and didn't even see Steve until she slammed into him and everything went flying out of her arms.

"Whoa, girl! Are you okay?"

Hot color flooding her cheeks at the sight of her bra and panties at his feet, she leaned down and snatched them up, then hurriedly reached for her other things. "I'm sorry. That was my fault. I wasn't paying attention to where I was going."

That much, at least, had been obvious, but he was kind enough to keep that thought to himself. Instead, he eyed the towel and clean clothes she clutched like a shield to her breast and arched a brow in surprise. "Where are you off to so fast?"

"A bath. There's a spring about fifty yards on the other side of the rise," she said, nodding toward the small hill that bordered the camp to the east. "I can't even think about eating when I'm this dirty."

Expecting him to make a teasing, flirty remark, she was surprised when his dark brows snapped together in a frown. "You're going alone?"

"Well, of course." She laughed. "I always take a bath alone."

His frown darkened; he clearly didn't see anything the least bit amusing about the situation. "You know what I mean, Lise. This looks like it's pretty wild territory. Do you think it's safe to go off by yourself?"

"It's not as if I'm hiking cross-country by myself to Sydney," she retorted. "I'm just going over the hill. If I get in trouble, all I have to do is scream, and the whole camp'll come running."

"That's true," he agreed. "*If* you have time to scream."

Her eyes searching his, Lise couldn't believe he was

serious, but he was as sober as a judge. She had, in fact, never seen him so somber. He was really worried about her! Amazed, she said, "C'mon, Steve, lighten up. I grew up here, remember? We've been coming to this same spring for roundup for as long as I can remember. There's nothing to worry about. It's as safe as a church."

Not convinced, Steve merely looked at her. "I'm going with you."

"Oh, no, you're not!"

His chin set stubbornly, he crossed his arms over his chest and looked at her. "Wanna make a bet?"

"Yes, dammit! I'm a big girl—in more ways than one. I don't need a baby-sitter."

"Too bad. Like it or not, you've got one."

They glared at each other like two gunfighters facing off in the middle of the street, waiting to see which one would blink first. Fuming, Lise wasn't sure if she wanted to kill him or scream, but in the end, she did neither. She'd be damned if she'd give him the satisfaction. Instead, she marched past him as if he wasn't there and headed straight for the spring.

He followed her, of course, just as she'd known he would, and that only irritated her more. Frustrated, she couldn't even enjoy the delicate beauty of the spring when they reached it. Untouched by man since she and her drovers had been there this time last year, the water was clear and cool as it bubbled up to form a deep pool in the middle of the desert. Wildlife—and cattle—came to drink at the far end of the large pool where it was more shallow, but it was here, where the water was deeper and the spindly desert trees hung protectively over it, that Lise always preferred to bathe.

When she looked at it now, however, all she saw was red. Whirling to face Steve, she snapped, "All right,

Yank, this has gone far enough! I am *not* taking a bath in front of you, so you can just turn around and head back to camp. I don't play those kind of games.''

''Neither do I,'' he said grimly. ''Trust me, sweetheart, the day you're naked in front of me, I won't be standing twenty feet away. I just wanted to make sure you'd be safe here.''

All prepared to argue with him, it was several long seconds before Lise heard him. Then his words registered and stole the air right out of her lungs. Gasping softly, she stood there, her hand pressed to her pounding heart, staring at him. ''What did you say?''

''You heard me,'' he growled. ''The day you're naked in front of me, I won't be standing twenty feet away. If you've got a problem with that, tough. I need to make sure you're safe.''

How could he be so confident? she wondered wildly. He didn't say *if* or *maybe someday,* as if it was still up for grabs whether anything ever happened between them. Oh, no, he was much more sure of himself than that. He said *the day you're naked in front of me*... As if it was a given that that day would somehow, some way, come to be.

And that stunned her. Because with nothing more than those few words, she could see herself in his arms, naked.

Flushed, her blood racing through her veins, she tried to push the image out of her mind, but it remained stubbornly before her, teasing her, pulling at her senses. Sure he must know what she was thinking, she pivoted, hot color staining her cheeks. ''All right, Superman,'' she said huskily. ''You did your duty—as you can see, the place is safe and sound. Now will you leave?''

For an answer, he stepped past her and walked around the pool, searching the entire area for any type of danger.

When he found none, he didn't return to camp, as Lise
had expected. Instead, he walked to a nearby boulder,
turned his back to the pool and sat down.

Stunned, Lise was sure her jaw must have hit the
ground. "You can't be serious."

"I won't look," he assured her, staring straight ahead.
"Go ahead and take your bath."

"Dammit, Steve—"

"I'm not leaving you alone here naked," he said flatly.
"I can either sit here while you bathe or join you, but
either way, I'm not leaving."

Lise took one look at the stubborn set of his jaw and
knew he meant every word. Nothing short of a bull-
dozer—or a single encouraging word from her, which he
wasn't going to get!—was going to budge him off that
damn rock.

So what was she going to do? Strip naked with him
sitting only a few feet away? Breathless at the thought,
she told herself she couldn't possibly do such a thing.
She'd never... What if he saw... He would think she
wanted...

Unable to finish a thought, she hesitated. Could she
trust him? She wanted to, but if he betrayed that trust...
Something that felt an awful lot like hurt squeezed her
heart. She didn't think she'd be able to stand it.

Her hand moving to the top button of her shirt, she
stared at his back for the longest time before she finally
said huskily, "I don't trust easily, Steve. Don't make me
regret this."

"I won't look, Lise," he promised her quietly. "I give
you my word."

She wanted to believe him, but still she hesitated, re-
counting to herself all the reasons she shouldn't do this.
He was practically a stranger to her, and what she did

know about him hardly inspired trust. He was a flirt, a man well experienced with women, a cowboy who never stayed anywhere long before the call of the wind tempted him to pack up and move on. For all she knew, he'd left a string of broken hearts behind him and betrayed every woman stupid enough to drop her guard with him. She wasn't stupid and never had been.

But recognizing who and what he was didn't seem to change anything. Deep down inside, where it counted the most, she trusted him. She hoped she didn't live to regret that.

With fingers that weren't quite steady, she continued to unbutton her shirt. And all the while, she stared unblinkingly at his back. She knew he had to hear the rustle of her clothes as she slipped them off, but true to his word, he never looked. Instead, he slumped comfortably on his rocky perch and watched the sun sink toward the horizon in the west.

Lise sighed—and released the breath she hadn't realized she'd been holding. "I'll hurry," she told him quietly, and eased into the water.

At the first sound of the water rippling against her naked body, sweat popped out on Steve's brow. Clamping his jaw on an oath, he sternly ordered himself to concentrate on the sunset, the low moan of the wind, the hardness of the rock he sat on—anything but Lise and what she was doing in the water. He was, however, fighting a losing battle. He glared at the western sky, but it was Lise he saw. Lise, undressing, easing her clothes down her body, revealing her soft flesh inch by inch, torturing him until he very nearly groaned with need.

Without a word, she tempted him. He'd never known another woman who could do that, and it was driving him crazy. One peek, he taunted himself. That was all he needed to put his fantasies behind him. But he'd given his word, and he stood by that. He had to. That was the kind of man he was. And nobody regretted that more than he did right at that moment.

His body tight with need, he couldn't have said later how long he sat there. Time, the desert, his mission ceased to exist. There was just Lise and the sound of the water as she bathed herself.

"I'm finished. Just let me get dressed and we can go."

Her husky words brushed over him like a caress, setting his nerve endings tingling and heating blood that was already red hot. A muscle ticking in his jaw, he swallowed a groan and said hoarsely, "Take your time."

Sleek and clean, her long wet hair streaming down her naked body, Lise stepped from the water and quickly dried herself with the towel she'd laid on a nearby rock. True to his word, Steve kept his back to her, but she still felt exposed. Hurriedly reaching for her panties, she stepped into them and grabbed her bra.

It was then that she saw the snake.

Chapter 6

She never meant to scream. She had a healthy respect for snakes, but she wasn't terrified of them. Normally, she would have seen in a heartbeat that this one wasn't poisonous, but she was distracted by Steve's presence and her own nakedness. And the small, strangled cry escaped her throat before she could stop it. That was all it took. In the time it took to blink, Steve whirled.

Wearing nothing but her panties and her bra, which she hadn't hooked yet, she felt the touch of his eyes on her bare skin and was sure she turned as red as a beet. Then he saw the snake. Swearing, he reached her side in three long strides, placing himself between her and the snake, and leaned down to snatch up a rock. With one quick, hard throw, he sent the snake slithering away from the spring and into the rocks.

"Are you all right?"

It happened so fast, she didn't even have time to react. When she stood there with a dazed look in her eye, he frowned and said sharply, "Lise? What's wrong? Are you okay? You didn't get bit, did you?"

"What?" His words abruptly registering, she blinked... and blushed to the roots of her hair. Dear God, what was she doing? She was practically naked and she wasn't even trying to cover herself! She had to be losing her mind.

Lightning quick, she snatched up the clean clothes she'd brought from camp, looking anywhere but at Steve as she tried to hook her bra and shield herself with her clothes at the same time. "I'm fine." She choked the words out. "It wasn't poisonous. It just startled me."

When she tried and failed to hook her bra for the third time and nearly dropped her clothes in the process, Steve had to suppress a smile. "Can I help you?"

"No!" Muttering a curse, she whirled, presenting him her back. "Just leave me alone. I can get it."

He didn't doubt that under most circumstances, she could easily handle dressing herself, but her fingers were suddenly all thumbs. If he didn't help her, they were going to be there a while, and it was starting to get dark.

That wasn't, however, why he stepped closer and reached for the ends of her bra to hook them together. Try as he might, he couldn't ignore her nakedness a second longer. Lord, she was magnificent! He'd seen her in her work clothes, in her nightclothes, and pictured her like this in his dreams a thousand times. And his imagination hadn't done her justice. She was beautiful. And there was only so much temptation a man could stand.

Gently pushing her hands out of the way, he felt her go still at the first touch of his fingers against her back and knew exactly what his touch did to her. Because her nearness did the same thing to him. Her skin was like satin under his hands, and with every breath he took, he inhaled the clean, enticing scent of her. It was enough to drive him out of his head with need.

Too late, he realized he should have found a way to draw out the clasping of her bra, but his brain didn't seem to be working any better than hers. Still, he couldn't step back, couldn't stop touching her. Placing his hands on her shoulders, he gently turned her to face him.

"Steve…"

Her husky protest slid over his skin like a caress, and for just a second, his fingers tightened on her shoulders. If circumstances had been different, he would have pulled her to the ground with him and made love to her right then and there. But as much as he ached for that, he knew it would have been a mistake. Not only could they be discovered at any moment by one of the other men, but she had him so tied in knots, he didn't know if he was coming or going.

And making love would only complicate those feelings. He might be skirting his orders, but until he had his head on straight and his emotions under control, he wasn't doing anything more than kissing and caressing her for the job. If she didn't trust him enough after that to tell him more about her father, making love wouldn't help the situation. Which meant, for now, at least, that he had to do the last thing he wanted to do. He had to help her finish getting dressed.

"Shh," he murmured. "It's all right." And sliding his hands down her bare arms, he covered her fingers, which clutched her blouse like a lifeline.

"I can do it."

"I know," he said with a crooked smile. "I just want to help you."

She shouldn't have. He was too close, and she was far too susceptible where he was concerned. Her blood was already humming, her senses reeling, just from the touch of his hands. If she let him help her dress, she didn't think she could be responsible for her actions.

But even as she opened her mouth to tell him she could do it herself, she couldn't bring herself to say the words that would make him step back from her. Not when she looked into his gray eyes and saw a need there that matched her own. Helpless to stop herself, she let her hands fall away from her blouse.

"Good girl," he said huskily, and gently guided her left hand through the armhole of her white cotton blouse.

What followed was the most sensuous thing Lise had ever experienced. With painstaking slowness, he eased her blouse up her arms to her shoulders, trailing his fingers across her skin in a whisper-soft caress that seemed to melt the bones in her body one by one. Shuddering, she drew in a steadying breath...and the faint, seductive scent of his cologne. He hardly touched her, yet she felt his touch to her very soul when he pulled her blouse across her breasts and slowly began to button it. With every brush of his knuckles against her breast, with the closure of every button, the fire inside her burned hotter and hotter.

It was torture. Sheer, unadulterated, wonderful torture. Watching Lise's blue eyes turn dark as midnight, Steve would have liked nothing better than to drag out the pleasure of the moment until they both groaned with need, but there was no time. The shadows were lengthening even as he buttoned her last button, and they'd been gone too long as it was. Obviously, no one at camp had heard her scream, but if the two of them didn't return soon, someone would come looking for them to make sure there wasn't a problem. And a fist knotted in his gut at the idea of anyone but him seeing her with her long, beautiful legs bare beneath the shirttail of her blouse and her cheeks flushed slightly with desire.

"It's getting dark," he rasped, and handed her her khakis. "We need to get back to camp."

He didn't help her with her pants—he didn't dare—but he still couldn't bring himself to step away from her. Standing close enough to touch, he watched her draw the slacks over her thighs and slender hips and swallowed a groan. Did she have a clue what she did to him? How sensuous she was? He'd been involved with his share of women, but none of them had ever driven him crazy the way Lise did by putting *on* her clothes.

His hands curled into fists to keep from reaching for her, he stood it as long as he could. But the second she had her khakis zipped and buttoned, he reached for her.

"Steve!"

"Don't ask me not to kiss you," he said, his voice husky, pulling her into his arms. "I'm not made of stone."

Her heart thumping crazily, Lise couldn't have denied him if her life had depended on it. She hadn't realized it, but ever since he'd kissed her the night of her birthday, she'd secretly been longing for him to do it again. Maybe then, she reasoned, she'd see it wasn't as magical as she remembered and she could let go of this foolish crush she had on the man.

But as his mouth came down on hers, she realized she wasn't fooling anyone, least of all herself. The minute he touched her, her heart thundered. The second his mouth covered hers, whatever defenses she had against him crumbled. With a quiet moan of need, she slipped her arms around his neck and melted against him, not caring that they were standing out in the open and one or all of her men could come across them at any moment. This was what she wanted, what she ached for.

Lost in the magic of his kiss and the heady sensations he stirred in her so effortlessly, Lise wanted the kiss to go on forever. She kissed him back with a hunger that matched his and was delighted when he groaned and held her tighter, as if he would never let her go.

The wonder of the moment, however, didn't last. The sun was quickly sinking toward the horizon, and once it went down, darkness fell quickly. Although she knew it was for the best, Lise was flooded with disappointment when Steve ended the kiss abruptly.

"C'mon," he said hoarsely. "We've got to get back to camp."

Dazed, her head spinning and her legs boneless, Lise took the dirty clothes and towel he stuffed into her arms without a word of complaint and followed him to camp. Later, she realized she must have looked thoroughly kissed, but she needn't have worried that the other men noticed. Those who weren't still eating were impatiently waiting for their chance for a bath. As soon as she and Steve came within sight of camp, they grabbed their towels and soap and made a beeline for the springs.

Her heart still beating like a drum, Lise couldn't have cared less about food, but she couldn't do her work tomorrow on an empty stomach, so she served herself a baked potato and one of the steaks Cookie had grilled for dinner and sat in front of her tent to eat. When Steve followed suit and sank onto a camp stool in front of his tent five feet away, she sternly ordered herself to ignore him. She might as well have told the wind not to blow. All her senses attuned to him, she was aware of every bite he took.

That's when she knew she was in over her head.

* * *

The camp settled down soon after Cookie did the dishes and shut down the chuck wagon for the night. He would be up first in the morning, so it wasn't surprising that he was the first to go to bed. Steve half expected the others to stay up for a couple of rounds of poker, just as they did every night at the bunkhouse, but everyone turned in early. One by one, the battery-powered lights in the tents went out, and by ten o'clock, the last cowboy had retreated to his cot and the camp was dead quiet but for the symphony of snores that echoed from the circle of tents.

At any other time, Steve would have been amused. But as he sat in his tent in the all-consuming darkness, the snores of his co-workers hardly penetrated his consciousness. The only tent he was aware of was the one to the right of his. Lise's. Was she asleep yet? he wondered. Or still awake, her body humming like his just at the memory of those hot, sensuous moments they'd shared at the springs?

He could still taste her on his tongue.

Groaning silently at the thought, he told himself to get a grip or he was going to make a first-class fool of himself. But as much as he tried to focus on his mission, Lise was all he could think of. Even though he'd returned to the springs after dinner for his bath, he could still smell her on his skin with every breath he took.

And he didn't have trouble admitting that worried the hell out of him. As much as he'd enjoyed women in the past and making love to them, he'd never let one get in the way of practicalities. With his job, he couldn't afford to—his life depended on it. So why was he letting Lise drive him crazy this way when she was so closely connected to Simon? She was his enemy's daughter, someone he didn't dare let down his guard with. And all he could

think of was how much he wanted to make love to her—
which was why he couldn't. He'd obviously lost his mind.

Remember why you're here, he told himself silently.
*All you have to do is remember that and the horrible
crimes Simon's committed, and you'll be fine.*

Usually it took nothing more than that to straighten out
his priorities and stiffen his resolve, but not tonight. Not
when Lise was sleeping so close that he could practically
reach through the walls of his tent and hers to touch her.
Just thinking about it made him hot.

Suddenly realizing what he was doing, he swore silently under his breath. He needed to accomplish his mission and get the hell out of there. Now. But he couldn't,
dammit! Not when Simon was still on the loose and could
show up at the station at any time. Like it or not, he was
stuck here for the moment, and there wasn't a damn thing
he could do about it.

Trapped and not liking it one little bit, he sat impatiently on his cot and watched the illuminated hands of
his watch slowly move. He had to check in with Belinda
and let her know what was going on, but with the way
sounds carried in the quiet of the bush, he didn't dare
make a call until he was positive everyone was asleep.

So he sat in the darkness for another hour, his ears
attuned to the night noises of the camp. Tent ropes flapped
in the wind, and in the portable corral that had been constructed for the horses, one of the mares snorted softly.
Occasionally, one of the men would mumble something
unintelligible in his sleep, but other than that, the camp
was quiet as a tomb.

Satisfied that he was the only one awake, Steve eased
out of his tent, only to pause, listening. All around him,
cowboys snored peacefully. That should have reassured
him, but he couldn't help wishing he'd brought a gun with

him. The agency had advised against it, however, and he knew they'd probably been wise to do so. Simon wasn't a trusting man. Steve didn't doubt for a second that the bastard had ordered his bags searched by someone in his employ the second he'd entered the country. Otherwise, he never would have been allowed to get anywhere near the station.

All his senses on alert, he headed for the springs, taking care to make sure he didn't trip over any tent guide wires in the dark. In the process, his foot landed wrong on a small rock and sent it skipping across the camp. In the quiet of the night, it sounded like a herd of buffalo running through the tents.

Idiot! He swore silently, freezing in his tracks. *Talk about bonehead mistakes!* Why didn't he just grab a pan from the chuck wagon and beat on it until he woke the whole camp?

Half expecting to be discovered any second, he had a story already worked out if anyone woke and asked him what he was doing out walking when he was supposed to be in bed. He'd just say he couldn't sleep in the strange surroundings, so he was going to walk to the springs to relax. It was a simple enough excuse, and nothing less than the truth. And the truth always made the best lie whenever you were caught somewhere you weren't supposed to be.

But the men—and Lise—continued to snore without interruption, and with a quiet sigh of relief, he continued toward the springs. This time, however, he was careful to make sure he didn't disturb any loose rocks.

Silence surrounded the springs, but Steve didn't make the mistake of thinking the place was deserted. In the cool quiet of the night, the desert animals came there to drink and were no doubt watching his every move. Moving cau-

tiously so as not to startle any of them, he stepped to the
edge of the springs and pulled out his phone card. Right
next to him, the water of the springs bubbled merrily,
which was why he'd chosen that particular location to
make his call. If anyone followed him from camp, they'd
have a hard time eavesdropping on his conversation.

"Hi, Mom," he said quietly when Belinda came on the
line. "How's Dad?"

"We're not quite sure," she said just as quietly. "That
new treatment you told me about in London doesn't seem
to be working. The doctors said we need to prepare ourselves for the worst and at least discuss funeral arrangements."

So Simon had gone underground, Steve thought grimly,
hence the funeral arrangements. If they were lucky, he
was on his way to the station even as they spoke, not that
that would do Steve any good. This far from the house,
Simon could fly in and out a dozen times and Steve would
never know it.

"I'm too far away to help you with that, Mom. In fact,
I don't seem to be much good to you at all. Maybe I
should just quit my job and come home."

He'd never asked to be pulled from a mission before,
and it stunned him as much as it did Belinda. For a long
moment, there was nothing but silence between them,
then Belinda said, "What's going on, son? Is something
wrong?"

Hell, yes, there was something wrong! he wanted to
growl. He couldn't concentrate, couldn't sleep, couldn't
remember his only reason for being there, for God's sake!
And Belinda knew it. That was why she'd felt the need
to call him son. With that one word, she'd reminded him
all too clearly of his cover and his mission.

Unfortunately, he knew what his responsibilities were,

but that didn't change the way he felt about Lise. All he could think about was kissing her, getting her into his bed, and that didn't bode well for his mission. If he didn't want to screw the whole thing up, he needed to get out of there while he still could.

But he couldn't just come right out and say that, not when there was even a remote possibility that his end of the conversation might somehow be overheard. "I'm just restless," he said, and hoped she understood. "You know how it is when you want something you can't have. That's all you seem to think about, all you want. And it frustrates the hell out of me. That's why I thought it might be time for me to come home, Mom. I could find another doctor for Dad who could get him back on his feet, then we could all get on with our lives."

His suggestion made perfect sense as far as he was concerned, but Belinda wasn't buying it. "Your dad doesn't need another doctor," she said firmly. "There's no time to find a replacement without causing problems. Anyway, the doctor he has is doing a wonderful job. I have complete confidence in him, and I'm sure the rest of the family does, too."

He didn't pretend to misunderstand. SPEAR was happy with the job he was doing and couldn't pull him without raising suspicions. Deep down, he'd expected as much, and he heard all the words she wasn't saying. The mission to capture Simon was bigger than any one person, and he couldn't allow his personal feelings to interfere with that. He was a better agent—and man—than that.

She was right, of course—she knew him too well. But even though he accepted her decision, he didn't fool himself into thinking it would be easy. Not after he'd held Lise in his arms when she was nearly naked and kissed

her senseless. After all, there was only so much a man
could be expected to put out of his mind.

The memory stirring needs he couldn't deal with at the
moment, he said roughly, "It's your decision, Mom. If
you're happy with the way things are, then we'll just go
on as we are. If you change your mind, let me know."

She wouldn't, and they both knew it, which meant he
was stuck. Like it or not, if he didn't discover any new
information on Simon soon, he would be forced to rethink
his decision not to seduce Lise to find out where her father
was. And everything inside him rebelled at the thought.
If he did decide to follow orders and go through with it—
and that was still a very big if—it would only be because
he was a professional and he'd made a commitment to
SPEAR. If his emotions were much more involved than
they should be, that was no one's business but his own.
Somehow, he'd learn to deal with it. *If* he made that decision.

"I've got to go," he said huskily. "Work starts early
in the morning. I'll call again when I can."

Hanging up, he returned his phone to his wallet and
quietly made his way to camp. Caught up in his troubled
thoughts, he never saw the observer who stood thirty
yards away in the thick shadows of the moonless night
and watched his every move.

She didn't sleep…at least, not peacefully. And it was
all Steve's fault. Every time her brain finally shut down
and she fell asleep, Steve crawled into her dreams. Time
and again over the course of the night, she relived those
hot, sensuous moments at the springs when he'd reached
for her. And time and again, she woke with her heart
pounding and her body hungry for his touch.

It was enough to drive a perfectly sane women right

over the edge. Frustrated, more tired than when she went to bed, she was in a bear of a mood the next morning, and it was all Steve's fault. He'd done this to her, he'd driven her to this, and she'd finally figured out why. He was playing with her. There was no other explanation. He was an attractive man with more experience in his little finger than she had in her entire body, and flirting came as naturally to him as breathing. He didn't mean anything by it—he was just teasing her.

And it had to stop. Because this wasn't fun for her anymore. She didn't have any defenses where he was concerned, and when he kissed her, she didn't want it to be a game. She didn't want him to tease her and touch her and kiss her just because he was bored and looking for a distraction. She wanted it to be for real, because he couldn't help himself, because he was as drawn to her as she was to him.

Instead, he was just passing time.

No more, she thought grimly as she pulled on her clothes, then stomped into her boots before heading for the chuck wagon for breakfast. She couldn't stand any more of this. It had to stop. Now!

He was the first person she saw when she joined the others at the chuck wagon, but he was involved in a conversation with Barney and made no attempt to join her when she took a seat with the rest of the men. Thankful for small blessings and the chance to eat her breakfast without having to confront him, she dug into scrambled eggs and bacon and coffee that was strong enough to choke a horse.

Breakfast, however, was not a meal that could be lingered over. Not when the sun was breaking over the horizon and they were burning daylight. By unspoken agreement, everyone finished at the same time, dumped their empty plates in the dishpan Cookie used to wash dishes, then hurried to the corral to saddle their mounts. It was time to go to work.

Lise had brought Thunder because he was an excellent cutting horse and could work for hours at a time without tiring. And there was nothing that he loved more than roundup. Snorting restlessly as she bridled him and threw a saddle blanket on his back, she could feel the excitement coursing through his big body. He was as anxious as she to get out in the bush. His ears were cocked forward, his big brown eyes sharp with intelligence. The second Lise settled on his back, he would be anxious to be off.

"Easy, big boy," she said softly. "We've got a full day ahead of us, so let's pace ourselves, okay? You'll get your chance to run later."

Appearing suddenly on the other side of Thunder, Steve grinned at her over the horse's back. "I just love it when you call me big boy. And here I thought you hadn't noticed."

He kept his voice down, thankfully, so the other men didn't hear, but that glint was back in his eyes, the one that always set Lise's heart thundering. With nothing more than a single look, he reminded her of last night and those heated moments she'd spent in his arms. Just that easily, he made her ache.

Horrified by how badly she wanted to feel his arms around her and his mouth on hers, she snapped, "Stop it, Steve! I mean it. I know you're just teasing, but find some other way to amuse yourself, okay? You don't have to flirt with me just because I'm the only woman within a hundred miles. I don't expect it or want it. Okay? Do we understand each other?"

Shocked, Steve understood, all right, and he didn't like it one little bit. She still thought he was like her father and was only attracted to small, petite women who were so fragile that they'd break if you looked at them wrong. And that infuriated him. He'd held her in his arms and kissed her like there was no tomorrow. Did she think he'd faked what she did to him? Did she really think he was that much of a bastard?

Hurt, more angry than he'd been in a long time, he should have turned and walked away before he did something stupid. But he'd be damned if he'd let her run him off like a dog with his tail between his legs.

Stepping around Thunder to join her on her side of the horse, he growled, "So you think I'm amusing myself, do you? That I couldn't possibly be attracted to you? Is that what you're saying?"

He reached for her, drew her up on her toes and saw her eyes widen in surprise. But she didn't back down. Oh, no, not Lise Meldrum. She threw up her chin and had no idea how much he admired her for that. He wasn't trying to intimidate her—he'd never do that!—but Lord, he liked a woman who stood up for herself!

Her eyes boldly meeting his, she retorted, "So what if I am? You can't deny you're a flirt."

No, he couldn't—he didn't even try. He liked women and he wasn't going to apologize for that. "That doesn't mean I'm not attracted to you."

"Quit saying that! You're attracted to cute little blondes, just like every other man, and that's something I'll never be. So quit making fun of me. I don't like it, dammit!"

They were practically shouting at each other and totally oblivious to the fact that they were drawing the eye of every man in camp. Even if he'd known, Steve wouldn't have cared. She thought he was making fun of her! That he was the type of man who would do such a thing.

Furious, he tightened his grip on her arms and drew her close, then closer still. His gray eyes glaring into her blue ones, he snarled, "I don't know who gave you such a poor opinion of yourself, but don't you ever insult yourself or me that way again. In case you hadn't noticed, lady, I want you, and that's not something a man can fake!"

Just to make sure she got the message, he hauled her flush against him, buried his hands in the wild mane of her hair and kissed her with all the hurt and anger raging inside him.

He couldn't, however, do anything to physically hurt her. The second his mouth covered hers, his temper died, and just that quickly, the kiss gentled and softened. Heat sizzled between them, and with a hungry murmur, he slipped his arms around her, cradling her against the entire length of his body, and deepened the kiss.

Every nerve ending attuned to the thundering of his heart against hers and the feel of his mouth against hers, Lise couldn't breathe, couldn't think, couldn't do anything but feel. And what he did to her made her feel wonderful. *He* felt wonderful. Hard and strong and steady as a rock. She wasn't a woman who needed a man to watch over her. She could take care of herself—she always had. But when he held her as if she was more precious than gold, she loved it.

Enchanted, she could have spent the next hour just kissing him. With a soft moan, she stood higher on her tiptoes and wrapped her arms around his neck, not caring that every one of her cowboys was watching the show. Nothing mattered but Steve...and kissing him.

She thought he felt the same way. She could have sworn he was just as caught up in the kiss as she was. But the second her arms circled his neck, everything changed. He stiffened, and before she could wonder what went wrong, his hands settled on her shoulders. A split second later, he abruptly set her away from him.

Stunned, still reeling from the punch of his kiss, she stared at him with eyes dark with need. "Steve..."

His eyes still hot with temper, he growled, "Save it. You've said more than enough already."

Without another word, he turned and stormed over to his mount, leaving her staring after him in chagrin. She'd offended him, and that was the last thing she'd meant to do.

Clearing his throat, Tuck said, "We're wasted enough time, people. Let's get to work."

He didn't have to say it twice. Everyone grabbed their mounts and stepped into the saddle. A few short seconds later, they rode out of camp just as the sun cleared the horizon. Normally, Lise would have been at the head of the group with Tuck, leading the way. But Steve had already taken a position at the older man's right flank, and he was studiously ignoring her. Hanging back, she clung to the rear and gave him the space he seemed to need.

She told herself that he wasn't the type of man to hold a grudge. He'd get over his anger. All she had to do was give him a little time to cool off, and he'd come around.

But one hour gave way to another, and another still, and he made sure that he didn't come anywhere near her. He joked with the other men as they worked, but whenever she joined in the conversation, he shut up like a clam and let the others do the talking. When they all returned to camp for lunch, he pointedly sat at the far end of the portable table Cookie had set up and pretended she didn't exist.

And the afternoon wasn't any better. He kept his distance as much as he could, and whenever he was forced to talk to her, which wasn't often, he kept the conversation strictly limited to work. There was no teasing, no flirting, and Lise was stunned to discover just how much she missed it and the mischief that usually danced in his eyes whenever they met hers. But it was when he called her Ms. Meldrum in a cool, distant voice that she realized just how much she had offended him.

She had to apologize. As they all returned to camp at the end of the day for supper, he didn't spare her so much as a glance, and she knew she had to find a way to mend fences with him. She wanted the old Steve back. In spite of the fact that he knew just how to push her buttons and seemed to relish doing that, she'd never felt so alive as when they were sparring with each other. That was the man she wanted back, the irreverent, devilish, fun-loving Steve, and if she had unthinkingly insulted him, then she would certainly apologize.

Not, however, in front of her men. The two of them had already put on enough of a show for the hands—whatever else they had to say to each other would be said in private. So she waited impatiently for supper to be over, then for the men to retreat to the springs for their baths. When Steve slipped into his tent to collect clean clothes before joining the others, she saw her chance.

The flap to his tent was open, but she didn't dare enter without his permission. Knocking quietly on the metal framework of the tent, she said softly, "Knock, knock. May I come in?"

For a moment, she thought he was going to turn her down flat. Glancing sharply over his shoulder, he scowled at her for a long, silent moment, considering, before he finally nodded curtly. "You're the boss. You can do any damn thing you like."

So he wasn't going to make this easy for her. Accepting

that it was no more than she deserved after the way she'd insulted him, she stepped across the threshold. "I don't blame you for being angry with me," she said huskily, gripping her hands together in front of her. "I realize now how I offended you, and I'd like to apologize. I never meant to insult you."

If he'd had a choice, Steve liked to think he would have held on to his anger and refused to accept her apology. Considering how susceptible he was to her, it would have been the smart thing to do and given him some emotional distance. And emotional distance, he was discovering, was something he desperately needed with the lady.

But he had a mission to complete. Like it or not, he wasn't going to be able to find out jack squat about Simon or his illicit activities if he wasn't talking to her. He needed her help. He still wasn't prepared to make love to her for the agency, but if her feelings for him became deeper than mere lust, he could use that to his advantage. Because a woman in love would tell a man just about anything he wanted to know.

His stomach knotted in distaste at the thought, and for the first time in all the years he'd worked for SPEAR, he hated what he had to do as an operative. There was, unfortunately, nothing he could do about that. He had to use her, and he felt guilty as hell about it. She was a good woman, dammit! And the only way he could make it up to her was to make her feel good about herself. He hoped after he was gone she'd remember that.

"I don't know what's wrong with the men around here," he said quietly, meaning every word, "but they must all be blind. You're an incredibly attractive woman. Why can't they see that? Why can't *you* see that?"

Tears welled in Lise's eyes at his words. Touched,

thankful that he was finally talking to her again, she found herself telling him things she'd never confided to anyone in her life. "Because no one's ever told me I was pretty before," she said huskily. "My mother was like a china doll, and my father was crazy about her. When she had new shoes, he'd carry her from the drive to the house so she wouldn't get them dirty. I can remember my mother laughing and throwing her arms around his neck, and I always wished Dad would do the same thing to me, but he never did. I thought it was because I wasn't small like my mother."

"Lise—"

"Looking back, I realize that he was so wrapped up in my mother that he couldn't see anyone else but her, but as a child, I assumed there had to be something wrong with me. And no one ever did or said anything to make me feel differently. I didn't get invited to the local dances. No one flirted with me the way you do. I could stand toe to toe with the boys and look them in the eye, and I guess I intimidated them. They didn't seem to think I was attractive, so neither did I."

She offered the explanation simply, without apology or anger, blaming no one, and it was all Steve could do not to sweep her into his arms, carry her to his cot and show her how she could ignite a fire in him that burned all the way to his soul. But if he did, he wasn't sure he'd be able to stop. So he took her into his arms and had to be content with kissing her like there was no tomorrow.

When he finally let her up for air, he was hot and hard, and she was clinging to him. Letting her go was the hardest thing he'd ever done. "One day soon," he promised her roughly, "I'm going to show you just how beautiful you are. And when I do, you'll never doubt yourself again."

Chapter 7

He didn't kiss her again for days.

His promise ringing in her ears, Lise found herself watching Steve every chance she got...and waiting. Waiting for the moment when he reached for her again, kissed her again, made good on his promise to show her just how pretty she was.

Just thinking about it made her heart turn over in her breast. How would he do it? she wondered, a shy smile of anticipation curling the corners of her mouth. Day after day, work brought them together, and although he didn't bring up the subject again, it was there every time their eyes met. And without saying a word, he made her want him.

Their relationship had changed subtly, in the most fantastic way, and she loved it. Oh, he still teased her, but she had a feeling that was for appearance's sake so the other men wouldn't guess how serious he was. She knew, though—she saw the dark promise in his eyes—and she couldn't sleep at night without dreaming of the moment when he would take her in his arms. This time, she promised herself, he wouldn't let her go.

On the fourth day of the roundup, the entire camp picked up and moved again, this time twenty miles toward the station. As soon as the tents, corral and chuck wagon were set up, everyone but Cookie immediately saddled up and went to work.

Riding into the bush with the men, Lise told herself she wasn't deliberately seeking out Steve. It was just coincidence that she and he both ended up checking a cross fence while the rest of the men began to round up the cattle. When they found a stretch of downed fence, it was only natural that they ended up repairing it together.

It was a relatively small job, one that could have easily been completed in less than an hour, but it took them twice that long. Setting new fence post and stringing barbed wire, they talked as they worked and never noticed the passage of time.

"So you went to school over the radio?" Steve said with a frown as he strung a second row of wire. "How did that work? Did you mail your homework in or what?"

"We had two-way radios that we used to communicate with the teachers at Schools of the Air," she explained as she helped secure the wire to the post. "This far from town, it's the only practical way to have a school."

Moving to the next section of fence that needed to be mended, she stopped suddenly, lifted her nose to the air and sniffed. "Mmmm. I smell roses."

"Yeah, right," Steve retorted, grinning. "We're in the middle of the desert. There can't be a rosebush within a thousand miles of here."

"Actually, there used to be one about a half mile past those rocks over there," she said, nodding at a strange assortment of rocks piled on top of each other like a small fort off to her left.

"What do you mean, used to be? If it's dead, you can't smell it. Hell, you couldn't smell it if it was alive, not if it's a half mile from here."

"This is the bush, Steve," she retorted with a wry smile. "The Aboriginals will tell you that a lot of strange things happen here. I don't know what it is about this area, but I know that my mother did plant a yellow rose-bush in the front yard of the cabin she and my father built when they first bought the station. The rosebush died before I was born, and my mother never tried to plant another one, but every time I get anywhere close to the cabin, I swear I can smell roses."

For a split second, everything inside Steve went still. Was this the cabin he'd found the receipts for in the computer? He'd assumed it was destroyed when the main house was built. Questions hammering in his head, he said casually, "I don't know what you're smelling, but it's not roses. Maybe your mother planted some other kind of plant."

"No, she learned her lesson with the roses. The water table in this area is really low. That's why my parents didn't build the main house here. They didn't realize how dry it was until they built the cabin."

"That must have been tough," he said, "living way out here without much water." Watching her like a hawk, he had to fight the urge to pump her for more information too fast. If he was too pushy, she might get suspicious and clam up on him.

"Actually, they were very happy at the cabin," she said absently as she concentrated on making sure the new fence they'd constructed was tight and sound. "My mother loved it there. That's why my father made sure the cabin was kept up all these years—he knew how much it meant to her.''

''You mean it's just like it was when they were living there?''

''I don't know,'' she said with a shrug. ''I've never been inside. No one has but my father.''

Bingo! Every nerve ending in his body on alert, Steve arched a brow at her. ''Why?''

''It's a special place,'' she replied quietly. ''My father goes there sometimes when he's home…to grieve.''

Steve sincerely doubted that. Another man might have still grieved for his dead wife after all these years, but Steve had a hard time believing that a cold bastard like Simon could have loved any woman that much. If he was going to the cabin by himself and not allowing anyone inside, he was hiding something, and it was a fair bet that it was records of his traitorous activities.

Finally! Steve thought in satisfaction. He was getting somewhere. Now all he had to do was to slip away from the others and search the cabin, and he wouldn't have to seduce Lise. When he eventually made love to her—and it was only a matter of time before that happened—it would be for himself.

Caught up in his thoughts and the fence repairs, he didn't notice that the wind had picked up until it suddenly threatened to blow his cowboy hat off. Grabbing it, he glanced up…and stopped dead in his tracks at the sight of the dark red cloud of dust swirling across the bush a half mile to the east. ''What the hell!''

At his side, Lise, looked up and went pale as a ghost. ''A dust storm! And it's coming this way. We've got to get out of here! Now!''

She didn't have to tell Steve twice. The urgency in her voice had him reaching for the reins to his horse and hers before the words were even out of her mouth. A heartbeat later, they were both in the saddle and riding hell-bent for leather, uncaring that they'd left their tools and fencing supplies behind them in the dirt.

There was no way they were going to outrun the storm, and they both knew it. Dust particles were already peppering them from the back, stinging their skin through their clothes, and the situation was quickly becoming desperate. They only had minutes before they would be engulfed by the storm, and camp—and the shelter of their tents—was still miles away.

"This way!" Lise said hoarsely, turning Thunder toward the rock formation three hundred yards away.

The wind rushed at them from behind with an angry snarl, tearing at their clothes and hair and half blinding them. Her heart in her throat, Lise hunkered down in her saddle and draped herself over Thunder's neck, urging him to go faster. Beside her, Steve did the same thing on his mount. They seemed, however, to be moving in slow motion. The storm was right on their heels, threatening to swallow them whole any second now, and the safety of the rocks never got any closer.

Just when Lise was sure they didn't stand a chance, time jumped into fast forward. They galloped into the circle of rocks and pulled up sharply as the full force of the storm hit. Before she could cry out a warning, the blowing sand blasted her, cutting through her clothes and filling her nose and throat. Choking, blinded by the thick dust, she slid off Thunder and clung to the saddle, coughing as she tried to find her bearings.

"There's a cave!" she called hoarsely to Steve, only to lose sight of him in the cloud of dirt. "Steve? Where are you? I can't see you."

"Here," he growled. Appearing beside her out of nowhere, he looked like a bank robber with his hat pulled low over his eyes and a handkerchief tied over his nose and mouth. "Hold on." And with no more warning than that, he swept her off her feet and strode through the storm like Rhett Butler carrying Scarlett up the stairs of Tara.

Lise buried her face against his throat. She never knew how he found the cave. The storm had caught her off guard, and she was totally disoriented. Not even sure which direction they were moving, she couldn't have found the cave if her life had depended on it.

Steve didn't have that problem. In a matter of moments, he stepped into the dark, cool confines of the cave. Only when they were far enough from the entrance to escape the blowing sand did he stop and set her gently on her feet.

"Are you all right?"

In the silence of the cave, his voice was deep and raspy. Shivering from their ordeal, Lise was thankful he continued to hold her tightly. She couldn't remember the last time she'd had such a close call, and she was still shaky. "Just give me a minute," she replied hoarsely. "I've seen dust storms before, but always from the security of the house. That was too close for comfort."

Steve agreed. Holding her close, he couldn't remember the last time a storm had blown up so quickly without him noticing it. It wouldn't have this time, he was forced to admit, if he hadn't been so distracted by Lise. She'd smiled at him and confided in him, and he'd forgotten what planet he was on.

And things weren't much better now. Outside, the storm continued to rage, howling like a banshee, but it was Lise who had his full attention. She was trembling, and that was nearly his undoing. She was a strong woman—she didn't get rattled very often. When she did, all he wanted to do was wrap her close and protect her.

Knowing that, he should have released her and put as much distance as possible between them. He ached to make love to her, but it wasn't going to be here, dammit. She was an innocent and deserved more than the dusty floor of a shallow cave.

Still, he couldn't bring himself to step away from her. Not yet. Tenderness tugging at his heart, he pulled his handkerchief from where it had slipped down around his throat and gently wiped the dust and sand from her face.

Blushing, she cringed in embarrassment and caught at his hand. "I must look like I've been rolling around in the dirt."

"You look beautiful," he said sincerely, and meant every word. He didn't care that she was covered in a little dirt—she had a natural beauty that would have found a way to shine through a mud mask.

And suddenly, it was very important that she know that. Pulling free of her hold on his wrist, he once again lifted his hand to her face, but not to clean it. Cupping her cheek in his palm, he said, huskily, "Look at me, Lise. I'm not kidding. I think you're the most beautiful woman I've ever seen in my life. You must know what you do to me."

Caught in the warmth of his eyes, she desperately wanted, needed, to believe him, but it was just so hard. He could hurt her so easily, and she didn't even think he knew it. "Steve—"

"Let me show you," he said softly, and leaned down to kiss her.

It seemed like she'd been waiting all her life for him to do just that. The second his lips touched hers, the cave, the dust storm blowing outside, the ground beneath her feet, dissolved. There was just Steve, and a kiss unlike anything she'd ever dreamed of.

Soft. His lips were so soft. With a sweetness that brought tears to her eyes, he kissed her slowly, gently, as if she was made of spun sugar and he only wanted to taste her with his tongue. And just that easily, he made her feel beautiful.

And it didn't end there. One kiss gave way to another, then another, and neither of them noticed the force of the storm blowing outside. Her heart hammering wildly, Lise moaned as his hands trailed over her back and hips, then slid around to her breasts. "Steve!"

"I know." His voice rasped. "Doesn't it feel good? You're so pretty, sweetheart. Let me touch you."

Her blood hot, her body throbbing with restless need, she couldn't deny him…or herself. Murmuring his name, she curled into his hand and kissed him hungrily.

Just that easily, she gave herself to him and had no idea how the trust she placed in him humbled him. He'd never met another woman like her. Strong and sweet, fiery and incredibly innocent, she was everything a man could want in a woman, and she drove him wild. She was the virgin, but it was *his* fingers that trembled when he reached for the buttons of her blouse. And it was his breath that lodged in his throat as he slowly slipped her blouse from her shoulders and saw the lacy bra that covered her breasts. Who would have expected lace from the oh-so-practical Ms. Meldrum?

Delighted, he arched a brow at her as he trailed a finger down the center of her breasts. "You surprise me, sweetheart. The other day, you were wearing cotton. Is this for me?"

Heat climbed into her cheeks, but she met his gaze boldly, her smile flirtatious. "Maybe. I like pretty things just as much as the next girl. Just because I work with cows all day doesn't mean I don't like lace.''

''I'll remember that,'' he promised, and leaned down to kiss the top of her left breast.

Her breath shuddered through her lungs, liquid heat streaked through her blood, and any further conversation between the two of them became impossible. Eager to touch and kiss him as he did her, she peeled his shirt off and felt her mouth go dry at the sight of his chest. She worked every day with men who often worked bare-chested in the sun—it took more than that to impress her. But then again, she'd never seen a man quite like Steve. Hard and sculptured and bronzed from the sun, he had the look of a Greek god. And she couldn't resist touching him.

Lifting her hand to his chest, she stroked him in wonder and felt him shudder under her fingers. Surprised he was so susceptible to her touch, she glanced up and found him watching her with eyes that were hot with desire.

''Do that again,'' he growled softly. ''I dare you.''

She'd been around cowboys too long to walk away from a dare. Especially when it felt so good. A half smile on her mouth, she said archly, ''What? Like this?'' and stroked him again.

With a low groan, he reached for her, and this time when he kissed her, there was nothing slow and easy about it. His mouth wet and urgent on hers, he unhooked her bra with a snap of his fingers. Before she realized what happened, her breasts tumbled free...into his waiting hands. ''Oh!''

''*Oh* is right,'' he groaned, caressing her with a soft touch that was guaranteed to drive her slowly out of her mind. ''That's it, sweetheart,'' he coaxed when she curled into his touch. ''Just let me love you.''

That was what she wanted, too, though she hadn't known how much until right then. She needed him to touch her, kiss her, love her until every thought, every breath began and ended with him. "Now," she murmured, kissing her way up his chest to his neck. "Love me now."

Steve told himself he could stop whenever he liked. But then she pressed a petal-soft kiss to a spot just below his ear and nearly brought him to his knees. What was left of his control shattered, and with a growl that came from low in his throat, he snatched her in his arms and brought her to the ground with him.

"Steve!"

Chuckling, he grinned at her. "I just love it when you say my name that way. Do it again."

She couldn't stop herself—not when his hands slipped to the snap of her jeans. "Steve."

"Oh, yes," he groaned and rolled to his back, taking her with him so she wouldn't be scraped raw on the rocky ground.

She opened her mouth to protest that that wasn't fair to him, but the words died unspoken on her tongue when he kissed her again, and the rest of his clothes and hers seemed to melt away. His hands trailed over her, caressing every dip and curve of her body, and just that easily, he made her burn.

Outside, the storm continued to rage, but it was the pounding of her heart and the roar of her blood in her ears that she heard when he touched her and made her want something she couldn't put a name to. Whimpering, aching, she moved restlessly against him, too breathless, too innocent to tell him what she needed.

But even as she struggled to find the right words, he understood. "Easy, sweetheart. That's it. Take it slow and easy. I'm right here,'' he murmured, kissing her tenderly as he protected them both. ''I'll take care of you. Just trust me.''

She did—more than she'd ever thought possible. Caught up in the sweet magic of his kiss, she welcomed him as he settled under her, then he was easing into her ever so slowly, and the rest of the world ceased to exist. There was only Steve and the heat and strength of him. He moved under her, and urgency fired her blood and coiled deep inside her. Her breath catching on a sob, she clung to him as her hips caught the rhythm of a dance she would have sworn she didn't know the steps to.

And Steve loved it. He'd known she had too much fire in her to be passive in his arms, but he'd never suspected just how giving she could be. She was an innocent—or at least she had been until a few moments ago—but she held nothing back, throwing herself into their lovemaking like a woman who knew exactly what she wanted and wouldn't stop until she got it. And she had no idea what that did to him.

''Lise, honey...'' Struggling to hold on to what was left of his control, he wanted to draw out the moment until neither of them knew their own name, but suddenly she stiffened in his arms, and with a startled cry of surprise, pleasure washed over her in waves.

And watching her, loving the feel of her coming apart in his arms, was Steve's undoing. His own body caught fire, and with a groan that came from the very depths of his being, he gave himself up to the all-consuming flames.

He was an idiot.

Lying with Lise cuddled close in his arms, Steve stared out of the cave at the dust storm, which was finally blowing itself out, and called himself seven kinds of a

fool. He'd gone too far, dammit! As long as he'd just
flirted with her and kissed her, he'd been able to convince
himself it was all part of his job. Granted, that hadn't
been something he was particularly proud of, but he'd
been able to live with himself knowing it was for SPEAR.
But he hadn't made love to Lise to discover information
about her father. He hadn't even thought of Simon—or
his mission. The only thing he'd been thinking of was
Lise—and the fire she'd lit in his belly.

He'd made love to her strictly for himself, which was
what he'd wanted, but it was too soon, dammit! He'd lost
himself in her arms, and he'd completely forgotten that
the only one he could truly trust was his contact at the
other end of the phone line.

Not Lise. As much as he'd wanted to let down his
guard with her, he never should have done it. Because
first, last and always, she was Simon's daughter. And
while Steve didn't think she knew anything about her old
man's terrorist activities, he didn't know that for sure.
Until he did, he never should have made love to her. After
all, blood was thicker than water, and she had a very
clever father. If she was just as clever, she could be up
to her neck in whatever Simon was doing.

He didn't want to believe it, not about Lise, and it was
that, more than anything, that scared the hell out of him.
She'd touched his heart in a way he hadn't expected, and
he couldn't afford to let that happen again. He would keep
his hands to himself, finish his mission and get the hell
out of there while he still could—before he did something
stupid. Like fall in love with her.

Her heart still thundering, Lise stared blindly out at the
dying storm and saw nothing but the last few moments
in Steve's arms. He'd been wonderful. Sweet, gentle,

tender. He hadn't rushed her like some sex-starved cowboy who'd been out in the bush too long, but instead, he'd drawn her slowly into lovemaking. And in the process, he'd made the moment so special for her that she'd been hard pressed not to cry.

But he'd never mentioned love, never talked about the future at all.

That might not have bothered a more experienced woman, but Lise wasn't experienced, and she'd be the first to admit it. She'd never made love before—she hadn't expected such a swirl of emotions to envelop her. She wanted hearts and flowers and pretty words. And she wanted a future. With him. And that absolutely terrified her. Everything was happening so fast! She felt like she'd stepped on a merry-go-round that was spinning out of control, and there was no way to slow it down or step off.

Was she falling in love with him? Was that why she was so confused? No. She couldn't possibly be. She'd only known him a matter of weeks. People didn't fall in love that fast—she should know. Her parents had been absolutely devoted to each other, and they'd known each other for six months before they'd realized they were falling in love. There had to be another explanation.

But the only one that came to mind was that she was falling in lust, not love, and she didn't even have to think about that one to reject it. She wasn't the type of woman who lusted after men—if she had, she'd have been involved with someone long before now. No, it was more than lust, she told herself, but not yet love. But it could be, and that was what worried her. She shouldn't be having these feelings for someone she knew so little about. Yes, he'd told her about his childhood, but how did he feel about children and commitment and marriage? If he gave his word on something, could she trust it? Could she trust *him?* Would he be there for her the way her father had always been there for her mother?

Would he be there for his child in a way her father had never been for her?

The traitorous thought came from out of nowhere to confuse her, but she didn't have an answer for that any more than she did for the rest of the questions buzzing around in her head. And answers were something she desperately needed right now. Answers about Steve, answers about herself and what she wanted for herself now and in the future. And there weren't any in sight.

She needed time to think, and she didn't have to wait long to get it. The storm blew itself out, and suddenly, Steve was as anxious as she to put some space between them. "We'd better get back to camp," he said huskily, breaking the tense silence that had fallen between them. "Everyone'll be worried about us."

Rolling away from her, he didn't give her time to argue, but simply reached for his clothes and hurriedly dressed without sparing her another glance. Seconds later, he stomped into his boots and grabbed his hat. "I'll see if I can find the horses."

He was gone before she could open her mouth to tell him she'd go with him, hurrying out of the cave as if he couldn't get away from her fast enough. Hurt, she tried to tell herself she was just being sensitive. If he was in a hurry, it was only because he knew the storm had no doubt caused a lot of damage. They could lie around like two lovers stranded on a deserted island another time. Right now, they had work to do.

And he was right, of course. Resigned, she hurriedly pulled on her clothes, wincing as the dirt and grime clinging to them scraped her sensitive skin. She longed for a bath, but the springs were miles away, and Steve needed her help. She tugged on her boots, then stepped outside to see what kind of damage the storm had done.

The fences she and Steve had spent the morning repairing were down again, but the horses, thankfully, hadn't gone far. They'd found shelter in the rocky outcroppings surrounding the cave, and Steve had collected them when she stepped outside. "How are they?" she asked huskily as he checked them for injuries.

"Dusty," he replied. "But not as skittish as I expected. I guess they're used to dust storms blowing up out of nowhere."

"It goes with the territory," she said with a shrug, making no apologies. "I'm just glad they didn't run off and leave us. It's a long way back to camp."

It was, in fact, ten miles, and they barely spoke to each other the entire way. Lise told herself she was okay with that—she wasn't in the mood for conversation anyway—but when they reached the camp, Steve couldn't seem to get away from her fast enough. Hurt, she told herself he was just pitching in and helping the others. The storm had come right through camp, knocking down tents and twisting them into a wild tangle. Clothes were scattered through the bush for a half mile or more, and the chuck wagon was covered in three inches of dust. The corral was down, and God only knew where the cattle were. It would take the rest of the day, and possibly tomorrow, to set everything straight.

She knew that, and was thankful that everyone immediately went to work rebuilding camp without having to be told. But she'd just made love for the first time in her life. There had been times in the past when she'd wondered what it would be like when she gave herself to a man, and not once had she ever thought that he would walk away from her afterward without a word—regardless of what was going on around them.

But that was exactly what Steve had done, and that devastated her far more than she'd expected it to. Did he think she wanted some kind of undying proclamation of love? she wondered, scowling at his back as he rode into the bush to pick up the clothes that were scattered to the four winds. Is that what this was about? Was he afraid that she wanted him to marry her now that she'd given him her virginity? Or did he just regret it and no longer want anything to do with her?

If that was the kind of man he was, then he wasn't who she'd thought he was. Pain squeezed her heart at that, but she knew it was better that she find out now than later. Determined to ignore him, she quickly turned her attention to the pans she was cleaning for Cookie while he swept dust from the chuck wagon.

She'd always considered herself a practical person, and putting Steve from her mind shouldn't have been difficult, not after the way he'd hurt her. The rat didn't deserve a second thought. But try though she might, she couldn't stop thinking about those moments in the cave when every thought she had began and ended with him.

Did he really regret making love with her? She had no experience to fall back on, of course, but she'd have sworn he was as caught up in their lovemaking as she was. So what happened? When had he started to regret it? Why? Had she said something, done something to offend him? She certainly hadn't meant to. He'd given her the most incredible experience of her life. Her heart turned over in her chest every time she thought of it. Surely he knew that. After all, he was the one with all the experience. He must have been able to tell.

But what if he hadn't?

The question snuck up on her from her blind side and stopped her in her tracks. Had she disappointed him somehow afterward? Was this what all the silent treatment was about? They'd both gone into the experience with expectations, and she had to believe that she'd somehow let him down. Otherwise, he'd be helping her clean the chuck wagon right now, flirting outrageously and waiting for another chance to get her alone.

What had she done? she wondered, worried. She'd never know until she asked him.

Another woman who'd just lost her virginity might not have had the courage to approach him when he so obviously wanted nothing to do with her, but she'd never lacked for courage before Steve Trace had come into her life, and she didn't intend to start now. If there was a problem, the only way to work it out was to talk about it.

Her mind made up, she set aside the large pan she'd been cleaning and dried her hands. Surprised, Cookie looked up from his sweeping and frowned. "Hey, you're not finished. Where are you going?"

"I'll be back," she assured him. "I've just got a little business I've got to take care of first."

"But—"

"I'll be right back."

She headed for the corral before he could say another word, leaving him grumbling in disgust as he turned to the chuck wagon. "That's okay. Take off like everyone else and find something else to do. Just don't complain when there's nothing but sandwiches for supper."

Quickly saddling Thunder, Lise wouldn't have cared if they had nothing but bread and water for the rest of the day. All she wanted was to talk to Steve. But when she rode out of camp a few seconds later, there was no sign of him anywhere. Surprised, she brought Thunder to a quick stop, scowling as she searched the area where she'd last seen him retrieving clothes and other items that had been blown to kingdom come by the storm, but she couldn't find him. Where the devil had he gone?

Thunder pawed the ground impatiently, but she only patted his neck absently and murmured, "Easy, boy. He's got to be around here somewhere. Give me a second to find his trail."

Riding to the last spot she'd seen him, she found his horse's tracks in the new coating of dust the storm had left behind and was surprised when she saw that he'd headed east. Since the storm had blown up in the east and moved everything in a westerly direction, there was nothing to retrieve to the east.

"Maybe he went to the springs for a drink," she muttered to Thunder. "That seems to be where he's heading."

His tracks didn't stop at the springs, but continued right on past them. Frowning in puzzlement, Lise searched the eastern horizon and finally spotted him in the distance, riding away from her.

He was headed for her parents' old cabin.

Later, she couldn't have said how she knew where he was going. She hadn't asked him to check out the cabin to see what kind of damage it had suffered from the storm, not when there was so much work to do at camp. But he was headed in the right direction, and common sense told her that's where he was going.

Why? she wondered, carefully keeping her distance as she followed him. There was no logical reason for him to take off for the cabin without so much as a goodbye. There was work to be done, dammit! So what the devil was he up to? She intended to find out.

Chapter 8

If anyone happened to see Steve riding away from camp, they would have thought he was searching the bush for items that had been blown away by the storm. In actuality, he was using the search to hide the fact that he was slowly, deliberately making his way toward Simon's cabin.

Thanks to the storm, things couldn't have worked out better if he'd planned them. The camp was a disaster area—not a single tent had been left standing, and it would take hours to set everything right. With so much work to do, no one had even looked up when he'd volunteered to ride out and collect the clothes scattered all over the bush.

That didn't mean, however, that he had hours to find the cabin and search it. He had thirty minutes—at the most—before someone noted his absence and possibly came looking for him, so he didn't have time to dawdle. Every instinct he had urged him to hurry, but he couldn't.

If someone saw him racing across the desert, that would
surely raise suspicions he didn't want to deal with. Better
to keep his pace slow, even though it ate up more time,
and appear to be searching for one of his shirts that had
disappeared in the storm. Then, if someone saw him and
demanded an explanation, he could pretend to be surprised that he'd wandered so far from camp.

It wasn't easy. He had to sit relaxed in the saddle, as
if he was bored with the job, and all the while, his eyes
searched the horizon for signs of the cabin. Lise had mentioned that it was a half a mile east of the springs. That
could cover a lot of territory. If he didn't find it soon,
he'd have to turn back and look another time.

Aware of every second that ticked by on his watch, he
was just about to give up hope when the sun glinted off
the tin roof of a small house in the distance to his right.
That had to be it! Chancing a quick glance over his shoulder, he saw nothing but red dirt and the bush behind him.
Relieved, he headed straight for the cabin.

Hanging well back and to his left, Lise wanted to sink
into the ground when he suddenly looked over his shoulder to see if he was being followed. She needn't have
worried. Still covered in dirt from the storm, she and
Thunder couldn't have faded into the terrain better if
they'd been dressed in camouflage. And Steve only took
time for a quick look behind him. If he hadn't been in
such a hurry, he would have surely seen her.

She wanted to believe that he'd just stumbled across
the cabin by accident, but she'd never been very good at
lying to herself. So maybe he was just curious, she
thought. She supposed she would be, too, if their positions
were reversed and she found herself in Wisconsin and had
a chance to check out his parents' farm. There was nothing wrong with wanting to see where a person was from.

But even from a distance, she could see it was more than curiosity that had led him to the cabin. He approached it almost like a thief scoping out the next place he was going to rob, and she couldn't begin to understand why. What did he hope to find? No one had lived there for years.

Questions nagging at her, she watched with growing indignation as he approached the front door. It was locked, for heaven's sake! What did he think he was going to do? Walk right inside like he owned the place?

That was, in fact, exactly what he did.

Stunned, Lise couldn't believe her eyes. One second he was standing at the door, and the next he was pushing it open. And for the life of her, she didn't know how. The cabin wasn't some abandoned shack that had been left to rot in the bush all these years—her father made sure it was kept in top-notch shape. It had a steel door and a dead bolt lock that would have given a skilled cat burglar pause. Yet Steve didn't even hesitate. With a flick of his wrist, he unlocked it.

A second after he stepped across the threshold, the door shut behind him, leaving him inside and her out. And that was the last straw, as far as Lise was concerned. Damn him, who the hell did he think he was? That was her parents' cabin. *Hers!* He had no right to be scrounging around in there when she'd never even stepped foot across the threshold! And she was going to tell him that right now! Urging Thunder forward, she headed straight for the cabin.

There was nothing there.

Standing flat-footed in the middle of the small one-room cabin, Steve couldn't believe his lousy luck. He'd taken a chance slipping away from camp, and for what?

Nothing, dammit! After what Lise had told him about the place, he was convinced Simon had a secret office set up there, but there wasn't a computer or desk or even a filing cabinet in sight. Instead, the cabin was furnished just as it must have been when Simon and his wife lived there, with an old-fashioned poster bed and dresser, an over-stuffed couch and matching armchair and an inexpensive chrome dinette set. If Simon had hidden any damning evidence there, it had to be under the floorboards or in the mattress because there wasn't any other place to conceal anything.

''Well, damn!''

He checked the entire cabin because appearances could be deceptive, especially where Simon was concerned, but the quick search soon proved to be nothing but a waste of time. The floorboards were tightly nailed in place, and the mattress and living room furniture were stuffed with nothing but their original padding. Like it or not, he had once again struck out.

Frustrated—and more than a little infuriated—Steve would have given just about anything to get his hands on Simon at that moment. If he hadn't known better, he would have sworn the bastard was on to him and had Lise tell him about the cabin just so he could sit back and laugh at the idea of Steve looking for something that wasn't there. Simon was that manipulative and sadistic.

But while Steve could believe that of Simon, he couldn't of Lise. If making love to her had shown him anything, it was just how open and honest and giving she was. She would never knowingly participate in such a scheme—she wasn't that cruel.

Deep down inside, every instinct he had told him he could trust her. She'd shown him the type of woman she was, and she was nothing like her father and never would be. He could let down his guard with her and not have to worry about her betraying him.

But even as he acknowledged all of that, he knew he couldn't allow himself to trust Lise. Because if he did, he'd have no defenses where she was concerned. Then where the hell would he be?

In love with her.

Not letting himself go there, he immediately steered his thoughts to the matter at hand. Simon and his capture. He had to remember that, focus on that—and find a way to forget what it was like to make love to Lise.

He might as well have ordered himself not to breathe.

Muttering a curse, he dug his phone card out of his wallet and swiftly placed a call to Belinda. Like a recovering alcoholic who desperately needed to talk to his sponsor, he needed her to help ground him and get his priorities straight.

"Get me out of here!"

He'd meant to at least greet her civilly, but the words popped out of his mouth before he could stop them. For a moment, there was nothing but surprised silence, then she said sweetly, too sweetly, "Having a rough day, are we? What seems to be the problem, son?"

He almost growled at her not to call him son. She was only a year or two older than he was, dammit, and he was in no mood to stick to his cover. Not when he was having a meltdown, which *never* happened to him!

"The problem, *Mother*," he said through his teeth, "is that I'm standing in the middle of Simon's cabin and there's not a damn thing here but a bunch of old furniture!"

"And that surprises you?"

Stunned that she even had to ask, he snapped, "Hell,

yes, it surprises me! Dammit, this was the one hiding place he had left I hadn't searched!''

''Who told you that?''

Confused, he frowned. ''What?''

''That the cabin was the one hiding place he had left,'' she repeated patiently.

''No one. Lise—''

''Is Simon's daughter,'' she interrupted quietly. ''Has something happened to make you forget that?''

His response should have been an immediate, ''No, of course not.'' Instead, there was a long pause that spoke more clearly than words. In the echoing silence, Belinda's voice was husky with concern. ''When you said you wanted out the other day, I thought you were overreacting to the situation. Now I'm not so sure. Are you all right?''

He knew what she was asking—had he been able to carry out his orders without letting his emotions get involved? No! he almost shouted at her. Couldn't she tell? Everything was screwed up, especially his heart, and he had no one to blame but himself. But that was about to change, he promised himself. It had to before he completely botched this assignment.

''No,'' he said flatly. ''I'm not all right. But I'm working on it. Talking to you has helped. Thanks.''

''I do what I can,'' she said simply. ''I take it you have nothing else to report?''

''Unfortunately, no. The cabin is a wash and there's still no sign of Simon. Though he could be at the main house right now for all I know.''

''He's not,'' Belinda replied. ''We're watching the place on radar. If a plane comes in, we'll know about it.''

That gave him some comfort, but not much. They both knew that Simon was too crafty to fly in if he thought the station was being watched. He'd drive in, and that would make him almost impossible to monitor since he could come from just about any direction. "Then all I can do for now is wait and watch," he told her. "I'll be in touch if I hear anything interesting. Bye, *Mom.*"

He hung up so quickly that Lise almost tripped over her own feet as she darted for cover around the corner of the house. Her heart pounding, she half expected Steve to come striding around the house any second and discover her, but he was obviously more interested in getting back to camp. A few seconds later, she heard the pounding of his horse's hooves on the hard ground as he rode away from the cabin, and with a sigh of relief, she sent up a silent prayer of thanks to God for giving her the sense to tie Thunder on the opposite side of the house.

The problem, Mother, *is that I'm standing in the middle of Simon's cabin and there's not a damn thing here but a bunch of old furniture!*

His words ringing in her ears, Lise frowned as she checked to make sure the coast was clear, then stepped onto the cabin's front porch as Steve disappeared from view. She'd arrived at the cabin just in time to hear him speaking to someone, presumably on a cell phone she hadn't realized he had, and nothing he'd said had made sense. What did he mean, he was standing in the middle of *Simon's* cabin? Who was Simon? This was her father's place, and his name was Art. Steve knew that—he was a friend of her father's, for heaven's sake! Her father had given him a job. And she had told him about the cabin and how her parents had lived there for the first few years of their marriage. Why did he think the place belonged to someone named Simon? And what had he expected to find there?

Anxious to find out for herself, she closed her fingers around the doorknob and felt like a child who was about to look in the closet where the Christmas presents were hidden. This place was off-limits to not only her, but to everyone on the station. In good conscience, she knew she shouldn't go in there.

But even as she told herself that, her fingers tightened around the doorknob and turned it. For as long as she could remember, it had been locked—she knew because she'd tried the handle out of curiosity every time she was in that area of the station—but this time, for the first time, it turned easily in her hand. Her blood thundering in her ears, she didn't fool herself into thinking that it had been that way when Steve had arrived. He'd obviously found a way to unlock it, and out of respect for her father's need for privacy, she should have locked it up without even looking inside.

But even though she knew that was the right thing to do, she couldn't. The cabin wasn't just her father's—her mother had lived there, too. Some of her things were still there, things that were Lise's last link to her. And she desperately needed to see them. Without another thought, she pushed open the door and stepped inside.

In the past, whenever she'd thought about the cabin, she'd always thought that if she ever got the chance to go inside, she would immediately feel the presence of her mother and her love. Instead, she felt nothing but curiosity. There was no special aura to the place, nothing that really touched her heart. The furniture was inexpensive and old, but it was in excellent condition and was, no doubt, arranged the way her mother had liked it.

All too easily, Lise could picture her father there, sitting on the sofa, his face lined with grief, shutting out the world, shutting out her. And it hurt. When her mother had died, it seemed like her father had died, too, and it shouldn't have been that way. Their grief should have drawn them together—instead, it had done the exact opposite, at least on her father's part. He'd withdrawn into himself, into the cabin, and there'd been no place for her there or anywhere else in his life.

And that hadn't changed with the passage of time. She didn't belong there, wasn't wanted there—over the years, her father had made that abundantly clear. He'd kept the place under lock and key, for heaven's sake, to keep her out! And she didn't go where she wasn't wanted.

Her pride urging her to leave, she turned to go only to remember Steve's frustrated phone conversation. Frowning, she glanced around, trying to figure out what he'd been looking for. But if he'd searched the place, she had to admit that he'd done it well. Nothing was out of place—everything was neat as a pin, just as her father had probably left it. So what had Steve been looking for? Money? Jewelry? In a deserted cabin no one had lived in for thirty years? She didn't think so.

This is the only hiding place he had left I hadn't searched...all I can do now is wait and watch...I'll be in touch if I hear anything interesting.

Snippets of his phone conversation came back to her, taunting her, confusing her. What had he meant when he said he'd searched all the other hiding places? Even if there'd been any—which there weren't!—being a hired hand on a station was hard work. They worked from sunup to sundown and had little time for anything but a game or two of poker at the end of the day. So when had he had time to search for anything?

Are you using the computer tonight? I still haven't found a treatment for my father....

Memories of all the times he'd used the computer in her father's study over the past week came rushing back, and the truth hit her right in the face. Dear God, how could she have been so naive? There was no mysterious illness—his father probably wasn't even sick! Steve had just come up with that excuse to get into the study and search it, and like an idiot, she'd fallen for it. The bastard!

Who was he? she wondered furiously. He obviously wasn't a friend of her father's. How could he be? He didn't know anything about Art Meldrum! From the moment he'd arrived at the station, he'd done nothing but ask questions about the station, her childhood, her father's comings and goings. She'd thought he was just curious, being a Yank and new to the country, but that obviously wasn't the case. Cringing, she wondered how she could have been so blind. Nothing about the man added up.

Which brought her back to square one. Who was he and what did he want?

The answer came far too quickly and drained the blood from her cheeks. From the time she was old enough to understand, her father had told her about the serious enemies he'd made when he worked in the mining business before he met and married her mother. He'd been trapped in a mining shaft and set on fire, and he'd been lucky to get out alive. To this day, his face was disfigured with scars from the burns and he wore a glass eye.

Because the men who'd tried to kill him had never been caught, he'd always warned her to be wary of strangers. There were dangerous men in the world who wanted to bring him down, and she shouldn't trust *anyone* at first meeting, regardless of who she thought they were.

Caution had been ingrained in her for as long as she could remember. So what had she done? She'd not only trusted Steve with the ranch records that were on the computer, but she'd also given him her innocence. Talk about a fool! She'd actually let him convince her that he teased and flirted and made love to her because he was attracted to her. What a joke. From the very beginning, it was her father he'd been interested in, her father he had some sort of twisted vendetta against. If she was the one who got hurt, then that, apparently, was just too damn bad. He had his own agenda, and he'd do whatever he had to, use whomever he had to, including her, to carry out the plans that had brought him to Pear Tree Station.

The hell he would! she fumed. If he thought she was going to stand by and let him bring her father down, he could think again. Two could play at his game. If he could spy on her father, she could do the same to him. She'd check him out, find out everything she could about him, then report to her father. Then Steve would be the one who was brought down, and it would be no more than he deserved. No one hurt her or her family and got away with it.

Satisfied that she would never let him hurt her again, she stepped out of the cabin and shut the door behind her, testing it to make sure it was locked. Still tied to the bush where she'd left him behind the cabin, Thunder greeted her with a soft whinny. Normally, she would have grinned and rewarded him with a rub on the nose and a treat, but not this time. All business, she untied him and stepped into the stirrup. "Let's go, boy," she said grimly. "We've got a rat to catch."

Heading to camp, she wasn't surprised to discover that Steve was still collecting the clothes and other items the storm had blown into the bush. Anger simmering in her as she watched him from a distance, she was tempted to ride out to him and tell him exactly what she thought of him. But that would only tip him off to the fact that she was on to him, and she had no intention of doing that. Not yet. Not until she knew who and what he was and could blast him with that. Then she'd throw him off the station for good.

Just thinking about that should have given her an immense amount of satisfaction. Instead, it did the exact opposite. Her heart hurt, and that only made her angrier. Her lips pressed into a flat line, she turned away, determined to ignore him until she had her emotions under control.

With so much work to do, that wasn't difficult. It took hours to set the camp up, then there was lost time to be made up rounding up the cattle and checking the area watering holes and fences. Work took them in opposite directions, and Lise didn't see Steve for the rest of the day.

By the time everyone returned to camp for dinner, they were hot and tired and dirty, and tempers were short. It had been a long day, and not surprisingly, no one was in the mood to talk. Silence hung over the camp like a shroud as everyone tiredly dug into the chicken Cookie had grilled over the campfire.

Every bone in her body aching with weariness and her appetite nonexistent, Lise knew she should wait until tomorrow to begin investigating Steve. She'd stewed over him all day and still couldn't quite control her hostility. But as she watched him lounge on a camp stool and eat dinner like he didn't have a care in the world, something in her snapped. Damn him, he had no right to look so comfortable when all she wanted to do was go off in a corner and cry!

"Hey, Steve," she called, forcing a tight smile that never reached her eyes, "how do you like your first bush roundup so far? Is it hot enough for you?"

"I'm getting by," he said easily. "It's not much different than Arizona and west Texas in the heat of the summer.''

''Oh, yeah, that's right,'' she said, pretending to just now remember the stories he'd told her about his past. ''You've worked in a lot of different places, haven't you?''

He shrugged. ''I like to move around.''

''Is that how you met my father? By moving around?''

It was a natural question, one that Steve had expected her to ask the first day he arrived at the station. She hadn't. So why, he wondered, was she asking him now? Had something happened to make her suspicious of him? Had she somehow discovered that he'd checked out the cabin?

Alarm bells clanging in his head, he studied her through narrowed eyes, but if she had doubts about him, she gave no sign of it. Her smile quizzical, she met his gaze head-on and waited patiently for his answer.

''Actually, we never met face to face,'' he finally said honestly, and wondered if he was being paranoid. She seemed fine. If she was asking questions he hadn't expected at this stage in the mission, it was probably because she was still coming to grips with what happened between them in the cave during the storm. She'd never made love before; she had to be feeling more than a little vulnerable right now. Considering that, he couldn't blame her for needing some answers about who he was.

So sticking to the truth as closely as possible in case Simon had already told her how they'd come to know each other, he gave her what answers he could that wouldn't blow his cover. ''I did some work for him through a friend, and when he heard I was looking for a job, he told me about the station and that you could always use a good hand. I'd never been to Australia, and I was looking for a change. This was it.''

''But your father was sick. Didn't you have any reservations about going halfway around the world and leaving your mother to deal with that alone?''

''He wasn't sick when I left,'' he replied patiently. ''And my mother didn't tell me how bad his condition was until he was doing better. By then, she didn't need me to come home, just help find a new treatment for him.''

Braced for more unwanted questions, he half expected her to grill him about the exact nature of his father's disease and the available treatment for it. If pressed, he could have provided a halfway decent explanation, but something he said must have satisfied her curiosity. In the blink of an eye, her mood, which seemed more than a little hostile, changed.

''That must have been difficult for you, being so far away from home and unable to do anything,'' she said quietly. ''If my father was that sick and in the States, I'd probably be a nervous wreck. How do you stand it?''

He shrugged. ''Work helps.'' Especially since his father was safe and sound and healthy as a horse in Wisconsin.

That returned the discussion to work and all that hadn't gotten done because of the dust storm. Listening to Lise question the rest of the men about the condition of the cattle they'd been able to round up, Steve breathed a silent sigh of relief. Obviously she believed him, or she never would have accepted his answers.

He was lying through his teeth.

The thought nagged at Lise all that evening and through the night, tying her in knots. Now that she'd had time to think about it some more, she was convinced she couldn't believe anything he'd said to her—not about his childhood, his parents, the kind of man he was. If he'd misled her about one thing, he could have lied to her about everything—especially about how he felt about her.

Pain squeezing her heart, she lay in her tent long after the rest of the camp had gone to sleep and couldn't stop herself from replaying those heated moments in the cave when he'd made love to her with so much tenderness. How much of that had been a lie? Which touch, which kiss had been real and which ones were designed to seduce her into giving him whatever information he wanted? Was he even attracted to her?

Tears stinging her eyes, she silently ordered herself not to go there, but it was already too late. The doubts she'd had her entire life about her own attractiveness washed over her, swallowing her whole and engulfing her in an old, familiar pain. And though she tried not to, she couldn't help but wonder if Steve would have done this to her if she'd been delicate and petite like her mother.

More miserable than she'd been in years, she didn't sleep. Through the screened door of her tent, she watched the moon rise and track its way across the night sky, then the first faint glow of dawn paint the eastern horizon. Long before Cookie had breakfast cooking on the campfire, she was dressed and ready for work.

She didn't need a mirror to know that she wasn't looking her best. Her eyes were red and swollen from the tears she'd fought all night, and she didn't doubt that she was as pale as a ghost—she always was when she didn't get enough sleep. The way she felt right now, she'd never sleep again. And that was all right with her. Because every time she closed her eyes, she could feel Steve's

arms slip around her and his mouth settle on hers. And it
hurt.

"You all right, Lise?"

"You look a little peaked."

"You're not coming down with something, are you?
Maybe you should stay in bed today and let the rest of
us pick up the slack. You don't want to come down with
something like that virus you caught last year. You could
end up in bed for weeks."

Embarrassed that her men noticed, she started to shrug
off their concern, only to hesitate when she noticed Steve
watching her through narrowed eyes. "Actually," she
said huskily, "I do feel a little sick. Maybe I should take
it easy today."

That was all she had to say to have Tuck, Nate and the
other hands swarming around her in concern.

"Here," Nate said gruffly, handing her a bottle of aspirin. "Take some of these. You look like you're running
a fever."

"You're supposed to feed a fever," Cookie growled,
and handed her a plateful of scrambled eggs that could
have easily fed three men.

"Give her some room," Tuck ordered with a scowl.
"Can't you see the girl needs some air?"

Touched by their concern and feeling guilty for mis-
leading them, Lise found herself suddenly battling tears.
"I'm fine," she said, her voice choked. "Maybe I just
need to lie down for a while."

"Someone should stay with you today," Steve said
gruffly. "You shouldn't be alone."

He hadn't meant to say anything. They'd barely spoken
since they'd made love, and she obviously wanted that to
continue since she'd taken every opportunity yesterday
and this morning to avoid him, but he was worried about

her, dammit! She was pale and drawn and looked like she'd blow away in a stiff wind. And he didn't know if that was because she was really sick or regretted making love with him.

Something lodged in his heart at that, paining him. The timing might have been all wrong for both of them, but he hated the thought of her regretting making love with him. It had been incredible for him, and he'd thought she felt the same. Maybe if he stayed with her, they could talk about it.

"I'll stay with her," Frankie said before Steve could open his mouth. "I don't mind."

"Any excuse not to work," Barney taunted with a shake of his head. "If anybody's going to stay, it should be Nate. He can't take the heat like he used to."

"Hey!"

"No one needs to stay behind," Lise said quickly before an argument could ensue. "It's not as if I'll be by myself. Cookie's here. If I need anything, I'm sure he'll be happy to help me."

"Damn straight," Cookie growled. Armed with a wooden spoon, he gave the lot of them a hard look. "Now that we've got that settled, you've got ten minutes to eat, then I'm going to start cleaning up. If you're hungry, you'd better grab a plate while you can."

He didn't need to tell them twice. They all rushed toward the chuck wagon. Watching Lise duck into her tent, Steve was tempted to follow her inside, but Cookie was standing guard, daring anyone to bother her. Reluctantly, Steve was forced to accept the fact that he didn't stand a chance of getting anywhere near her today. Not when everyone was feeling so protective of her. He kept his distance and joined the chow line.

If he could hold her just once, he knew they'd both

feel better. But she didn't come out of her tent, and he didn't get another chance to talk to her. Breakfast was wolfed down, and all too soon it was time to get to work. Horses were bridled and saddled, and ten minutes later, everyone rode into the bush to round up the cattle. Steve was left with no choice but to go with them.

Lying on her cot, Lise would have liked nothing better than to go back to sleep and forget the world. But when she heard the others ride out of camp, she knew this might be the only chance she got to search Steve's things. So as soon as the last man rode off and the only sound in camp was that of Cookie doing dishes, she quietly stepped out of her tent.

Another woman might have made no secret of what she was doing, especially with Cookie, whom Lise trusted with her life, but she couldn't be quite that brazen. She knew it was stupid, but she didn't want anyone else to think as badly of Steve as she did. So she stood outside her tent for what seemed like an eternity, watching Cookie at the other end of the camp as he went about his morning routine, and sighed in relief that he was too occupied with the dishes to notice her. Humming softly to himself, he turned his back to her as he washed a large skillet, and Lise quickly took advantage of his distraction. Soundlessly, she darted to Steve's tent and disappeared inside.

Her heart pounding, she stood just inside the tent opening and told herself there was no reason to feel like a thief in the night. She wasn't going to steal anything, just find out who the real Steve Trace was. And there was nothing wrong with that. If he hadn't lied to her, she would have accepted him for the man he'd said he was, and none of this would have been necessary.

* * *

It only took a single glance to verify that his tent was just as sparsely furnished as hers. Other than a canvas cot, there was nothing in it but the duffel bag that held his clothes.

Hesitating, she stood there for what seemed like an eternity, not sure that she could do this. In the end, however, she knew she had no choice. She wasn't going to get the truth from Steve, so she had to find it for herself. She stepped over to the duffel bag, which sat on the ground at the foot of the cot, and went down on one knee to examine its contents.

The second she touched his neatly packed clothes, she felt as if she was somehow betraying him. Her palms damp and her stomach churning with nerves, she glanced guiltily at the tent flap, half expecting to find Steve standing there, glaring at her in outrage, but he was nowhere in sight. If she hadn't already been kneeling, she was sure her bones would have dissolved in relief. Hurriedly, she turned to the duffel bag and quickly went through it.

She didn't know what she expected to find, but when the search turned up a wallet and passport that verified the man she'd given her virginity to was, indeed, Steve Trace, Lise didn't know if she was relieved or disappointed. She didn't know much more than she'd known before, just his name and that he had reasonably good credit, if the handful of credit cards in his wallet was anything to go by. There had to be more to the man than that, though.

Frowning, she examined his wallet carefully and had just about decided that there was nothing of interest when she suddenly discovered a hidden flap behind the compartment that held his driver's license. And in it was a neatly folded piece of paper. Her heart slamming against her ribs, she quickly pulled it out and unfolded it.

In case of emergency, please contact Henry Trace, Route 1, Box 25, Laurel Heights, Wisconsin.

A phone number was scrawled after the address, but Lise hardly noticed. So his parents really did live in Wisconsin—at least he hadn't lied about that. That didn't, however, mean that he'd told the truth about anything else. After eavesdropping on his conversation at the cabin, she knew for a fact that he was no friend of her father's. So who was he? She wouldn't rest until she found out.

Chapter 9

Steve liked to think he wasn't a stupid man. Years ago, when he'd first started working for SPEAR, he'd learned he couldn't trust anyone but himself. That, apparently, hadn't changed, he realized at lunch when he stepped into his tent. Since he'd left camp after breakfast that morning, someone had been there. He'd been careful to take note of where his duffel bag was sitting that morning, and it was no longer in the exact same spot. Someone had not only moved it a quarter of an inch to the right, but he didn't doubt that they'd gone through it. And it didn't take a rocket scientist to figure out who the culprit was. Only two people had stayed behind that morning when everyone had ridden out of camp. Lise and Cookie.

He knew he was in trouble when he jumped at the chance to blame Cookie for the deed.

Dammit, he had to stop this. He had to stop assuming that Lise was an innocent in the game they were playing. She wasn't. She couldn't be. There was a reason Simon

had left her in charge of the station, and that was that he
could trust her above all others to protect his interests.
How many times did Steve have to be reminded of that
before he accepted the fact that she was the last person
on the entire station he could trust?

Irritated with himself, he stepped out of his tent and
looked around for Lise, sure that she was watching to see
if he'd discovered his tent had been searched. There was
no sign of her anywhere.

"Where's Lise?" he asked Chuck with a frown when
the two of them fell into step on the way to the chuck
wagon. "She's not still in her tent, is she?"

"Yeah. Cookie took her a tray, but she didn't want it.
I guess she's really sick. She doesn't usually turn down
food."

Concerned, Steve couldn't help but feel guilty. While
he'd been blaming her for searching his things, she'd been
lying in her tent, too sick to even care about eating.
"Maybe I'll stop in and say hello," he said huskily. "It
sounds like she's feeling pretty miserable."

"Go ahead, if you like, but I'd grab something to eat
first if I were you," he warned. "With three people out,
we're really going to be shorthanded this afternoon, and
Tuck wants us to get back to work as soon as possible."

Surprised, Steve arched a brow at him. "Three people?
Who else is sick? I thought it was just Lise."

"Didn't you hear? Barney got a nasty cut on his hand
from some rusty wire when he was riding fence, and Frankie twisted his foot when he tried to get a heifer out of a
mud hole she was stuck in."

"You're kidding! When did this happen?"

"About an hour ago. Tuck's pretty disgusted with them
for being so careless. We were already a man short without Lise—now we've got to pick up the slack for two

more. They'll both be out the rest of the day and maybe tomorrow.''

His mind working furiously, Steve hardly heard him. So Lise and Cookie hadn't been the only ones in camp all morning. Just how serious were Barney and Frankie's injuries? he wondered. There was no question that Barney's cut hand had to be tended to—that wasn't the kind of thing you ignored if you valued your life—but a simple cut wasn't anything that should have taken him out of commission. He should have been able to return to work after it had been cleaned and bandaged, as long as he was careful to wear his work gloves. So why hadn't he? Had he spent what was left of the morning searching Steve's tent, instead?

And what about Frankie? A twisted ankle didn't sound like much of a reason to lay off work, especially for someone built like Frankie. He was as big as a house, for God's sake! He shouldn't have even have blinked at a twisted ankle. He sure as hell shouldn't have come hobbling into camp for first aid when there was so much work to be done. So why had he? Had he hoped to do a little snooping while everyone was gone?

Suddenly not sure of anything, Steve swore softly. Well, that was just great. Now instead of having two people in camp he couldn't trust, he had four. Hell. Disgusted, he joined the other men for lunch, but he had little appetite for the pork chops Cookie had grilled. He ate what was on his plate, but he could have been eating a bologna sandwich for all the notice he gave it. All he could think about was someone going through his things.

He wasn't worried that the searcher might had found something. The phone card was virtually undetectable from his other credit cards, and he'd been careful to make sure everything else in his wallet and personal belongings supported his cover. Even the address and phone number that he'd hidden in his wallet had been set up by SPEAR, so it wouldn't do Lise or whoever had gone to the trouble to search his tent any good to investigate the phony address and phone number they'd found. They would both check out.

No, it wasn't the information the searcher had found that bothered him. It was the searcher himself. If it wasn't Lise, who was it? Who was suspicious of him? And why? How far would they go to find out who he was?

Questions swirling in his head, he glanced casually around to see where Frankie and Barney were and found them at the chuck wagon with Cookie, finishing lunch. Looking a little the worse for wear, they didn't spare him so much as a single glance, and neither did Cookie. That left only Lise, and she was still in her tent.

He should confront her just to see if she could look him in the eye. It would have been the smart thing to do, and he knew it. But there was a good possibility that she really was sick, so for today, at least, he could give her the benefit of the doubt. When she was feeling better would be soon enough to find out if she was spying on him for her father.

The decision made, he returned his empty plate to Cookie, then retrieved his mount from the corral and rode out of camp with some of the other hands. He didn't have to look behind him to know that someone watched him with hostile eyes—he could feel them drilling into his back.

Stepping out of her tent just as several men rode out of camp, Lise recognized Steve's tall, broad-shouldered form leading the way toward the horizon and felt her heart constrict with pain. If she needed any proof that their lovemaking had meant little to him, he'd just given it to her. He'd known she wasn't feeling well and he hadn't even taken time to stop by her tent and see how she was when he came in for lunch.

"Lise? Are you all right?"

Sudden tears stinging her eyes, she dragged her gaze from the horizon and found Nate studying her worriedly. "I just got some dust in my eye," she said. "It's nothing."

Nate followed her gaze to the departing men, but although his eyes narrowed on the lead rider, he only said, "How are you feeling? You still don't have much color in your cheeks."

"I think I was just out in the sun too much yesterday," she replied huskily. "I'll be better after I rest some."

As far as hints went, that was a pretty strong one, and Nate was not an obtuse man. Not pressing her, he said gruffly, "I guess I'd better get back to work, then, and let you go back to bed. If you need anything, just call Cookie. He'll take good care of you."

His usually easygoing grin noticeably absent, he strode to the corral, where Tuck was checking one of the shoes of his mount, and growled, "The Yank hurt Lise."

Tuck's head came up sharply at that, his brows knit in a scowl. "What? How?"

"I don't know," he muttered, "but those were real tears in her eyes when she watched him ride off with Preston and Chuck. If he took advantage of her, I swear I'll break his face."

Tuck gave him a hard look. "You think he did that?"

Nate considered, then nodded shortly. "Yeah, I'm afraid so. And it stinks. Don't get me wrong—I like the Yank. I thought it was great when he flirted with Lise. It was about time somebody appreciated her. But she was an innocent, and he knew it. He went too far.''

"Then maybe it's time we had a talk with him," Tuck retorted grimly. "He might get away with making the ladies cry in America, but he's damn sure not going to do it here.''

Satisfied, Nate nodded. "Good. I'll round up some of the boys.''

The windmill was old and rusty and in sorry shape. But it was the only source of water for ten miles, and it was badly in need of repair. After strapping on a tool belt, Steve climbed up the metal tower to work on the motor, cursing the sun as it beat down on him, broiling him alive. It was a sweltering day, without a cloud in the sky, and hotter than hell. Even through his leather gloves, he could feel the heat radiating off the metal in waves.

Later, he couldn't have said how long he was twenty feet off the ground, cursing the windmill's old motor and sweating like a pig. At first, he thought the motor was frozen and incapable of being repaired, but after oiling every movable part he could find, the huge fan finally, reluctantly, groaned and started to move.

"All right!" he shouted to the wind. "It's about damn time!''

Grinning like a fool, he scrambled down the tower feeling like he'd just built the space shuttle with a screwdriver. Given the chance, he might have danced a jig, but the second he stepped down from the tower, he discovered he had visitors. And they didn't look very happy to see him. In fact, they looked downright hostile.

Surprised to see Nate, Tuck, Chuck and Preston glaring at him like he was roadkill and already starting to smell, he eyed the four of them cautiously. Had they somehow found out who he was? Was that what this little meeting was all about?

Alarmed, he greeted them with an easy smile, but on the inside, every muscle was tensed for action. "Hey, guys, what's going on? I thought you were rounding up the cattle this afternoon."

"It's time we had a little talk," Nate said flatly. "About Lise."

"You hurt her," Preston said quietly, resentment glinting in his eyes.

"No—"

"Don't bother to deny it," Tuck growled. "Nate saw her crying at lunch."

"And it's all your fault," Chuck added with a rare show of temper. "I've been here two years, and Lise never cried once in all that time. Not until you came and started hitting on her."

"I wasn't hitting on her—"

That was as far as he got. All his attention focused on Chuck and appeasing his anger, he never saw who threw the first punch. It caught him on the side of the jaw, and before he could even mutter a curse, fists were flying from every direction.

Steve liked to think that he was fairly tough—in his line of work, he had to be. When the need arose, he could throw punches with the best of them and hold his own. But Muhammad Ali would have had his hands full when the odds were four against one. Especially when the four closing in on him thought they were protecting the innocence of a woman they cared about. He didn't stand a chance.

That didn't mean he just gave up. After all, a man had some pride. So for a few moments, at least, he gave as good as he got. But he was fighting a losing battle, and they all knew it. For every punch he landed, at least three connected with various parts of his body. He grunted in pain and kept swinging. He was still swinging when a rock-hard fist caught him in the temple. Lightning swift, darkness fell like a shroud over him. Without a sound, he crumpled to the ground.

He was late.

Watching the others gather around the chuck wagon to eat, Lise frowned. Steve wasn't usually the first one in line when the dinner bell rang, but he wasn't the last, either. He usually came riding in with some of the other guys, and after a hard day's work, he could put the food away with the best of them.

So where was he? she wondered, gnawing on her bottom lip. Everyone had come in except him, and it was long past quitting time. Her gut told her something was wrong.

"Has anybody seen Steve?" she asked as she joined the chow line. "He should have come in by now."

For a moment, she didn't think anyone was going to answer her. Silence threatened to stretch into eternity. Then Nate said gruffly, "Maybe he realized the work's too hard for him. He wouldn't be the first cowboy to walk off the job when it got to be more than he could handle."

If they'd been talking about anyone but Steve, Lise might have found a way to accept that. The work *was* hard, and the pay was nothing to write home about. Over the years, more than one cowboy had ridden out to check fence and just kept on riding. Not Steve, though. She couldn't believe that of him. He truly seemed to enjoy the work, and she couldn't see him walking away from it—or her—without a word. He wasn't that kind of man.

And Nate knew that as well as she did. So why was

he suddenly spouting such garbage? "All right," she growled, including the entire group in the scowl she aimed at Nate. "What's going on? And don't look at me like you don't know what I'm talking about. Something stinks here, and I want to know what it is. Where's Steve?"

For a moment, she'd didn't think anyone was going to tell her. Exchanging speaking glances, the men shuffled their feet like guilty little boys. Frustrated, and getting more worried by the minute, Lise didn't know which she wanted to do more, shake them until their teeth rattled or fire the lot of them.

"Don't make me ask again," she warned.

She rarely lost her temper, but she didn't have red hair for nothing, and her men knew it. They looked at each other again. Finally, it was Chuck, the youngest of them all, who had the courage to speak up. "He's out at old Nelly," he mumbled, referring to the old windmill that they'd all worked on—and cursed—at one time or another. "He hurt you, so some of us thought it was time he was taught a lesson."

Outraged, Lise couldn't believe he was serious. "You beat him up?"

"Well, not by myself. Anyway, he hurt you! Nate saw you crying."

"So that gives you the right to beat him up? That gives all of you the right to step in and be judge and jury without so much as a by your leave? How dare you!"

Fury burning in her eyes, she couldn't believe their audacity. She may have decided that she couldn't trust Steve, but that was her business, dammit. *Hers!* "Whatever is going on with me and Steve has nothing to do with any of you," she said coldly. "Do you understand? When I need your help, I'll ask for it. In the meantime, you'd better pray that he's not seriously hurt. Because if he is, whoever's responsible for hurting him can pack their bags and get out.''

Not giving them time to so much as mutter a protest, she turned to Cookie and growled, ''Go get your first aid kit and meet me at the truck. I'm going to need your help getting him back to camp.''

Turning to her tent without another word, she collected the bedding from her cot and hurried to the pickup truck that was used to tow the chuck wagon. Cookie was waiting for her there with his first aid kit and the keys. ''I'll drive,'' he said before she could say a single word. ''Let's go.''

Lise was too worried about Steve to argue. Silently, she walked around the truck to the passenger door.

Sick with worry, Lise didn't remember much of the ride to the windmill. Staring straight ahead as the countryside whizzed past, all she could see was images of Steve's battered, broken body lying in the dust at the foot of the windmill. If he was hurt...

''He's going to be okay,'' she told herself and Cookie firmly, and tried to believe it. But when they finally reached the windmill and her searching eyes immediately found Steve lying in a crumpled heap, just as she'd pictured him, her heart stopped dead in her chest. With a strangled cry, she was out of the truck and running toward him before Cookie had even brought the truck to a stop.

''Oh, my God! Steve! Can you hear me?''

He didn't move so much as an eyelash.

Terrified, Lise dropped to her knees in the dust beside him and reached for him with trembling fingers. He was, thank God, breathing, but that was about all he had going for him. His face was bruised and swollen and bloody from the blows he'd taken, and his knuckles were scraped raw.

"Quick, Cookie, bring me some water and the smelling salts. And a blanket. We need to get him out of the dirt."

Cookie wasn't the kind of man who ever got in a hurry, but he was beside her in seconds, checking Steve's wounds with expert hands. "Nothing seems to be broken," he said matter-of-factly, "but he took some hard punches. Here, let's get him on his back and see if we can bring him around."

With gentle hands, he rolled Steve onto his back on the blanket he'd spread out next to him, then uncapped the smelling salts and waved the bottle under his nose. "C'mon, Yank," he muttered, "you've slept on the job long enough. It's time to wake up."

His brain smothered in darkness, Steve drew in the sharp scent of the smelling salts and winced. Throbbing with pain, he groaned and turned his head away. "Don't!" he muttered. "I've told you everything I know."

"Steve? Are you okay? Can you hear me? It's Lise."

From a distance, Steve thought he heard Lise calling him, but he couldn't be sure. Images swam in and out of his head, confusing him, and with a muttered curse, he growled, "The bastard slipped away again! Just like a rat in the dark. I don't know how the hell he does it. I've got to call Belinda—"

He started to turn, only to groan as the slight movement sent a white-hot pain rippling through his head. Dragging in a sharp breath, he tried to hang on to consciousness, but he was fighting a losing battle. Darkness descended like a sudden, unexpected storm, and there was no place he could run to to escape the thick, black clouds that swallowed him whole. Without a sound, he slipped back into unconsciousness.

"Steve!" Worry knitting her brow, confused by his mumblings, Lise wanted to ask him who Belinda was, and the man who was like a rat in the dark, but he couldn't hear her. "We've got to get him back to camp," she told Cookie huskily. "Let's do it now, while he's unconscious, and it won't hurt him so much."

They had their work cut out for them. Steve was a big man, and though Lise was strong for a woman, she only had Cookie to help her, and he wasn't even as tall as her shoulder. She didn't know how they were going to find the strength to lift him.

Cookie, however, had no such worries. Quickly backing the truck up to where Steve lay, he told Lise, "You take his feet."

"But that's the lightest end. You can't—"

"I can," he said firmly, and motioned her to move to Steve's feet.

Later, Lise didn't know why she ever doubted him. From the time she was a little girl, Cookie had had a magical, mystical power about him that she'd never understood. He could do things that no one else on the station could do, and whenever she asked him how he did such things, he always smiled mysteriously and said it was the way of his people.

This time was no different. She didn't know how he did it, but within minutes, he had lifted Steve into the back of the truck, and with very little help from her. She knew he had to use some kind of mind over body control, but there was no time to ask him about it now. Climbing into the back of the truck, she settled down beside Steve as Cookie once again slipped into the driver's seat. Within seconds, they were racing back to camp.

* * *

Slowly regaining consciousness, Steve opened his eyes to discover himself in his tent, with Lise and Cookie hovering over him worriedly. Disoriented, he frowned and only then remembered the little run-in he'd had with Nate and Tuck and the others. Immediately, he struggled to sit up. "I'm all right," he began, only to groan and collapse on his pillow as sharp, shooting pain streaked through his battered and bruised body.

"You're a strong man," Cookie told him solemnly. "After the beating you took, you shouldn't even be able to move."

Gritting his teeth against the pain, Steve grimaced wryly. "Gee, thanks for the compliment. I'm flattered."

"You're lucky to be alive," Lise told him, worry clouding her blue eyes. "Chuck told me what happened. I'm sorry."

"For what? You didn't do anything."

"No, but my men did, and I feel responsible. I promise you it won't happen again."

He accepted that with a nod, but they both knew why her men had felt compelled to give him a thrashing. Ever since they'd made love, it seemed like they'd been at odds. Obviously, he had done something to hurt her, and they needed to talk about it, but Steve had no intention of having that kind of discussion in front of Cookie. And the old man wasn't going anywhere. Hovering at Lise's side like a watchdog, he wasn't the least impressed with the hard look Steve shot him.

Frustrated, Steve growled, "Don't worry about it. I'll be back on my feet in no time."

Not waiting to be asked, Cookie said, "A week. No sooner."

Steve wanted to argue, but he had a sinking feeling the

old man was right. Nate and Tuck and the others had done
a good job of working him over. Even his teeth ached.
"We'll see about that. I'm a fast healer."

Lise rolled her eyes. If that wasn't just like a man. Why
was it so difficult for them to admit that they were hurting? It wasn't a character flaw, for God's sake! They
didn't have to be strong all the time.

But that's just what Steve would do, she realized, if
she didn't find a way to get him out of there. He'd fight
her efforts to keep him in bed, in spite of the fact that
was obviously where he needed to be, and the first time
she turned her back, he'd go back to work.

What if he had a blood clot? she wondered worriedly.
He had bruises all over his body. If he went back to work
too soon, a blood clot could develop and kill him.
Couldn't it?

Unsure, unwilling to take the chance, she said, "No,
we won't see about it. As of this moment, you're on sick
leave for the next week. And just to make sure you do
what you're told and rest, I'm taking you back to the
house."

"What? But what about the roundup? You're needed
here."

"The guys'll get by without me. And the roundup ends
next week. By the time you're back on your feet, it'll be
all over with."

If Lise needed any proof that she was doing the right
thing, she got it when he scowled like a little boy who'd
just been told he couldn't have another piece of candy.
Smothering a smile, she said, "Now that we've got that
settled, I just need to collect a few things from my tent,
then we can go. Cookie, would you make a pallet in the
back of the truck, please?"

"I don't need a pallet!"

He might think that now, but Lise knew he wouldn't be able to make it all the way to the house without needing to lie down. To keep the peace, however, she only said, "Fine. You don't have to use it. But it'll be there if you need it."

He didn't like it, but there wasn't a hell of a lot he could do about it since she was the boss. Pride forcing him to hide how much he was hurting, he rolled stiffly out of his cot and slowly, painfully, made his way to the truck as she conferred with Tuck, leaving him in charge of the men and finishing up the roundup over the course of the next week.

Less than five minutes later, Lise drove out of camp with Steve in the back of the pickup. Standing by the chuck wagon, a frown knitting his dark brow, Cookie watched them until they disappeared from view. Like Tuck and Nate and the rest of the men, he'd seen the way Lise opened up like a flower whenever the Yank flirted with her, and he didn't mind admitting that had him worried. He loved her like a daughter, and he couldn't stand around with his hands in his pockets while she got hurt. Unlike the rest of the men, he didn't have to use his fists to protect her. He had other means.

Stepping into his tent, he found the special phone his boss had given him that allowed him to keep in touch with him anywhere in the world. Quickly dialing the number he knew by heart, he waited only until he heard the familiar voice at the other end of the line before he said, "I think we've got a problem between Lise and the Yank."

Steve didn't remember much about the long drive back to the house. Less than a half mile from camp, he found it impossible to sit up anymore, and with a ragged sigh, he let go of his pride and collapsed on the pallet of blankets Cookie had made for him. The padding helped, but not much. The station road was little more than a rough dirt track, and Steve felt every jarring bump and dip. It was nearly as bad as getting beat up all over again.

Drifting in and out of consciousness, he lost track of time and where he was. Lying flat on his back, he stared at the night sky and wished the world would stop moving. When it finally did, all he wanted to do was lie right where he was for the rest of the night.

Before he could close his eyes and drift back into unconsciousness, however, a woman was leaning over him, urging him to get up. "C'mon, Steve, you have to help me. I can't get you into the house by myself."

Not recognizing her, he frowned. Who was she? And why was she calling him Steve? That wasn't his name. Was it? "What house? Where are we? I need to call Belinda."

Lise winced at that. There was that name again. Belinda. Who was she to him? And why, when he was feeling so miserable, did he call for her? Was she some long-lost love? Or a wife he'd walked away from somewhere and still loved?

Pain lanced her heart at the thought, but she didn't have time to worry about that now. "You can call Belinda later," she promised. "After you're feeling better. Right now, we've got to get you in the house. Can you sit up?"

Lise didn't know if it was the promise that he could call his precious Belinda or that her words registered and he realized she really did need his help to get him inside, but he gritted his teeth and struggled to sit up. It wasn't easy for him. The second he started to move, his body cried out in protest. He groaned, but didn't let the pain stop him. Sitting up without help, he swung his legs over the tailgate of the truck.

''That's it,'' she said, hurriedly scrambling to his side to slip her arm around his waist. ''Put your arm around my shoulder. Now we're going to take it slow and easy. There's a guest room downstairs, off the study. Just hang on a few more steps and we'll be there.''

It was more than a few steps, but if Steve noticed she wasn't quite truthful about that, he didn't say anything. All his attention apparently focused on putting one foot in front of the other, he let her guide him inside. And all the while, the weight of his arm on her shoulder grew heavier and heavier as he leaned on her more and more.

If the guest room had been five more steps, Lise didn't think they would have made it. Steve had used the last reserves of his strength and was stumbling by the time they reached the threshold. Two steps into the room, he started to fall, and Lise knew there was no way she could catch him. Luckily, she didn't have to. The bed was right there. He fell across it with a groan and didn't move again.

''Steve?''

Unconscious, he didn't twitch so much as an eyelash. And that, Lise decided, was probably for the best. Getting him out of his clothes was, no doubt, going to be quite painful. Wishing she could spare him that, she determinedly went to work on the buttons of his shirt.

''Dammit to hell, I knew the bastard was playing both sides against the middle! Lying piece of trash. He's going to burn in hell for this—I'll make sure of it.''

Jolted out of a sound sleep, Lise jerked awake, her heart thumping crazily, and then realized she must have fallen asleep next to Steve in the guest room after she'd stripped him of his clothes and bathed his wounds. Even now, just thinking about it, she wanted to cry. His poor bruised body—

"Belinda? Dammit, where are you when I need you? Get your ass in gear and answer the damn phone!"

Worried sick, Lise didn't even wince at the mention of Belinda's name. He'd rambled on about her several times while she was tending his wounds, then he'd slipped into something that sounded an awful lot like Spanish. When he'd switched back to English, he'd complained that he hadn't been able to bring a real gun with him—he had a feeling he was going to need it.

At any other time, Lise might have been disturbed by that. But there was no time for that when she was so worried about him. He'd taken a real beating. Any other man would have been in desperate need of a hospital, but he was somehow still hanging tough. In his more lucid moments, she was able to get some aspirin down him to ease the pain, but he was still hurting. And that meant she was hurting, too. Because she was falling in love with him.

The truth crept out of the darkness of the night to steal the air right out of her lungs. No! she wanted to cry. She couldn't possibly love him. She didn't know anything about him—except that he was a man she couldn't trust. For reasons she couldn't begin to understand, he wanted to bring her father down. How could she love a man who wanted to hurt her father?

She had to be mistaken, she told herself. She was attracted to him, that was all. If she was in love, it was just with the idea of being in love. They'd made love, and she'd allowed herself to get caught up in feelings she had no business feeling. She couldn't, wouldn't make that mistake again. Because the time was quickly approaching when she would have to call her father and tell him her suspicions about Steve. Then her father would fire him, and he would be gone.

Not yet, she thought, swallowing a sob. She couldn't lose him just yet. Not when this was the only time they would ever have alone together. One week—that was all she was asking for—to take care of him and spend nearly every waking and sleeping moment with him. What could it hurt? Then she would do the right thing and call her father.

Her decision made, she checked to make sure he was resting as comfortably as possible, then laid down beside him. She'd just rest until he needed her again, she thought, and closed her eyes with a contented sigh. Almost immediately, she was asleep.

The night passed in wave after wave of dark colors. Drifting in and out of consciousness, his body racked with pain, Steve thought he was dreaming. He had to be. Lise was there beside him in bed, at her house, and she was wearing a powder blue nightgown that would have made his mouth water if he hadn't been hurting so badly. And she seemed to know that. Her blue eyes soft with understanding, she bathed and soothed and eased his every discomfort with a gentle touch, and he never had to say a word. She knew where he hurt.

And when he finally drifted into an exhausted sleep, she still stayed by his side. He could feel her beside him in his dreams, stretched out next to him, stirring only when she felt him stir. Then, once again, her hands were there to ease his pain as she murmured to him quietly.

Heaven, he thought sleepily. He'd died and gone to some kind of weird heaven.

* * *

The sun was already climbing into the sky when Steve came slowly awake the next morning. His entire body throbbed with a dull ache, but the fog shrouding his brain had finally lifted. The second he opened his eyes and saw Lise asleep on the bed beside him, jagged, blurry images of the night—and the beating—came rushing back. He had little memory of the drive from camp to the house, but he remembered every blow of the thrashing he'd taken, and who'd hurt him.

Stay away from Lise. The message had been loud and clear, the threat behind it impossible to ignore. *Or else.* If he didn't take the hint, the price he paid would be much worse than a beating.

He liked to think he was a man with more than his share of common sense. He didn't need another beating to know that he was outnumbered, and this was a battle he couldn't win. So the wise thing to do was to bow to the power of persuasion and leave the lady alone.

He knew that, accepted that and didn't for a minute fool himself into thinking he was going to be able to do that. Not now that he'd made love to her. He still didn't trust her and didn't know if he ever would. When he got back on his feet, he'd arrest Simon the first chance he got, and he'd take Lise down with Simon if he found out she was involved in her old man's activities. But until that happened, he knew he wasn't going to be able to stay away from her. Not yet.

He didn't know how she'd done it, but she'd stolen his heart right out of his chest. And right or wrong, that was something he was going to have to live with.

Chapter 10

"Are you comfortable? Can I bring you anything?"

"I'm fine, Lise. You don't have to keep waiting on me this way. I can get what I need."

"No! You need to rest. I'll get some more books from the study for you."

Afraid that if she ever let him get out of bed he would go back to work before he was completely healed, she hurried to the study for several of the mysteries her father collected. She was back almost immediately with the last three he hadn't read. Who would have guessed he was such a voracious reader? Over the course of the last few days, he'd consumed everything he could get his hands on.

"Here you go," she said brightly. "After you finish those, you can read the labels of the canned goods in the pantry. You've read everything else."

Grinning, he made no apologies for the fact that he

liked to read. "I could go back to work, you know. I'm feeling much better."

"Tomorrow," she said promptly. "We'll see how you're doing tomorrow."

She'd put him off for the past three days with the same excuse, and each day, it was harder to keep him in bed. She believed he was feeling better, but he still looked awful. Covered in bruises that seemed to grow worse with the passage of time, he was now every conceivable shade of purple and green. So she kept refusing to let him go back to work and spent her days taking care of him and finding ways to keep him entertained.

And with each passing day, they grew closer.

They didn't talk about it—they didn't dare!—but Lise knew he was as aware as she was of the quiet intimacy that was developing between them. She touched him, and her heart pounded. His fingers brushed hers, and she only had to look into his eyes to know that he was remembering, like she, those hushed moments in the cave when they'd made love.

It was a dangerous game they were playing, and no one knew that better than Lise. She hadn't forgotten that he was her father's enemy and had apparently come here to bring him down, but she couldn't worry about that right now. They had these days stolen out of time, and for a little while, at least, it was easy to pretend they were the only two people in the world. There was no subterfuge, no secrets, no lies. He was simply Steve Trace, cowboy from the States and the man she was falling in love with. Nothing else mattered. There would be time enough to call her father and tell him what was going on once Steve was completely healed and back on his feet.

As hard as she tried to pretend otherwise, however, they were quickly running out of time. Four days after they arrived at the ranch, she could no longer ignore the fact that he was just about back to his old self. Oh, the bruises were more colorful than ever, but they would disappear with time, and he'd regained his strength. He insisted on getting out of bed, and spent the day restlessly following her around the house, helping her cook and clean while he grumbled that he had nothing to do. Left with no choice, Lise was forced to concede that he really was ready to go back to work.

And it broke her heart. She was losing him, and there was nothing she could do about it. Loyalty and love for her father forced her to warn him about the traitor in their midst, and once she did that, she knew she could kiss Steve goodbye. Because even though she ran the station, her father wouldn't tolerate any kind of betrayal from an employee once he found out about it. He would get rid of him so fast, Steve wouldn't know what hit him. And once again, she would be alone. Just as she'd always been.

Her heart already heavy with the loss of what might have been, she couldn't fight the sadness that engulfed her. By the end of the day, all she wanted to do was escape to her room and cry her eyes out. She didn't, however, because her pride would never allow her to wallow in self-pity. So she forced a bright smile and acted as if she was thrilled that he was better and they both could get back to their regular routines.

"I talked to Tuck this afternoon," she told him over dinner. "He and the boys are just about through with the roundup. They should be dragging in here sometime tomorrow afternoon. The day after that, my father's flying in for the barbecue we always have to celebrate the end of the roundup. After that, you can go back to work."

She wasn't brimming over with enthusiasm at the idea, but Steve couldn't say he blamed her. He didn't want this time they had together to end, either. But if Simon was expected the day after tomorrow, everything would end then.

He had to call Belinda and let her know what was going on, but he couldn't bring himself to do it just yet. Time was slipping through his fingers, and he wanted to grab onto it with both hands. Later, he promised himself, he would call Belinda. After dinner.

But after dinner, he helped Lise clear the table and do the dishes, and all he could think of was that this was probably their last night together. When they finished the dishes and both grabbed the dish towel at the same time to dry their hands, he instantly began to pull her toward him. Suddenly, nothing seemed so important as touching, holding her, kissing her.

His eyes alight with promise, he said, "I want you."

His boldness shocked her. "We shouldn't," she gasped. But when he pulled gently on the towel, tugging her toward him, she didn't let go. "Steve—"

"I love it when you say my name all soft and sexy like that," he growled, pulling her into his arms. "Say it again."

"Oh, Steve."

He assured himself he just needed a kiss, but the second his mouth settled on hers, he knew he'd never again be content with just that when he had her so close. Need clawing at him with sharp talons, he tangled his hands in the fiery strands of her hair and took the kiss deeper. And still it wasn't enough.

The guest room was just steps away. With a little urging on his part, he could have had her there in ten seconds flat. But he needed more than that. He needed to make love to her in her room, her bed, so that she would remember him there long after he was gone.

Dragging his mouth from hers abruptly, he whispered, "Let's go upstairs to your room. I want to make love to you."

Aching for him, needing him more than she needed her next breath, Lise wouldn't have argued if he'd said he wanted to make love to her on the roof. Taking his hand, she led him upstairs to her bedroom.

She started to turn the light on, but his hand was there before hers in the dark, stopping her. "The moon's out," he said huskily. "That's all we need."

All her attention focused on him, she'd never noticed the moonlight streaming through the open window and across her bed. It looked like something out of a romantic dream. A soft breeze stirred the gossamer curtains at the window, and the bedding was already turned back, revealing her favorite lace-trimmed sheets and fluffy pillows. With no effort whatsoever, she could see the two of them lying there together, making love.

"Steve."

That was all she could say, just his name, but he must have sensed the longing in her heart. With a quiet murmur, he leaned down and swept her off her feet. A heartbeat later, he carried her to the bed and laid her in the middle of the mattress. Before she could call his name again, he followed her down, his mouth tender and urgent on hers as he reached for the buttons of her blouse.

She loved the feel of his hands on her. He was so gentle, so tender, she could have wept with the sweetness of it. Her clothes disappeared with a whisper in the night, and just that easily, she was bathed in moonlight. She could feel the touch of it on her skin, setting her aglow as his hands moved slowly over her, exploring every inch of her.

Need settled low in her belly, and with a soft moan, she kissed him hungrily and ached for more. She needed to touch him as he touched her, to trace the long, hard length of him with her hands and commit every second of their loving to memory. Because this was probably the last time she would ever get to love him.

Her heart flinched at the thought, and she quickly pushed it aside. She wouldn't think of that now. She couldn't let the loneliness of the future ruin the wonder of this precious moment. They had today, and that was all she would think of—the two of them together.

With eager hands, she pulled his clothes from him so she could touch him as she longed to. Then with slow, deliberate strokes, she set about driving him slowly out of his mind.

It didn't take much.

The man was amazingly sensitive to her touch. She only had to draw her fingers down his back and over his hips to drag a groan from him. A kiss on the side of his neck made him shudder. Delighted, she would have kissed her way down his chest to his thundering heart, but he stopped her before she'd hardly begun. With a low growl, he rolled onto his back, taking her with him in a dizzy rush that had her gasping in surprise.

"Steve!"

"There you go again," he said with a raspy chuckle. "Say it again."

She couldn't deny him. With her lying on top of him, his hands had access to every inch of her, and he delighted in taking advantage of her position. He touched her in places she would have sworn weren't the least bit sensitive, then his mouth followed the trail his hands had set. Just that easily, he had her calling his name.

"Steve. Oh, Steve!"

He might have been able to hang on to what was left of his self-control if she hadn't chosen that moment to touch him just the way he was touching her. But she was a quick learner, and with a touch that was petal soft, she ran her fingertips over him lightly, slowly, seductively. Pleasure streaking through him, loving what she was doing to him, he told himself he could handle this. Then her mouth joined in the teasing. In the time it took to draw in a sharp breath, she had him right where she wanted— groaning and out of his mind for her.

There was no time for teasing after that. His blood roaring in his ears, his heart hammering against his ribs, he hurriedly took care of protection, linked his fingers with hers and rolled her under him. She was still gasping when he slid into her.

"Steve!"

No woman had ever come so close to bringing him to release simply by calling his name. She moved under him, with him, and what was left of his self-control unraveled. He was on fire for her in the moonlight. Just her. His breath tearing through his lungs, he raced with her through the darkness, every nerve ending in his body tight with need. Then, just when he thought he couldn't last another second, she shattered.

Her cry of release was his undoing. Following her over the edge, he wanted to tell her how much he loved what she did to him, what they did to each other, how no one had ever destroyed him so completely. But in the end, he could only manage one word. Just her name. "Lise."

*   *   *

This was killing him.

He watched her slip out of the bedroom dressed in nothing but his shirt to get them a snack from the kitchen, and he couldn't help but feel like the lowest heel on earth. When Simon flew in the day after tomorrow, Steve was going to bring her and her father's world tumbling down. And although he knew he was doing the right thing, the only thing he could do, that didn't make him feel any better. He'd gone and done the one thing he'd sworn he wasn't going to do. He'd fallen in love with her, and it was tearing him apart.

How had he let this happen?

He wanted to believe she'd deliberately said or done something to seduce him, but looking back on his time at the station, he was forced to admit he'd been taken with her from the first moment he'd laid eyes on her. And the attraction had only grown stronger with each passing day.

When Simon showed up, though, it would end.

If he'd had a choice of whether to bring the bastard down or not, that might have changed everything. But there was no choice—not where Simon was concerned. He wasn't just a danger to Jonah and the entire SPEAR organization, he was a threat to everything that was good and right in the world, and he had to be brought down. At any cost. Even if that cost was the love of a good woman.

And she was, Steve knew, a good woman. If she was caught up in her father's nefarious dealings, he had to believe it was only because she didn't realize the extent of the bastard's wickedness. When the truth finally came out and she discovered just what kind of man Simon really was, maybe then she wouldn't blame Steve too much for his part in his downfall.

But even if she hated his guts, he still had a mission to complete.

Slipping out of bed, he pulled his wallet from his jeans, found his phone card among his credit cards and pressed in the code for Belinda. When she came on the line, there was no need to talk in code. Lise would be downstairs for some time, out of earshot, and he couldn't take a chance that Belinda might misunderstand. "Simon will be home the day after tomorrow for a barbecue he always gives after the roundup," he said flatly. "I want backup waiting nearby, no more than ten minutes away."

"I'll wait for your signal," she assured him. "Where are you now?"

"The main house," he replied, and told her about the beating he'd suffered at the hands of Lise's men. "I'm all right, but I think it's fair to say I've convinced the other men that I'm after Lise. They don't have a clue why I'm really here."

"And what about Lise? How is that going?"

"Fine. She doesn't suspect anything, either."

He would have sworn his voice was perfectly normal, that he didn't give his feelings away by the slightest change in intonation, but Belinda was nothing if not sharp. "I didn't think that she did—you're too good an agent to give yourself away. It was your relationship with her that I was really asking about. You've grown closer, haven't you?"

He didn't bother to deny it. What would be the point? "I'm handling it."

"That's what I'm afraid of," she said dryly. "You're getting too close, Steve. You're in love with her, aren't you?"

"I told you—I'm handling it."

"I'm trusting you to do that, but I'm reeling you in," she told him. "You're in danger of losing your perspective, and that's when covers get blown. You've got forty-eight hours to complete your mission, then I'm pulling you."

At any other time, he would have argued with her, though it would have done little good—she was his contact, and it was part of her job to make that call. But in this particular case, forty-eight hours would be more than enough time to complete his mission. This time, he was sure Simon would show up.

"Whatever you say, Mom," he answered. "You're the boss."

Standing pale and shaken in the hallway with a tray full of snacks, Lise heard every word of Steve's side of the conversation and felt her heart drop to her knees. For days now, she'd been pretending he was the man she needed him to be, a man she could trust. And all this time, he'd been waiting for the chance to heal so he could make his move. A move, she thought bitterly, that had nothing to do with her. The only Meldrum he wanted was her father.

Simon will be home the day after tomorrow.... I want backup waiting nearby, no more than ten minutes away.... I think it's fair to say I've convinced the other men that I'm after Lise. They don't have a clue why I'm really here.

Over and over again, the hurtful words replayed in her head, words she never would have heard if she hadn't rushed to return to his side, and it was all she could do not to cry out in pain. How could the man who had just made love to her so tenderly be such a monster? Was he really that cold? Even now, she didn't want to believe it, but he couldn't have been clearer if he'd carved his words in stone. She was nothing to him. Nothing.

She had to warn her father.

Devastated, she knew she couldn't put it off any longer. Steve was going to have men waiting for him. If she didn't warn him, he'd walk right into a trap.

No! her heart cried out. She couldn't stand by and let that happen. Her father didn't deserve that. He might not be the most attentive father in the world, but at least he wasn't a monster like Steve. She had to call him. Now!

The decision made, she soundlessly made her way downstairs and hurried into the study. Taking time only to set the tray of snacks on the desk, she quickly snatched up the phone and punched in the number of her father's cell phone.

"Lise!" her father said in surprise, answering the call before his voice mail could take it. "I wasn't expecting to hear from you until tomorrow. What are you doing home so soon? Is there a problem or did the roundup finish ahead of schedule?"

"Actually, Dad, there *is* a problem," she said shakily. "You can't come home for the barbecue."

They didn't have the kind of relationship where they joked around or played tricks on each other—they weren't that close. Which in this particular case was an advantage. He knew immediately that she was serious.

"What's wrong?"

At his grim tone, tears welled in her eyes. How was she going to tell him that he was being betrayed by someone he considered a friend? "It's Steve."

"Steve Trace?"

Swallowing the lump in her throat, she said huskily, "Yes. He's not your friend, Dad."

"No, he's not," he agreed. "He did a favor for me

once, and I returned it by giving him a job. What's going on, Lise? What's he done that's got you so upset?''

Her heart breaking, she had no choice but to tell him. ''I think he was sent by some of your old mining enemies. Before the roundup, when he was just supposed to be using the phone in your study, I caught him on the computer.''

''Why? Did you question him about it? What was he after?''

''No, I didn't question him. I thought it would be better to wait and see if he made a comment about it, which he did. He said he was trying to find some information about how to treat a medical problem his father has. But then he broke into the cabin.''

If anything would set her father's back up, she knew it was that. She didn't have to wait long for his reaction.

''Oh, really?'' he said silkily.

''I don't know what he was looking for, but I think he must have searched the place. I followed him and overheard him on his cell phone. He was mad because he hadn't found anything and kept talking about someone named Simon. Do you know who that is?''

For a minute, she didn't think he was going to answer her. Cold, empty silence echoed across the phone line, and there was something about the very nature of it that chilled her blood. Suddenly frightened and not sure why, she said hesitantly, ''Dad? Are you all right?''

No, he wasn't. So SPEAR had invaded his home space. No doubt, Jonah thought he finally had him cornered. Like hell! Jonah and his agents were the ones who were coming down. All he needed was a little more time.

''Don't worry about Mr. Trace,'' he finally said coldly. ''I'll take care of him.''

''But he's set a trap for you! I overheard him on the

phone just a minute ago. He didn't say what his plans are, but there are other people involved. They're going to be waiting for you when you fly in for the barbecue. Please don't come, Dad. I really think they're going to hurt you.''

''I've got it taken care of,'' he repeated. ''Continue with the barbecue, as scheduled, and leave Steve to me.''

He hung up without another word, just as he always did. Lise knew she shouldn't have been hurt—her father never seemed to have time to say goodbye, and she'd gotten used to that over the years—but this time, it was like a slap in the face. She was only trying to protect him, dammit! The least he could have done was take a few more minutes to reassure her before he hung up. She was worried about him.

That's just his way, a voice in her head said. *You know how he is. Don't take it personally.*

She'd been telling herself that for as long as she could remember, shrugging off her father's coldness by reminding herself that he treated everyone that way so there was no reason to think he'd gone out of his way to be cold just to her. This was the man he'd become after her mother died. Knowing that usually made it easier for her to accept his indifference, but this time, it didn't help. He could have at least thanked her for warning him.

There was, however, no time to dwell on her hurt feelings. Not when Steve was in the bedroom, waiting for the snack she'd promised him. By now, he'd no doubt started to wonder where she was. How, she thought wildly, was she going to face him without him guessing what she'd been up to? She'd never been any good at hiding things—her face was too expressive. He'd take one look at her and know she'd been up to something suspicious.

''Act normal,'' she told herself sternly. ''You just made

love, for heaven's sake! Distract him with a couple of
kisses and he won't have time to look at your face.''

That sounded good, but as she started up the stairs, she
was a nervous wreck. Her heart was in her throat, and her
hands were shaking so badly she was sure she was going
to drop the tray of snacks she'd almost forgotten at the
last minute. She dragged in a deep breath, released it
slowly and forced a smile. She didn't have to look in the
mirror to know that it was strained, but considering the
circumstances, it was the best she could do.

''Here we go,'' she said brightly as she stepped into
the bedroom to find him still in her bed, looking strong
and sexy against her white sheets. ''Sorry I was gone so
long, but I couldn't find the crackers. Every time I think
I know where things are in the kitchen, Cookie moves
things around. He's one of those people who needs
change all the time to keep life interesting.''

She knew she was chattering, but she couldn't seem to
stop. ''So what would you like? We've got cheese and
crackers, some of Cookie's shrimp salad, and brownies.
The salad's delicious. Cookie uses this special secret sea-
soning—''

''Are you all right?''

No! She wanted to cry. She was a basket case, and if
he didn't stop looking at her so worriedly, she was going
to collapse in a heap and confess everything. ''Actually,''
she lied huskily, ''I'm feeling a little dizzy. I think I must
be coming down with something.''

That was the only excuse she could think of on the
spur of the moment to explain her odd behavior, and too
late, she realized it was the last thing she should have
said. The words were hardly out of her mouth before he
hurriedly jumped out of bed. Stark naked, he quickly
moved to take the tray from her.

''Why didn't you say something?'' he scolded. ''You should have called me—I'd have carried that upstairs for you. Here—let me have that.''

Quickly taking the tray from her, he set it on a table by the window, then turned to help her into bed. ''Do you have a fever?'' His hand settled on her forehead. Just that easily, he heated her blood. ''You are a little warm,'' he said with a frown. ''Have you got any aspirin in the bathroom? Hang on, and I'll get you some.''

''No. I'm sure I'm fine—''

She might as well have saved her breath. He didn't give her time to argue, but simply disappeared into her private bathroom. A few seconds later, he was back, not only with the aspirin and a cup of water, but also a damp washcloth. ''This'll make you feel better, I promise.''

Lise didn't think she would ever feel better again, but that was something she could hardly tell him. Dutifully, she downed the aspirin, then eyed the washcloth suspiciously. ''What's that for?''

''Your head,'' he replied promptly. ''Lie down.''

''You don't have to baby me, Steve. I'm fine. Really. I probably just took the stairs too quickly.''

''You look awfully pale,'' he argued. ''Lie down and let me take care of you.''

That was the last thing she wanted—and the one thing her heart longed for. Torn, she hesitated, feeling more vulnerable than she'd ever felt in her life, but in the end, she couldn't resist letting him fuss over her. Obediently, she leaned back.

''Good girl,'' he growled softly, and gently set the damp folded washcloth over her forehead and eyes. ''Just rest and try to go back to sleep. I'll be here all night if you need me.''

Tears sprang to her eyes at that, but with the washcloth

across half her face, he couldn't see them, thank God—
or how badly her heart was breaking. And even if he
could have, she doubted that he would have cared. After
all, she was just a convenience he used to get to her father.

Swallowing the sob that rose in her throat, she felt him
lie down beside her and draw the covers over the two of
them, and it was all she could do not to turn into his arms
and cry her eyes out. Life just wasn't fair sometimes. It
seemed like she'd waited all her life for a man who didn't
give a flip that she wasn't petite and blonde. A man who
cherished her and made her feel special…and loved. And
now that God had finally sent her one, he only cared about
two things—bringing her father down…and a woman
named Belinda. And that hurt.

Why, she wondered, couldn't he have been a cold, unfeeling monster who didn't care about anyone but himself? Then he would have been easier to hate. But it was
hard to dislike a man who was so solicitous of her. Even
as she struggled with her secret tears, she felt him gently
stroke her hair, then lift the washcloth to check her temperature.

Lying perfectly still, not moving a muscle, she should
have told him to stop. She was only torturing herself by
letting him continue. But knowing that, she still couldn't
bring herself to say anything. Not yet. Not when his touch
felt so good. She just needed a few more moments.

Caught up in the wonder of his gentle care, she couldn't
have said exactly when she fell asleep. One second, she
felt the stroke of his hand over her hair, and the next, she
couldn't stay awake. With a silent sigh, she drifted into
sleep, loving the feel of him next to her.

She didn't sleep long. Her dreams wouldn't let her.
Over and over again, her brain replayed her conversation

with her father. *I've got it taken care of...leave Steve to me.* What had he meant by that? Her imagination supplied all sorts of answers, and each one chilled her to the bone, making it impossible for her to sleep. She'd never heard her father sound quite so cold before. If he'd spoken of her that way, she'd have been scared to death. And that worried her. Surely he wouldn't hurt Steve. Would he?

Images haunted her dreams, and she came awake to find Steve leaning over her, trying to soothe her as she tossed and turned restlessly. "It's okay, sweetheart. Everything's going to be okay."

Her heart pounding, she stared at him searchingly in the moonlight. "What happened?"

"You were calling my name in your sleep," he said huskily. "Are you okay?"

If his concern wasn't genuine, he should have been acting in Hollywood. Tears stung her eyes, and she prayed he couldn't see them in the darkness. "I guess I was dreaming," she said thickly. "I don't remember."

"How are you feeling? Can I get you anything? Some soup? Crackers? Gardenias?"

Reaching over, he stroked her hair again, and that was nearly her undoing. She doubted that there was any kind of flower for a thousand miles, but if she asked for some, she knew he would find a way to get them for her. And that only confused her more. One second, she was sure he was there to hurt her father, and the next, he was treating her like she was the most precious thing on earth. Who was this man, really? Would she ever know now that she'd called her father?

Second thoughts hit her from all directions. She whispered, "No. I don't need anything. Just some rest."

And a chance to turn back the clock. She buried her face in the pillow and wondered, too late, if she'd made

a horrible mistake by calling her father. What if she'd
misunderstood that conversation she'd overheard from the
hallway? Her father was going to come in and squash him
like a bug, and he might be totally innocent.

Sick at the thought of what she might have set in motion, she didn't know what to do. She didn't want her
father hurt, but she didn't want Steve hurt, either. Dear
God, what had she done?

Chapter 11

She should have called her father back and told him she'd made a mistake. She wasn't very good at lying, but she could have found a way to make him believe her. All she had to do was convince him she'd misunderstood what she'd seen and heard. How difficult could it be?

All that night and the next morning, guilt nagged her. It would take all of two minutes to make the call, she told herself. But just the thought of trying to get a lie past her father made her sick to her stomach. He'd see through her in a heartbeat. And he wasn't a man who tolerated being lied to. She told herself there had to be another way.

But none presented itself, and finally, she was reluctantly forced to admit she had no choice. She had to make the call. The only problem was every time she tried to slip away to the study to make the call in private, it seemed Steve was right there, blocking her path. Before she knew it, the morning was gone.

And she'd heard nothing from her father.

Trying not to panic, she told herself that wasn't necessarily a bad thing. Since she'd talked to him last night, he'd had time to think about her warning and had probably decided she was being paranoid. *That* was why she hadn't heard from him. He wasn't going to do anything.

Clinging to that thought, she heard vehicles in the drive and glanced out the front windows in time to see Tuck and the others pass on their way to the barn and bunkhouse. Thank God, she thought with a sigh of relief. Everyone was back, her father was nowhere in sight, and life could return to normal. All she had to do was get through the barbecue tomorrow.

There was, she supposed, still an outside possibility that her father might not show at all. Granted, he'd never missed a barbecue yet, but for some reason, things were different this year. He was more distracted than usual, and even though the barbecue wasn't until tomorrow, he should have been home by now. He loved the roundup, and in the past, he'd always showed up several days before it ended to get in some work with his favorite cutting horse and the cattle. But not this time. The odds seemed to be in her favor that he wouldn't show at all.

And for the first time in her life, she truly hoped he wouldn't. She hadn't known the man she'd talked to last night. He'd been so cold and hard that she'd felt like she was talking to a stranger—and a very menacing stranger, at that—and that scared her. In spite of the fact that she and her father had never been close, she'd always felt like she knew who he was. Until last night. He'd sounded like he was capable of anything, and that had her worried.

"It looks like you survived the last week taking care of the Yank," Cookie said from the doorway to the living room. "How'd it go?"

If circumstances had been different, she might have

told him about her father and Steve and the concerns twisting in her gut. After all, he'd practically raised her, and there'd been a time in the not too distant past when she'd felt like she could completely trust him and her father and every other man in her life. Not anymore. She didn't know if she was changing or everyone else was, but she wasn't the trusting innocent she'd once been. From now on, she decided, she'd keep her own counsel.

So she forced a smile as she turned to face Cookie and told him nothing more than he could see for himself. "Just fine," she said easily. "Steve's finally back on his feet, so I imagine he's gone out to the barn to help the others unload everything. He'll be going back to work after the barbecue. So how'd the last week go? I guess you didn't have any more problems or I would have heard something."

"We could have used a break in the heat, but other than that, everything went like clockwork," he said just as casually, giving away little of his thoughts. "Has your dad arrived yet? I thought he'd be here by now."

"Not yet. I talked to him last night, but he didn't say when he'd make it in. I got the impression, though, that it wouldn't be until tomorrow."

Deliberately changing the subject to the barbecue, she said, "I thought maybe we could prepare some things ahead of time so tomorrow won't be so hectic, so I've already made the fruit salad. What else would you like for me to do? Fix the marinade or make dessert?"

Cookie was justifiably proud of his barbecue, so Lise wasn't the least bit surprised when he immediately said, "You do the dessert. I'll handle the marinade." He didn't let her or anyone else touch his marinade.

Relieved that she'd successfully distracted him, she

said dryly, "No problem. I'll take the easy way out and grab a couple of frozen pies from the freezer."

They spent most of the rest of the afternoon cooking and setting up tables on the patio, and Cookie didn't ask her again about her father. When hours passed and there was still no word from him, she tried to take that as one more sign that he really wasn't going to show. Still, one question continued to haunt her. What if he did?

Just thinking about what he might do to Steve because of what she'd said chilled her to the bone. What if he really did hurt him? Could she live with herself?

No.

The answer came swift and sure and made her sick to her stomach. She couldn't stand by and do nothing while her father took Steve apart. Even if that meant incurring her father's wrath. She had to get Steve out of there before her father got back. Then he wouldn't be hurt.

In the process of cleaning the oversize serving dishes that would be used tomorrow, she knew she didn't have any time to waste. Abruptly, she walked off the job and headed for the back door.

Cookie looked up from the stove with a scowl. "Hey, where're you going?" he growled indignantly.

Her thoughts on Steve, Lise only waved absently and kept walking. "I'll be back as fast as I can. There's something I have to do."

She didn't wait for him to reply, but stepped outside and strode toward the barn. At different times over the course of the afternoon, she'd caught sight of Steve working around the corral and barn and wasn't surprised to find him still there long after the others had stopped to wash up for the evening meal. He had taken nearly a week of sick leave at one of the busiest times of the year, and he was the type who would feel guilty about missing work while everyone else slaved in the hot sun. Now he was trying to make up for it.

Finding him in the barn cleaning the rifles that had been taken on the roundup, she said without fanfare, "I need to talk to you."

Never lifting his eyes from his work, he said, "I'm almost finished here. I'll be with you in a few minutes."

"Someone else can do that later," she replied impatiently. "Right now, I need you to put that away and hitch one of the horse trailers to my truck. There's an auction over in Matilda tomorrow I want you to take some colts to. If you leave within the hour, you should make it there by midnight. I've already made a reservation for you at the King's Inn. Call me when you get there."

Surprised, Steve looked at her. What the devil was she talking about? The barbecue was tomorrow, and Simon was coming in. He wasn't going anywhere. "You expect me to go to Matilda? *Tonight?*"

"Yes, I do. There's an auction tomorrow—"

"So? Auction houses have them all the time. What's so all-fired great about this particular one?"

"It's the best in Western Australia," she responded. "With everything that's been going on, I completely forgot about it. Horse buyers from all over the country will be there. If we're lucky, we can sell a good number of colts. Which is why you have to leave *now,*" she insisted.

Since when had she become so desperate to sell horses? Steve wondered with a frown. It wasn't like they were overrun with them. They were working a cattle station, for God's sake. They needed every horse they had.

His gray eyes narrowing suspiciously, he growled, "What's going on, Lise? If I didn't know better, I'd swear you were trying to get rid of me."

"Don't be ridiculous." She sniffed indignantly.

"Nothing's going on. I don't know why you think there would be. I just need those horses in Matilda by eight o'clock in the morning, and I want you to take them. What's so difficult to understand about that?"

Difficult, indeed, he thought with a snort. Delivering the horses wasn't the problem. It was her story, dammit. It didn't add up, and he wanted no part of it. "Nothing," he said flatly. "Except that I'm not going."

He couldn't have surprised her more if he'd slapped her. "You're refusing to go?"

"You're damn straight, I'm refusing. You said yourself I didn't have to go back to work until after the barbecue, so that's what I'm doing. If you really want those horses in Matilda tomorrow, I'm sure Tuck will be happy to take them for you."

No one had ever openly refused to obey one of her orders before. "I didn't tell Tuck to go," she snapped, outraged. "I told you. *Told*, Steve," she stressed. "I didn't ask. That means you don't have a choice in the matter if you intend to keeping working on this station. So what's it going to be? Are you going to Matilda or not? The choice is yours."

"I already told you. I'm not going."

She was so furious, steam was practically coming out of her ears. At any other time, Steve might have been amused that he could push her buttons so easily, but there was nothing amusing about her present behavior. She wasn't the type to throw orders around and play the heavy-handed boss. That just wasn't her way. So what the hell was going on?

"Then you can pack your bags."

If she thought she could manipulate him that easily, she quickly discovered she'd underestimated him. "Go ahead and fire me," he taunted, as angry as she. "But

I'm not going anywhere until you tell me what this is all about. And don't give me that garbage about the auction. What's really going on? Are you afraid I'm going to embarrass you in front of your father or what? Is that why you're trying to get rid of me? Just tell me the truth and get it over with!''

She shouldn't have. If he hadn't been so stubborn and he'd followed orders the way he was supposed to, she wouldn't have had to. All he had to do was go to Matilda. But no! He dug in his heels, then he wouldn't even let her fire him properly! She'd never known a more frustrating man in her life.

Furious with him, afraid for him, she took the rifle from him and barely resisted the urge to throw it across the barn. ''All right, you want the truth, I'll give it to you!'' she snapped as she practically threw the rifle on the workbench. ''I don't know who you are or who sent you, but I know you're not a down-on-your-luck cowboy looking for work. You came here for one reason and one reason only—my father.''

''Who the hell told you that?''

''You did!''

''I did not!''

''Well, not to my face, no.'' When he scowled at her, she told herself she'd be damned if she'd apologize for eavesdropping. He was the one who'd been lying for weeks, not her! ''I heard you on your cell phone last night when I went downstairs to get some snacks,'' she said defiantly, ''so don't try to pretend you don't know what I'm talking about. I know you're setting some kind of trap, dammit, and *so does my father!*''

She should have known he wouldn't admit it. A man like him didn't admit anything until his back was to the wall and he had a gun at his head. His gray eyes flinty, he just glared at her.

And for reasons she couldn't begin to understand, that hurt far more than she'd thought. After what they'd shared, she'd expected at least some version of the truth. Tears gathering in her eyes, she said, "I didn't know what else to do. I couldn't just stand by and let Dad walk into a trap. I was afraid you were going to hurt him. So I called him."

When he looked at her and didn't say a word, she turned away, pain squeezing her heart. "You have to leave," she said huskily. "My father was furious last night—I've never heard him so cold. He didn't tell me what he was going to do to you, but you can't stick around here to find out. If something happened to you..."

When her voice broke, Steve desperately wanted to believe she cared. But she wouldn't be the first woman to try to trick him into confessing his mission by pretending not only to have feelings for him, but that she know all about his little *secret*.

Hesitating, he watched her head for the door and told himself she was just guessing. She couldn't have possibly heard him last night—he'd hardly spoken above a whisper, and only then after he was sure she'd gone downstairs.

But even as he argued with himself, he knew she wasn't lying. She knew too much of what had been said last night—this wasn't just a shot in the dark to see if she could hit something. And she truly cared about what happened to him. She wasn't faking that. If he knew anything about the lady, it was that she was honest when it came to her emotions—and everything else, for that matter. He didn't know how it happened, how he'd *let* it happen, but he'd come to not only love her, but trust her.

And while it was too soon to say if that was a mistake, for tonight, at least, he believed her. "Wait," he said sharply. "We need to talk."

But even as the words left his mouth, he heard a plane overhead and knew they may have just run out of time. "Dammit to hell!"

"Oh, my God, it's my father!" Lise cried, recognizing the familiar drone of her father's small jet. Pale and shaken, she ran to him and grabbed his arm. "You've got to get out of here! Hurry! Go out the back way. You can escape in the bush."

"Come with me!"

Shocked, she looked at him as her father's plane banked overhead to land at the station airstrip in the distance. "Steve..."

"Russell," he growled. "My real name is Russell Devane. And your father's is Simon. He leads a double life, Lise. I'm sorry I had to deceive you, but I didn't have any other choice. Simon's a dangerous man—he's responsible for terrorist activities all over the world."

"No!"

"Yes!" Aware of each tick of the clock, he hurriedly told her about SPEAR and her father's attempts to bring it and Jonah down. "He's evil, Lise. You owe him no loyalty. Come with me."

Torn, she hesitated. Did he have any idea what he was asking of her? What kind of choice he was asking her to make? He was talking about her father, for God's sake! All her life, she'd wanted his love. Was it possible he was really that kind of monster?

Yes.

Later, she couldn't have said why she believed him, especially after the way he'd lied to her. But there was a ring of truth to his words that struck a chord deep in her heart. Suddenly, a lot of things made sense that never had before.

"Take Thunder," she said quickly, tugging him toward the door that opened onto the corral. "He's the fastest horse we've got. I'll bridle him while you get his saddle."

Instead of grabbing a saddle, however, he reached for his wallet. Confused, she frowned. "What are you doing?"

"Calling for backup," he replied grimly, and pulled what looked like an ordinary credit card from his wallet. Pressing on the series of numbers that appeared to be the account number, he patched through a call to his people. "Belinda, the devil's in hell."

There was no need to say more, and without another word, he hurriedly returned the space-age device to his wallet. But when he looked up, it wasn't the phone Lise commented on, as he'd expected. Instead, she said with a small smile, "Belinda's someone you work with."

It wasn't a question, but an observation. There was little point in denying it, he nodded curtly. "She's my SPEAR contact. She'll have backup here within fifteen minutes."

Relieved, Lise only heard the first part of his response. There was no other woman, no other love. Belinda was the woman he kept in contact with when he was on a mission.

Then the rest of his words registered as she heard her father's plane touch down on the runway. "Fifteen minutes! Oh, God! You can't wait that long. You've got to get out of here!"

Her heart pounding and her only thought to help him get safely away, she rushed to the corral, only to freeze as she automatically glanced at the airstrip. Even before the plane had rolled to a complete stop, armed guards began to pour from it like soldiers invading a foreign land. Dressed in desert camouflage and carrying automatic weapons, they looked combat-ready and deadly.

But it was the man who appeared after the hired thugs at the top of the gangplank who caught her attention and turned her blood to ice. It was her father—or at least, the man who was dressed all in black and held an automatic rifle in his hands like he'd been holding it all his life looked like the man she'd always called Father. But this wasn't the Art Meldrum she knew. By his stance alone, he looked as cold and ruthless as the devil. And that terrified Lise.

"He'll kill you if he gets the chance." She didn't know how she knew, but at that moment, she realized her father was capable of anything, including murder. He always had been—she hadn't let herself see that because she'd needed his love so badly.

"Take Thunder and head west," she said hurriedly as she grabbed the stallion by his bridle and quickly led him into the barn. "It'll be dark soon. Then you can call your people to pick you up."

Russell knew she was right. Help was never going to arrive in time. He had to get out of there. But even as he quickly saddled Thunder, everything inside him rebelled at the thought of leaving Lise behind. "I'm not going without you," he said flatly. "C'mon."

"But Dad'll come after you for sure, then," she argued when he reached for her. "Save yourself."

"No, dammit! I'm not leaving you."

He urged her onto Thunder's back, but before he could step into the stirrups to mount behind her, he heard a sound from the doorway and turned to find Cookie standing there with a pistol that was aimed right at his heart.

"Get out of here, Lise," the older man growled, never

taking his eyes from Russell. "I'll take care of this riff-raff. You go greet your daddy."

"Don't hurt him, Cookie," she pleaded. "I mean it. Put the gun down and let him go."

His finger on the trigger, every muscle tight with tension, Cookie shook his head. "I can't. He's not any good, Lise. I knew that the moment I met him—which is why I've been keeping my eye on the bastard. Somebody had to look out for you while your daddy was gone so you wouldn't get hurt."

"I'm not hurt," she insisted. "Look at me! Do I look like I'm hurting?"

Her arms wide, she sat perfectly at ease on Thunder's back and dared him to find anything wrong with her. Reluctantly, he had to admit she looked fine, but that didn't change what he had to do. "That doesn't mean a damn thing. He's got you so in love with him, you're not thinking straight. Get off the horse and tie him up. We'll let your father decide what's to be done with him."

"No! Dammit, Cookie, this is none of your business!"

"The hell it's not. I've been watching over you for Art since you were a little girl."

Caught up in the argument with Lise, he never saw Russell reach for the rifle he'd been cleaning earlier. But Lise did, and although she loved Cookie like a second father, she didn't say anything to warn him. She couldn't, not when her father's men would be closing in any second. This was Russell's only chance to get away.

"I appreciate that," she said huskily as tears gathered in her eyes. "But I'm not a little girl anymore."

Russell grabbed the rifle, and swung it with all his might. The pistol in Cookie's hand went flying into the dark, shadowy recesses of the barn. "Son of a bitch!" the older man swore, and turned to find the gun.

Russell didn't wait to see more. Lightning fast, he vaulted onto Thunder's back behind Lise, who immediately dug her heels into Thunder's flanks. Startled at the rough treatment, the horse bolted for the open door to the barn like a racehorse heading for the finish line.

"Stop!"

"Let her go, you bastard!"

"I'll shoot!"

Behind them, Simon's armed men came running, shouting angrily after them, but they were too late. A shot rang out, but it fell a hundred yards short. Their hearts pounding, Russell and Lise raced into the bush.

For a long moment, the sound of the horse's hooves faded in the distance. Then Simon began to swear in a hard, cold voice that his hired thugs knew all too well. Warily, they watched him in silence.

"How the hell did this happen?" he demanded icily. "You knew he was in the barn—I checked with Cookie before we landed. Why didn't you capture him? Were you waiting for a personal invitation or what? Dammit to hell, I want some answers, and I want them now!"

"It's my fault," Cookie said gruffly, stepping out of the barn as the station cowboys came running from the dining hall at the ruckus. "I thought I could catch him by surprise and hold him off with a pistol until you got here, but he surprised me and knocked it out of my hand. Before I even knew what hit me, he grabbed Lise and rode off."

"Who did?" Nate demanded with a scowl. "What's going on?"

Not one to miss an opportunity, Simon saw the concern in his eyes and those of the other ranch hands and took advantage of it. "The new hand, Trace, just kidnapped Lise and took her into the bush."

"What!"

"The bastard!"

"Let's get him! Tuck, get the ammunition from the gun cabinet."

Pleased that his employees were not only loyal to Lise, but easily manipulated, Simon said, "I appreciate your enthusiasm, men, but you need to know that Steve Trace is a dangerous man. I didn't know it when I hired him, but he's wanted in the Caribbean for murder. So be careful out there. He won't hesitate to kill anyone who gets in his way."

"He's got Lise," Barney said flatly. "I don't care if he's killed a dozen men. We can't let him get away with that."

"That's right," Tuck growled. "Check the rifles and make sure he didn't sabotage them."

After that, no one needed to be told what to do. The horses were saddled, rifles checked, ammunition retrieved from the gun cabinet in the house and distributed among the cowboys. Within minutes, every man on the station was astride his mount and ready to ride. Grim with determination, they—and the men Simon had brought with him—were armed with enough firepower to take on an army.

Leading the way into the bush, Simon had a difficult time holding back a smile.

His arms around Lise's waist, Russell bent low over Thunder's neck and urged the horse faster. The sun had finally slipped over the horizon, and darkness was quickly falling, but not fast enough for Russell. They'd outwitted Simon for now, but Russell didn't fool himself into thinking the bastard wouldn't come after them. He could practically feel Simon breathing down his neck.

Glancing at the sky, he prayed. *Come on darkness. Don't fail me now.* All he needed was time. Time to evade Simon while SPEAR closed in. And darkness would make that a hell of a lot easier.

Listening for the sound of pursuit—and the arrival of his backup—Russell breathed into Lise's ear. "How long can he keep up this pace?"

"He's carrying a double load," she replied huskily. "Maybe another mile or two."

Russell swore under his breath. That wouldn't give them nearly enough time, but it would have to do. All his attention focused on Thunder's pace and breathing, they rode on.

Later, he couldn't have said when the light began to fail. One minute, he could clearly see where they were going, and the next, he couldn't. "All right! It's about damn time."

"They'll never find us now," Lise said excitedly, easing back on Thunder's reins until she slowed him to a walk. "We did it! Oh, Russell!"

He hadn't realized how long he'd been waiting for her to call him by his real name until then. Something went through him, rippling right through his heart, and when she turned in the saddle and threw her arms around him, he could have held her like that for hours.

Simon, however, had different ideas. Just as Russell leaned forward to kiss her, she stiffened, her gaze moving past him to the dark horizon behind them. "Oh, God!"

At her horrified whisper, he jerked around to see what had caught her attention—and swore like a sailor. He'd underestimated Simon. Russell had stupidly thought Simon would have to let them go once darkness fell and

it became impossible for his men to follow their trail. He
should have known the bastard was too ruthless to let a
little thing like darkness stop him. Instead, he'd set the
bush on fire.

"Son of a bitch!" he muttered. "We've got to get out
of here! That thing's going to spread like wildfire in this
wind."

Even as he spoke, the wind caught the flames that
danced on the horizon, and between one heartbeat and
another, the fire had taken on a life of its own. The dry
plant life of the bush fed the flames like alcohol. Flaring
into a raging inferno, the fire raced through the night toward them.

Her heart pounding crazily, Lise told herself it couldn't
possibly reach them. But even as they watched, the wind
shifted slightly. Suddenly, Lise could have sworn she
smelled the smoke from where they stood. Thunder
agreed. Shifting under them, he whinnied nervously.

There was no time to soothe him, no time to do anything but run for their lives. Turning, she urged the horse
forward, and he leaped to do their bidding in spite of the
fact that he was nearly spent. His long, powerful legs
stretching out, he carried the two of them deeper and
deeper into the bush.

The three of them were, however, running a race they
couldn't win. Mother Nature didn't play fair, and suddenly, the wind that had been blowing steadily from the
southeast was swirling all around them. Caught by the
capricious breeze, flames skipped ahead of the main fire
like pebbles across a lake, lighting little hot spots along
the way. With a roar, new fires were all around them.
Within minutes, they were outflanked, and the flames
were in danger of flaring out of control.

They were trapped.

"Son of a bitch!" Russell muttered as Lise pulled back on Thunder's reins and turned him in a circle, searching for a way out. There was none. "The bastard has us surrounded."

Her heart in her throat, Lise had never been more frightened in her life. "No! This has to be a mistake. My father knows I'm with you. He wouldn't deliberately put me in danger. It's the wind. It fanned the fire out of control."

"Your father set the fire," he snapped. "In this wind, he had to know we couldn't outrun it."

"It was just so he could see us," she said desperately. "He didn't know this was going to happen."

Russell heard the pain in her voice, the hurt, and wished he could make this easier for her, but he couldn't. She had to know who and what her father was. "I know you don't want to hear this," he said roughly, "but don't kid yourself into thinking your father will back off because you might get caught in the cross fire. *He doesn't care!* He'll sacrifice anyone—even his own daughter—to destroy SPEAR."

"No!"

"Yes, sweetheart. I told you—he's an evil man. I can't tell you how many people have died because of him. He's ruthless. Once, when we almost captured him in Brussels, he threw a man in front of a train to get away. Then there was the letter bomb that blew up in a D.C. post office. Ten people died that day—and they all had families. Do you think that bothered him? The very next day, he sent another bomb, this time to a U.S. senator. If the authorities hadn't been on alert because of the previous one, even more people would have been killed."

Cringing, Lise paled. She knew Russell wasn't lying to her, but she didn't want to believe her father was so bad.

The man he described was a devil. "You can't know for sure that my father was responsible for that," she said desperately. "Anyone could have sent that."

"Simon made sure everyone knew he was involved. He taunted SPEAR with information that no one but the maker of the bomb could know. He wanted people to know that he did this. He has no conscience, Lise. You have to believe me. He has connections with terrorists all over the world."

He told her things that appalled her, plots and schemes and brutal, fiendish ploys that had wreaked havoc all over the world. And her father had been behind every one of them. He gave her dates and times, not to mention a list of the lives and businesses that Simon had destroyed without remorse.

Chilled to the bone in spite of the warmth of the night and the blasting heat of the approaching fire, Lise shivered, sickened. She didn't know this man he called Simon. She only knew Art Meldrum, and while he had always kept her at a distance and treated her with little more than indifference, she'd never thought he was capable of the kind of atrocities Russell described.

There was, however, no chance that this was all some kind of awful mistake. Russell was too passionate, too outraged. He'd come halfway around the world to capture the man he called Simon, and he wouldn't have done that unless he was sure he had the right person. And then there was the fire. That spoke for itself.

No, her father and Simon were one and the same.

That should have devastated her. But as she listened to the crimes Simon had committed all over the world, she realized that deep down inside, she'd always known her father was capable of just about anything. The coldness he'd always shown her wasn't due to grief over her mother's death—that was who he was. Cold, unfeeling, without compassion. If he'd never shown her any emotion, it was because he'd never cared about her.

And that was all right, she realized. All this time, she'd thought she loved him, but it was difficult to love someone who gave you no emotion in return. What she'd loved was the idea of having a father who was crazy about her. She'd longed for that for years and foolishly thought that one day it was going to magically happen. It hadn't, and it never would.

Relieved that he had never loved her and never tried to make her love him, she said huskily, "I believe you. I guess I should thank him for never showing me much attention."

"He did you a favor," Russell replied. "He could have turned you into the same kind of monster he is."

Instead, he was going to kill her. So much for small favors.

"Don't give up," he said, reading her mind. "We're going to make it through this."

Lise desperately wanted to believe him, but they were quickly running out of options. "I thought Belinda was going to send someone to help you. Where are they?"

"I wish to hell I knew," he said grimly. "It's got to be the fire. They can't find us in all this smoke."

So they were on their own, at least for now, and the fire was closing in on them fast. They were almost completely surrounded. Only one spot remained open—a small break in the flames that led back to their pursuers.

Thunder danced nervously as the hot, billowing smoke reached them, stinging their eyes and lungs. Coughing, nearly blinded by the smoke, she choked. "Now what?"

In a matter of minutes, the fire would cut off their last

exit. If they didn't take it and face Simon and his posse, they would die.

Left with no choice, Russell growled, ''Let's go face the music.''

Chapter 12

Even if her father didn't love her, Lise tried to convince herself he wouldn't blatantly hurt her or Russell in front of a dozen or more men. He might be madder than hell at her for siding with a man he considered an enemy, but he wasn't stupid. He'd deal with them in a civilized manner.

Still, tension knotted in her stomach at the very idea of facing him now that she knew who he really was. He was a terrorist, for heaven's sake! All these years, while she'd been at home, running the station and waiting for him to come back so they could finally establish a father-daughter relationship, he'd been travelling around the world blowing up buildings and killing people. And she'd never known.

There was, however, no time to dwell on that now. Urging Thunder into a gallop, they headed straight for the last small break in the wall of fire that surrounded them. Smoke and heat slapped them right in the face. Her eyes streaming with tears, Lise didn't realize until they were racing for the gap that it had already closed up.

"Oh, God! Oh, God!" she muttered. They needed to stop, but they were going too fast. Horrified, her heart in her throat, she opened her mouth to scream, but it was too late. Behind her, Russell stiffened as Thunder prepared to jump. Before she could do anything but gasp, they were soaring.

Flames licked at them, hotter than the fires of hell, singeing skin and hair and clothes. Her lungs burning, Lise slammed her eyes shut, sure she was going to die. But then they passed through the smoke, and fresh wind hit them in the face. With a jolt, Thunder landed on the other side of the fire.

They were safe! It all happened so fast, Lise didn't know if she wanted to laugh or cry. Tears blinding her, she pulled back on Thunder's reins and had hardly brought him to a stop when she whirled in the saddle and threw herself into Russell's arms. "We did it! My God, we did it!"

"Lise—"

Laughing, she kissed him fiercely, only to pull back with a grin and exclaim, "I thought we were goners there for a second. Did you feel the heat? It was incredible!"

"Lise, honey, we're not out of the woods yet."

"What are you talking about? Of course we are! The fire's behind us—"

Something in his stiff manner hit her then, and in the glow of the fire, she finally saw the warning in his eyes. Suddenly more afraid than she'd ever been in her life, she glanced around...and froze. Her father's mounted mercenaries—and her own cowboys—had them surrounded. Nearly a dozen guns were pointed right at the two of them.

"Put your hands over your head," her father said coldly, nudging his horse forward. "Now."

When he pointed his rifle right at Russell's head, Lise felt her heart stop dead in her breast. She'd thought she'd grown used to her father's scars long ago—she'd never known him any other way—but in the glow of the fire, his disfigured face seemed to throb with fury. He looked like a monster, capable of anything. "Dad—"

"Stay out of this, Lise," he growled. "This doesn't concern you. Don't make me say it again, Trace."

Russell wasn't a fool—he knew better than to argue with a madman with a gun. Without a word, he raised his hands above his head.

"Smart man." Simon sneered in approval. "Too bad you weren't smart enough to mind your own business. Dismount. Slowly!" he snapped when Russell started to slide over Thunder's hindquarters. "Don't make any sudden moves. I wouldn't want to shoot you."

That was exactly what he wanted to do, and everyone there knew it. Russell, however, didn't plan to make it easy for him. If Simon was going to kill him, it would be without provocation. So he did as he was told and carefully dismounted. Raising his hands above his head again as soon as he was on the ground, he turned to face his captor with a mocking grin that was guaranteed to irritate the hell out of him. "That makes two of us, *Art*. I don't want you to shoot me, either. So what can I do to change your mind?"

"Nothing," he growled. "No one betrays me and lives to tell about it. If I were you, I'd make peace with my maker." And with no more warning than that, he raised his rifle and took aim.

"No!"

Later, Lise never remembered moving, but she jumped

from Thunder's back and stood directly in front of Russell, daring her father to pull the trigger. "You're not going to do this," she said furiously, her blue eyes glinting with outrage. "I won't let you."

The rifle pointed steadily at her, Simon didn't so much as blink in surprise. "Step out of the way, Lise."

"No."

"He's not the man you think he is."

If she hadn't been so furious, she would have laughed at that. "And you are? Yeah, right! Tell me another one."

For a moment, she thought she saw something flicker in his one good eye, something that might have been regret, but then she realized that was just wishful thanking on her part. His expression never changed. "I don't know what you're talking about," he said flatly.

Hurt, she couldn't believe his arrogance. He actually thought she was going to meekly accept that? She didn't think so! "Then maybe I should explain. Does the name Simon mean anything to you?"

"No. Should it?"

Staring at him, wondering how she'd ever thought she knew him, let alone loved him, Lise had to admit that he was good. He didn't flicker so much as an eyelash when she mentioned the name he was known by all over the world. Undaunted, she said, "Then let me tell you a little something about him. He's a terrorist. According to what I've heard, he's killed and maimed and destroyed the lives of just about everyone he's touched, and he couldn't care less. His objective seems to be to bring down a secret organization that combats evil in the world, and he doesn't care who he has to hurt to accomplish that."

Aware that the ranch hands were listening to her every word with avid interest, Simon swore silently and quickly tried to regain the upper hand by playing the aggressor. "So? What does any of this have to do with me?"

"You're Simon."

"Don't be ridiculous," he retorted icily. "Everyone here knows who I am."

"No, they don't. They only know who you pretend to be when you're home. And how often is that, Dad? Once a month? Maybe less? I know—you have business that keeps you away. A lot of men have to travel for their work, but they still manage to come home occasionally. You don't. Why? What are you hiding?"

"Nothing! Your mother—"

"Is dead," she cut in coldly, uncaring if that infuriated him. "Don't you dare claim that you can't stand coming here because of your grief. You don't come home because you're too busy playing the devil around the world."

"This is all nothing but a pack of lies!"

"No, you're the lie," she said. "Everything about you is a lie. You don't care about the station. And you certainly don't care about me. You never have. And everybody knows it. Ask them," she taunted, nodding toward her cowboys. "They've got eyes. They all know you're cold and unfeeling. But then again, I guess you have to be. Anyone that's soft enough to care about human life wouldn't be able to throw someone in front of a moving train, would they?"

Raging on the inside, Simon told himself he didn't have to worry. Lise could rant and rave all she wanted to, but she was wasting her breath. He had a respectable name in the outback—he'd gone to considerable expense and effort to make sure of that—and no one was going to believe such wild tales about him. Especially when there was no proof to substantiate them.

But even as he tried to take comfort from that, he

glanced around at the ranch hands, some of whom had been working there since Lise was a baby, and couldn't miss the sudden suspicion in their eyes. Too late, he realized their allegiance was to Lise. Instead of looking at Trace as if he'd just crawled out from under a rock, *he* was the one they were glaring at with hostility.

Suddenly, the numbers had changed, and he didn't like them. He still had Cookie and the men he'd brought with him in his corner, but that was it. The ranch hands would protect Lise, and Trace, too, for that matter. And that infuriated him. They all worked for him, dammit! *He* was the one they owed their loyalty to, not Lise and a backstabbing loser like Steve Trace!

He was enraged at the idea of being cornered and outnumbered, and he wasn't a man who put his trust in others when he was in a bind. Taking matters into his own hands, he brought his rifle up with lightning speed and fired—right at Lise.

It all happened so fast, Lise didn't even realize he was aiming at her until she felt the bullet slam into her right shoulder like a fireball from hell. Knocked off her feet, she screamed and fell backward, grabbing at her shoulder with fingers that trembled.

"My God, he shot her. He shot his own daughter!"

Taking advantage of the surprise he'd created, Simon dug his heels into his mount and sent him racing wildly for the fiery bush. Before anyone could move, he'd disappeared into a huge, billowing cloud of black smoke.

Outraged, the men of Pear Tree Station snapped up their guns and aimed them at the hired thugs who were about to take off after Simon. "Hold it right there, sleazeballs," Tuck growled. "You're not going anywhere. Nate, take Barney and Frankie with you and see if you can run the bastard down. The rest of us will take care of these dirtbags.''

He didn't have to tell them twice. Leaping into action, their faces grim with determination, they turned as a unit and raced after Simon.

"Lise? Are you okay? Here, honey, let me see." Dropping to his knees beside her in the dark, his face pale with concern, Russell saw the blood spreading through her blouse and swore fiercely. "The son of a bitch! Tuck, help me," he called sharply as he applied pressure to the wound. "We've got to get her back to the house!"

Her shoulder on fire, tears stinging her eyes, Lise caught weakly at his hand. "Go after Simon. Don't let him get away."

"I'm not leaving you," he said fiercely. "Don't ask that of me."

"But Simon's getting away. He'll head for the plane. Call Belinda. You have to stop him."

His face carved with worry, Russell reached for his wallet and jerked out his phone card, uncaring that the others were watching. If they didn't know by now that he wasn't one of them, it was time they found out.

"Where the hell are you?" he growled when Belinda finally came on the line. "Lise has been shot, and Simon got away. He's bound to be headed for his plane. Do what you have to to stop him."

"The fire threw backup off course," she explained. "They'll be right there."

"See that they are," he growled, and hung up, all his attention once again focused on Lise.

Fanned by the high winds, the fire had intensified and was now raging out of control, racing across the bush. Russell never spared it a glance. Still lying on the ground where she had fallen, Lise was pale as a ghost in the light cast by the fire. Worried sick, he kept his hand tight against her shoulder. And with every beat of her heart, her blood leaked between his fingers.

Unseen in the night, a squadron of helicopters approached the ranch like a swarm of locusts, using the cover of darkness to conceal their position from enemy eyes. Simon, however, heard their rotors beating at the smoky air and knew who had sent them long before he saw them. SPEAR. Sanctimonious bastards, he thought grimly. So they thought they could catch him, did they? Better men than they had tried and died regretting it. This time would be no different.

Uncaring that he'd nearly ridden his horse into the ground, he whipped it with the reins and raced for the house just as the first chopper came into view. By the light of the fire, it looked like a black demon in the night sky. His heart hammering against his ribs, he knew he could be seen from the air—the compound was lit up like a Christmas tree—but he had the advantage. He was still out of range of their firepower, and he knew the place like the back of his hand. His enemies didn't.

Ruthlessly demanding his spent mount give its all for him, he rode it into the ground and didn't care that the horse was half dead from exhaustion by the time they reached the barn. It had served its purpose. Not sparing the poor animal a second thought, he jumped from the saddle and ran to the main power switch, which was located on the outside wall of the barn. With one downward thrust, he cast the entire compound—house, barn and landing field—into darkness.

Triumphant, he laughed, but it was a short-lived victory. The total darkness he'd hoped for was ruined by the fire raging a half mile from the house. Running the length and breadth of the horizon, it set the night sky aglow. From where he stood in the shadow of the barn, he could clearly see where his plane sat on the landing strip. Even though he was dressed in black, he would be just as visible the second he came within thirty feet of the jet.

"Damn!"

Furious, there was nothing he could do but run for it. And he didn't have a hell of a lot of time to waste. If he gave the choppers time to land, they'd surround his plane and cut off his escape. Swearing, he took off at a dead run, weaving in and out between the barn and outbuildings like a dark shadow running from the hounds of hell.

When the first bullet whizzed past him, he felt the heat of it graze his cheek. Ducking, he cursed and zigzagged across the runway while a hail of bullets rained down from the sky.

A lesser man might have surrendered rather than chance getting shot, but he'd avoided capture too many times in the past to worry about a little gunfire. He threw himself up the gangplank just as the first chopper landed and armed SPEAR operatives spilled from it.

"Steady," he told himself as he ran to the cockpit and prepared to take off. "There's no reason to panic. You've got them right where you want them."

He hurriedly started the engine of the small jet and taxied down the runway, away from his pursuers. Long seconds later, his wheels left the tarmac as he took off. The helicopters gave chase, but there was no way they could keep up with the power of his jet. Laughing, he left the station far behind and soared into the sky. Once again, he'd evaded SPEAR.

She was dying.

Russell could practically feel Lise's life force slipping

through his fingers, and it struck terror in his heart. He couldn't lose her! Not now that he'd finally found a woman who meant everything to him. Didn't she know he'd been waiting his entire life for her? He had to tell her!

His hand still pressed to the gaping wound in her shoulder, he bent over her and said hoarsely, "Lise? Don't you die on me, sweetheart. You hear me?"

"I'm okay," she whispered faintly.

"You damn well better be," he growled. "I love you, and I'm not losing you, dammit!"

Tuck ran up with Preston while Chuck held Simon's thugs at gunpoint. "How is she?"

"Fading fast," Russell answered, worried out of his mind. "We've got to get her back to the house. Take off your shirt. This has to be bandaged before we try to move her."

Lightning quick, the older man peeled off his shirt and tore it into strips, one of which he hurriedly folded into a thick bandage. "Ready?" he asked Lise. "We're going to have to tie this down tight. It's going to hurt."

"Do it," she said, bracing herself. "I can take it."

She was a strong woman, but not even she could withstand hard pressure on a gaping gunshot wound. The minute Tuck pressed the bandage into place, she screamed, stiffening against the white-hot pain that ripped through her shoulder. In the end, however, she couldn't fight it. Without a sound, she wilted, unconscious.

"Dammit to hell, Tuck, she's passed out! You hurt her."

"No," he retorted, "her father hurt her. I'm just trying to keep her from bleeding to death. Mount up. I'll hand her to you."

Terrified for her, Russell grabbed Thunder's reins and

vaulted into the saddle. He'd barely settled into the stirrups before the older man was handing Lise to him. Limp as a dishrag, she collapsed against him without a sound. Scared to death, Russell didn't wait to see more. Spurring his horse, he bolted for the house.

Russell never remembered much about that ride. Tuck stayed behind to help Chuck escort Simon's mercenaries to the house, so Russell was alone with Lise as he galloped across the bush in the night. A half a mile away, he saw the lights of the compound flare on and didn't have time to wonder if Simon had gotten away. Right now, the only thing that mattered was Lise. He wouldn't lose her. His face grim with determination, he headed straight for the house. It was the longest ride of his life.

The compound was crawling with agents when he finally galloped into the light, but Russell only saw one man. "Jeff!" Russell shouted hoarsely. "Thank God! Lise has been shot. You've got to help her."

In a split second, three pairs of hands were there to take her from his arms. Jeff Kirby, a tall, good-looking man who, at twenty-four, still showed the lankiness of youth in his face and body, was a medical student currently getting field training for his planned medevac specialty. Young in age but old in the ways of the world, he took one look at the bloody bandage strapped to Lise's shoulder and immediately took charge. "Let's get her inside—there's a downstairs bedroom. Somebody get my bag. Easy!" he barked when the men accidentally jostled Lise's shoulder and she moaned. "She's in enough pain already. Be careful."

Suitably chastised, the men carried Lise inside and deposited her on the bed. After washing his hands in the nearby bathroom, Jeff stepped into the bedroom and scowled. "Where's my bag?"

"Here," Tish Buckner said from behind him in the hallway. "I had to get it from the chopper." Tish was the senior agent in charge of the search of the compound. Her eyes met his for a long moment as she held his medical bag out to him, then she glanced past his shoulder to Russell, who was hovering close by Lise, refusing to leave her side. Nodding grimly at him, Tish said, "It's good to see you again, Russell. From what I've heard, you've done a good job here."

"Not good enough," he retorted bitterly. "I couldn't protect Lise when she needed me, and I don't know what the hell happened to Simon."

"He gave us the slip in the smoke," Jeff told him flatly as he quickly moved to the opposite side of the bed to inspect Lise's wound.

"He turned off the compound lights, and by the time we spotted him, he was already halfway to his jet and out of range," Tish added in disgust. "Once he took off, the choppers couldn't keep up."

Lise moaned, shifting under Jeff's hands as he inspected the wound. As pale as the bedsheets, she groggily opened her eyes and stiffened at the sight of a stranger bending over her. Alarmed, her eyes flew from him to the small, pretty woman standing at the foot of the bed. They were both dressed all in black and looked too much like the hired thugs her father had brought to the station with him. "Who...?"

"It's all right, sweetheart," Russell said quickly, taking her hand. "This is Jeff Kirby and Tish Buckner. They're with SPEAR. Jeff's a medical student—he's going to take care of you. How do you feel?"

"Like I got hit in the shoulder with a flamethrower," she said faintly, wincing. "My father shot me, didn't he?"

Nodding, he said, "I knew he was a bastard, but I never thought he'd hurt you, Lise. Not like that. I'm sorry."

"Don't blame yourself. How could you be expected to know that when I didn't know it myself? I'm his daughter, for God's sake! He left me to die." Suddenly remembering the fire, she blanched. "Oh, God, the fire! We've got to do something."

"It's already being taken care of," Tish assured her. "Your neighbors volunteered their water trucks, and now that the wind has died some, the fire's not spreading so quickly. It's under control."

"So just relax and let somebody else worry about the station," Jeff added. "Right now, we want to get you patched up and back on your feet. And that's going to be easier than I first thought. The bullet appears to have exited cleanly, and I don't see any bone fragments. Let me give you something for the pain, then I'll clean the wound and bandage it for you."

Her entire shoulder throbbed, but Lise didn't realize how badly it was hurting until Jeff gave her a shot. Within minutes, the pain eased to a dull, bearable throb. Relieved, Lise could have cried. "Thank you!"

"Jeff'll fix you right up," Tish said confidently. "He's an excellent doctor."

She smiled at Jeff, and something passed between them, something intimate and private that Lise doubted Tish was even aware was reflected in her expressive brown eyes. But Lise saw it and blinked in surprise. Jeff might have the eyes of an old soul, but he couldn't have been older than his middle twenties. Tish, on the other hand, had to be at least ten years his senior, in spite of the fact that she looked no more than thirty. With her olive complexion and glossy, dark brown hair, she was very attractive, but there was a maturity about her that only came with age.

And it showed when she realized Lise was watching the two of them together. With the blink of an eye, she hid whatever was between her and Jeff and became all business again. "I know this has to be difficult for you, Lise. Unfortunately, I can't make things any easier for you. Your father was able to escape, so it's my job to make sure he hasn't hidden anything here. I had to order my men to tear the place apart."

Even as she spoke, Lise could hear the groan of wood as floorboards were pried up and furniture dismantled as SPEAR agents went to work searching for every possible hiding place. Lise couldn't blame them. After the way her father had betrayed her, she'd have been right in there with them, looking for whatever she could find to incriminate him, if she hadn't been shot. "Do what you have to do," she said huskily.

Relieved, Tish said, "Thanks. If you can think of someplace in particular he might have hidden his records, we'd appreciate it."

Lise would love to have helped her, but there was little she could tell her. "Sorry," she said with a grimace, "but he really didn't spend a lot of time here. Other than his study, the only place I can think of is the cabin he built for my mother when they first married."

"Russell mentioned that he'd already searched it, but we had to go through it again and take it apart. The team I sent to go through it should be back shortly."

The words were hardly out of her mouth when they heard the sound of a helicopter approaching the airstrip. "That'll be them now," Tish said. "Excuse me."

Hurrying out to meet with her men, she left Lise in Jeff and Russell's care, only to return moments later with a disgusted look on her face. "It looks like we struck out at the cabin and here at the house."

"What about the barns and outbuildings?" Jeff asked. "You know how crafty Simon is. For all we know, he could have a secret basement out there somewhere that no one would think to look for."

"I tried searching them before the roundup," Russell said, "but it was difficult with the other hands always around."

"It's probably a waste of time," Tish said, "but we can't leave any stone unturned. I'll tell the men."

She started to turn away when the cell phone clipped to her belt rang. Frowning, she quickly answered it. "Yes?"

"Simon made it to the Perth airport before he ran out of gas," a male voice said in her ear. "He caught a flight to New York."

"Damn!"

"Leave the search to the others—they'll finish up, then return to the States and report to headquarters. We need you to follow Simon now. Take a chopper to Perth. There's a private jet waiting to take you to New York."

Outside, a chopper fired to life, signaling that there was no time to waste. "I'll leave immediately," she said, and hung up. Across the room, her eyes met Jeff's. "Simon's on his way to New York. I've got orders to follow him."

Orders were orders. There was nothing left to say. With a nod of goodbye, she turned and walked out.

When Jeff watched her until she disappeared from view, Russell arched a brow in surprise. Interesting. Was there something going on here that he didn't know about? Curious, he almost asked, but another look at Jeff's face and he shut his mouth with a snap. Jeff was hurting, and it was none of Russell's business why.

"Now that Lise is going to be okay, I'll get back to the search," Jeff said huskily. Digging into his bag, he produced a bottle of antibiotics and another of pain pills. "Keep your arm in a sling, and take the antibiotics for the next ten days. Your shoulder will tell you when to take the pain pills. If you have any problems, have Russell call me. I'll be here the rest of the night."

He could search from then until doomsday, but Lise knew he and the others wouldn't find anything. Art— Simon, she corrected herself with a grimace—was too smart to hide anything on the station. There were too many people milling about, and he wouldn't take a chance that someone might stumble across something incriminating when he wasn't there to protect it.

Still, it was the SPEAR agents' job to look, so she said, "Thank you, Jeff. I don't know what I would have done if you hadn't been here."

"We would have flown you to Perth," Russell told her, "and that could have been damn dicey with the way you were bleeding. Thanks, man," he added gruffly to Jeff, offering his hand. "I owe you."

"I'm just doing my job," Jeff replied, returning his handshake. "Sometimes, it works out better than others."

He left then to join the search, and suddenly, for the first time in what seemed like hours, Lise and Russell were alone. Their eyes met, then danced away. Her heart thumping crazily, Lise told herself to say something, but all she could think of was that Russell's mission was complete. He would probably be leaving in the morning with the other agents. Just the thought of that caused a pain in her heart that was a hundred times worse than the one in her shoulder.

Say something, a voice in her head urged. *You can't just let him walk away. Say something, for God's sake!*

She should have asked him where he was going from there, if he thought he would ever come back to Australia, but those questions never entered her head. Instead, she asked, "Did you mean it?"

Another man might have pretended he didn't know what she was talking about, but Russell met her gaze head-on. "Yes," he said gruffly. "I love you. I think I fell in love with you the moment I met you. Not," he added before she could say anything, "that I expect you to feel the same way. All things considered, I wouldn't blame you if you hated me."

Surprised, her heart pounding crazily in her breast, she frowned in confusion. "Why would I hate you?"

"Because I used you to try to get information about Simon," he said simply. "I was just doing what I had to, to do my job, but I still flirted with you so you'd trust me and tell me what I needed to know."

"Even when we made love?"

"No!" Horrified that she even had to ask that, he sank down on his knee next to the bed and took her hand. "When we made love, that was for me," he said huskily. "For us. It had nothing to do with my job. I was falling in love with you and it scared me to death, but I couldn't stop myself."

Tears flooded her eyes at that. "Oh, Russell." She choked, tightening her fingers in his. "That was just the way I felt, too, and I didn't know what to do about it. No one had ever made me feel the way you did, and I was afraid you'd break my heart when you left."

"Oh, sweetheart, I would never do that to you." Leaning over, he kissed her hungrily and wished he could hold her the way he longed to. But her hurt shoulder prevented that, so he had to be satisfied with just a kiss. "I love you," he murmured, cupping her face in his hands. "I would never do anything to deliberately hurt you."

"I love you, too," she said softly, unable to stop the tears that spilled over her lashes. "I don't want to lose you."

"Once I fell in love with you, that was never a possibility." His face somber, he took her hand again and gave it a reassuring squeeze. "There's something you should know, sweetheart. Even before I came to Australia, I was thinking about retiring from SPEAR."

"What? Why?"

"Don't get me wrong," he said quickly. "I believe in the agency and what it does, but I've been doing this for a long time now. I'm tired of the constant moving around. I want to put down roots somewhere and settle down. I thought maybe I'd go to Wisconsin and buy a farm, like my parents. What do you think? Would you be interested in marrying me and being a dairy farmer's wife?"

Her heart expanding with love, Lise would have gone to the moon with him if he'd asked. But before she could tell him that, there was a knock at the door, and they both looked up to find Jeff standing in the doorway. "Sorry to interrupt," he said gruffly, "but I just wanted to let you know we didn't find anything in the barns and outbuildings. Headquarters wants us to extend the search to the rest of the station, so we're going to be taking off in a few minutes, then head for Perth sometime tomorrow morning. Are you coming, Russell?"

Lise's heart stopped cold in her breast, but she needn't have worried. "No," he said without hesitation. "I'm calling it quits. I'll report to headquarters later to make it official, but for now, I'm staying here."

"I wish you luck then," Jeff said with a short salute. "Both of you."

With a final nod, he disappeared from the doorway as quickly as he'd appeared, and almost immediately, they heard the helicopters fire to life on the airstrip. Long seconds later, they lifted into the night sky and fanned out over the station.

The silence left by their leave-taking was ripe with promise. His gray eyes smiling into hers, Russell arched a brow at her. "Well?"

Feeling like her heart suddenly had wings, Lise couldn't seem to stop smiling. There'd been a time when she'd thought she'd never be able to forgive him for using her to get to Simon, but that was before she knew just how wicked her father was. Desperate situations called for desperate measures, and Russell the SPEAR operative did what he had to do to catch a dangerous terrorist. It was Russell the man who had made love to her, however. And it was that same man who made her fall in love with him.

Her heart in her eyes, she reached for him, needing his arms around her when she told him she would marry him. "I love you with all of my heart," she said huskily. "Yes, I'll marry you. As for Wisconsin, it sounds wonderful, but what about the Pear Tree Station? It's mine, you know."

Surprised, he said, "It is? I thought it was Simon's."

"He had it put in my mother's name when they married, and it became mine when she died. Now I know why. He didn't want it traced to him."

"Son of a bitch," Russell growled. "He hid behind his own wife and daughter."

"He won't do it again," she promised. "Even if I'd let him—which I won't—he'll never come back here now that SPEAR knows about the place. So how do you feel about Australia? Would you be terribly disappointed if we owned and operated a cattle station here instead of a dairy farm in Wisconsin?''

Wondering how she could even ask that, he grinned and kissed her. ''Are you kidding? Cows are cows. I love it here. Especially with you beside me. That's all I need.''

''Me, too,'' she said huskily, and realized that she'd never spoken truer words. As long as she had him beside her, nothing else mattered. Love shining in her eyes, she turned into his arms. It was the only place she wanted to be.

*   *   *   *   *

Next month, look for

THE WAY WE WED

by Pat Warren,
as Intimate Moments' exciting

A YEAR OF LOVING DANGEROUSLY

series continues.

Turn the page for a sneak preview....

Chapter 1

The late afternoon sun was quite hot along the Pacific coast of southern California even in mid-April. Jeff Kirby felt his shirt sticking to his back as well as the dampness of his jogging shorts, but he ignored both. Running on the hard-packed sand of the beach at the foot of Condor Mountain Resort and Spa was something he looked forward to each time he returned. His shoes hit the ground with staccato precision, spraying clumps of wet sand as he made his way north alongside the frothy waves. Some distance out, seagulls artfully dived into the sea in search of a late lunch.

Glancing at a cloudless blue sky, Jeff felt glad to be alive, grateful for each day. A near-death experience will do that to a person, he decided. He'd come a shade too close for comfort last year and didn't ever want to repeat the ordeal. Yet he was increasingly aware that the work he did, the job he'd chosen, would ultimately put him in danger more often than not. He knew that, yet chose to stay.

Jeff's adoptive father, Easton Kirby, had once been one of the top field agents for SPEAR, a secret government agency that dated back to the Civil War and was rumored to have been founded by no less than Abraham Lincoln himself. But a devastating personal incident had all but turned East into a recluse, a man haunted by his own demons, one who holed up in his room at Condor and withdrew from all who cared about him.

Until the night he'd encountered a fourteen-year-old boy who'd run away from his latest in a series of foster homes, a boy as damaged and needy as East was. That boy's name was Jeff.

They'd both been the walking wounded back then, but each had managed to overcome a disturbing past, to bond with one another and learn to care, to trust again. After a slow healing time, East, who'd been twenty-five ten years ago, only eleven years older than Jeff, had adopted the boy and taken over the running of Condor Mountain Resort as a civilian employee. Only occasionally these days did either of them speak of those past terrible years.

Through most of his teen years and later, Jeff had met or heard about several agents—men and women—who'd been badly hurt in the line of duty, some physically, some emotionally. A few had even died. But with the arrogance of youth, he'd felt certain none of those things would happen to him. He'd quickly shot up to a height of six feet, lean and muscled from training sessions and working out regularly. He'd felt confident, invincible, ready to take on the world.

Until the day he'd been kidnapped, buried alive and left to die.

Slowing his steps, Jeff came to a stop, breathing

deeply. He bent over, bracing his hands on his knees, letting his body cool. That episode had changed him forever.

Jeff frowned as his thoughts drifted to another matter, one equally if not more important to him: Tish Buckner. Skirting a moss-covered rock, he wondered why the course of love never ran smoothly. He'd met Tish last year at Red Rock Ranch in northern Arizona where he'd gone to recuperate after his ordeal, and he'd fallen for her fast and hard. She was a SPEAR agent who'd come to take a refresher course on her vacation because she wasn't the type for lazing about. But their road to happiness had been filled with stumbling blocks right from the start and, sadly, they'd gone their separate ways. Running across her in Australia a few weeks ago had been a lucky break, but they'd had too little private time. He'd pretty well convinced her they should try again when the call had come in that Tish was needed along with several other SPEAR agents. A traitor known as Simon, who'd been orchestrating all sorts of treasonous acts against the country and framing the head of SPEAR for them, had been traced to New York. Tish had quickly boarded a helicopter after receiving orders to follow Simon. But she'd promised to meet with Jeff to talk more as soon as her assignment ended.

This time he'd make her see that they belonged together, Jeff vowed as his steps brought him back to the foot of the majestic resort where he paused. It was part of the Monarch Hotel chain owned and operated as one of SPEAR's legitimate business enterprises. The lobby floor of Condor offered moneyed guests a luxurious retreat with a magnificent view and a cosmopolitan atmosphere with a renowned chef holding court in both restaurants.

He was nearly to the landing that led to the stone stairs of the terrace dining room when he spotted his dad standing by the waist-high railing.

As Jeff hurried up the last few steps, he couldn't help wondering what had put that very serious look on his father's face. From the beginning, they'd shared a remarkable intuition about one another that was usually right.

Jeff felt a worried frown form as he stepped onto the terrace. "What's wrong?" he asked East.

East was openly studying him, as if gauging how best to deliver bad news.

Finally Jeff could stand it no longer. "What is it?"

"There's been an accident. In New York." The everpresent shadows in East's brown eyes seemed to darken to near-black. "Several agents were checking out a warehouse where Simon was reportedly stockpiling weapons. A bomb went off."

Jeff felt the blood drain from his face. "Tish?" He managed to get her name out, his voice strained. *Oh, God! Not now, please.*

"She's in the hospital, unconscious." East reached over, placed a hand on his son's shoulder and squeezed hard.

"The prognosis?" Jeff asked as a terrible weight took up residence in his chest.

East shook his head. "No one knows."

Jeff was not a man who could wait for answers. He had to take action, to find out for himself. "What hospital?"

East handed him a notepad where he'd jotted down the phone number. "Metropolitan General in Manhattan."

It took Jeff some time to get through to the right floor, the right nurses' station. Tish was in surgery, he was told, her injuries quite serious, but the nurse wouldn't elaborate. Trying to stay in control of his emotions, Jeff scrubbed a hand across his face. "I've got to go there," he said as he hung up the phone.

East handed him a sheet of paper. "You're booked on the red-eye out of LAX. Get ready and I'll drive you to the airport."

Jeff prayed that he wouldn't get to her too late.

INTIMATE MOMENTS™

presents a riveting 12-book continuity series:

a Year of loving dangerously

Where passion rules and nothing is what it seems...

When dishonor threatens a top-secret agency, the brave men and women of SPEAR are prepared to risk it all as they put their lives—and their hearts—on the line.

Available April 2001:

THE WAY WE WED
by Pat Warren

They had married in secret, two undercover agents with nothing to lose—except maybe the love of a lifetime. For though Jeff Kirby tried to keep Tish Buckner by his side, tragedy tore the newlyweds apart. Now Tish's life hung in the balance, and Jeff was hoping against hope that he and Tish would get a second chance at the life they'd once dreamed of. For this time, the determined M.D. wouldn't let his woman get away!

*Available only from Silhouette Intimate Moments
at your favorite retail outlet.*

Where love comes alive™

Visit Silhouette at www.eHarlequin.com   SIMAYOLD11

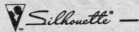

Silhouette —

where love comes alive—online...

eHARLEQUIN.com

your romantic books

♥ Shop online! Visit Shop eHarlequin and discover a wide selection of new releases and classic favorites at great discounted prices.

♥ Read our daily and weekly Internet exclusive serials, and participate in our interactive novel in the reading room.

♥ Ever dreamed of being a writer? Enter your chapter for a chance to become a featured author in our Writing Round Robin novel.

• • • • • •

your romantic life

♥ Check out our feature articles on dating, flirting and other important romance topics and get your daily love dose with tips on how to keep the romance alive every day.

• • • • • •

your community

♥ Have a Heart-to-Heart with other members about the latest books and meet your favorite authors.

♥ Discuss your romantic dilemma in the Tales from the Heart message board.

your romantic escapes

♥ Learn what the stars have in store for you with our daily Passionscopes and weekly Eroticscopes.

♥ Get the latest scoop on your favorite royals in Royal Romance.

All this and more available at
www.eHarlequin.com
on Women.com Networks

SINTA1R

a Year of Loving dangerously

If you missed the first 8 riveting,
romantic Intimate Moments stories
from *A Year of Loving Dangerously*,
here's a chance to order your copies today!

#1016	**MISSION: IRRESISTIBLE** by Sharon Sala	$4.50 U.S.☐ $5.25 CAN.☐
#1022	**UNDERCOVER BRIDE** by Kylie Brant	$4.50 U.S.☐ $5.25 CAN.☐
#1028	**NIGHT OF NO RETURN** by Eileen Wilks	$4.50 U.S.☐ $5.25 CAN.☐
#1034	**HER SECRET WEAPON** by Beverly Barton	$4.50 U.S.☐ $5.25 CAN.☐
#1040	**HERO AT LARGE** by Robyn Amos	$4.50 U.S.☐ $5.25 CAN.☐
#1046	**STRANGERS WHEN WE MARRIED** by Carla Cassidy	$4.50 U.S.☐ $5.25 CAN.☐
#1052	**THE SPY WHO LOVED HIM** by Merline Lovelace	$4.50 U.S.☐ $5.25 CAN.☐
#1058	**SOMEONE TO WATCH OVER HER** by Margaret Watson	$4.50 U.S.☐ $5.25 CAN.☐

(limited quantities available)

TOTAL AMOUNT	$ _____
POSTAGE & HANDLING	
($1.00 each book, 50¢ each additional book))	$ _____
APPLICABLE TAXES*	$ _____
TOTAL PAYABLE	$ _____
(check or money order—please do not send cash)	

To order, send the completed form, along with a check or money order for the total above, payable to **A YEAR OF LOVING DANGEROUSLY** to: **In the U.S.:** 3010 Walden Avenue, P.O. Box 9077, Buffalo, NY 14269-9077; **In Canada:** P.O. Box 636, Fort Erie, Ontario L2A 5X3.

Name: _____

Address: _____ City: _____

State/Prov.: _____ Zip/Postal Code: _____

Account # (if applicable): _____ 075 CSAS

*New York residents remit applicable sales taxes.
Canadian residents remit applicable
GST and provincial taxes.

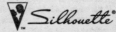

Visit Silhouette at www.eHarlequin.com

AYOLD-BL8